Dennis L Citrin

Fatal Error

ISBN: 1450524907
ISBN-13: 9781450524902

Chap 1

Large cell lymphoma. Stage four. In her brain *at twenty nine.*

Winnie Brown was terrified, with good reason.

Her doctor, David Stern said it was curable, that she could survive and see her twins grow up. But the treatment was rough.

She went through it all. She endured months of chemotherapy that caused sores in her mouth and throat, making every bite of food painful. Her once beautiful face was bloated and distorted by high dose steroids. She lost of all of her hair, head and body. She experienced never-ending fatigue and diarrhea that drained all of her strength. Her sleep was disturbed by the agony of shingles over much of her back.

It was worse, much worse than Doctor Stern had described.

Through it all, supporting her and Robert, always patient and sensitive, always encouraging and upbeat was her doctor.

She sometimes thought that she would not be able to handle it, but her doctor was always there for her.

He gave her chemotherapy. He allayed her fears. He listened to her, answered her questions and celebrated with her and Robert when all of her tests came back showing she was cancer-free.

Then he killed her.

Chap 2

"I may be late tonight Andi," said David as he finished a quick cup of coffee.

"You know that Mondays are always real busy in the clinic, and I have to go over my presentation for San Diego."

He spoke casually, and didn't notice *the look* that crossed his girl-friend's face.

David and Andi Kaplan shared a high-rise condo in Lincoln Park. They had lived together for nearly two years, and things were not going well.

David's life revolved around his work. He was totally involved in it. He loved the intellectual challenge of practicing cancer medicine at the highest possible level. Emotionally he was a deeply sensitive man who was driven to help people. He loved being a doctor. He would be the first to admit that his professional life kept him very busy and fulfilled.

Andi felt cheated. She enjoyed her work as a computer programmer at the Board of Trade but her job was much less intense than David's. His patients and research kept him away from her for long hours. Worse, even when they were together he often seemed distant and distracted.

Yesterday had been a complete disaster, and Andi was still silently fuming. She really looked forward to their weekends as precious time they shared.. Sunday afternoon they had tickets for the Chicago Symphony. They were going with her best friend Julie and her husband Sandy, but at eleven that morning David got paged.

He frowned as he read the message.

"Looks like I've got to go in, Andi. It's one of my bone marrow transplant patients."

"On a *Sunday?*" asked Andi.

David shrugged as he pulled on his jeans.

"People get sick all the time, Andi. You know that it's never been a nine to five job."

He slipped on a dark blue cashmere turtleneck.

"I'll try and be back by two. I'll call if I'm going to be late." He smiled. "We'll still make the concert."

She turned her head away as he tried to kiss her goodbye. If David noticed he didn't say anything.

He didn't make it back by two. At the hospital he was caught up in a difficult situation. One of his lymphoma patients who had received a bone marrow transplant six weeks earlier needed emergency surgery, at a time when his immune system was dangerously low. It was touch and go for hours, but eventually David felt that his patient was stable enough for him to go home.

He breezed in at nine o'clock. On the very evening that Andi had invited her parents round for dinner. At seven.

"Hi everyone ," said David, "sorry I'm late."

He kissed the top of Andi's head, "How was the concert?"

Three angry people looked at him in silence. Andi's parents had always liked David, but after listening to two hours of their daughter's tearful complaints about him, they weren't exactly friendly.

"I didn't go, David," said Andi stiffly, "I waited all afternoon, but you didn't call."

"Oh, I'm sorry," said David innocently, "it was crazy for a time there. I had a guy who was really sick. I kind of assumed that you would know I couldn't get out in time."

He looked with interest at the table.

"I haven't eaten all day, what's for dinner ?" he asked.

Andi burst into tears and ran from the room.

Andi's mother shook her head, "You could have called her, David."

David looked uncomfortable.

"I'm sorry. I guess I got caught up in things. The guy I went in to see was really in a bad way. It took hours to get him in shape for surgery. I didn't have a chance to call."

"And you're the only doctor who could look after him?" she asked.

David shrugged, "He's my patient. It's my job."

Any further discussion was interrupted by his pager.

"Excuse me I've got to answer this," he said, escaping to the kitchen. As he cradled the telephone to his ear, he checked the refrigerator. It was pretty empty. Andi had dumped the remains of dinner in the garbage disposal.

"I am definitely up shit creek with Andi!" thought David, as he spoke with the hospital.

Hanging up the phone, he made himself a cheese sandwich and returned to the dining room. A red-eyed Andi was back, sitting with her angry parents.

"Look, I'm sorry I didn't call, Andi. I was really busy, and time just got away from me. You know how it is."

Andi didn't say a word, but her expression didn't change.

"No, she doesn't know how it is, and neither do we."

Andi's mother did the talking for the group.

"You're always too busy, David. Your first responsibility should be to Andi, not some stranger. Frankly it was very selfish of you. We've always put family first. I don't know if you understand that!"

"Well, that's the problem, right there," thought David, *"Do I really consider Andi the number one priority in my life?"*

His thoughts were easy to read. Andi burst into tears and ran to the bedroom again.

"We should go, Jackie," said Andi's father.

They left without another word.

The evening was not a success. David ate his sandwich alone, and slept on the couch in the living room. Andi kept their bedroom door tightly closed.

Chap 3

Andi went to sleep very angry, and woke up angry. So it didn't take much to set her off on Monday morning. David's ill timed remark about San Diego was all the spark.

Andi had been furious when David told her a month earlier that his paper had been accepted for presentation at the National Lymphoma Meeting in San Diego, on the very day when her aunt Linda was getting married in Highland Park.

The reminder that David would not be there for her and her family ignited all of her simmering resentment.

"How many times does this happen? All my other friends, their husbands or boyfriends are always there,' she said angrily, "I'm always by myself. I'm tired of people asking, *where's David?*"

David made a conciliatory gesture.

"Look, I'm sorry about yesterday, it was wrong of me not to call."

Andi was not impressed, "All you think of is that damned hospital and your patients. You're never there for me when *I* need you."

David looked at his watch, "I'm sorry, Andi. I have to go. Can we talk about this tonight?"

Andi shook her head, "I want to talk about it now. I don't see why you can't give up the conference for Linda's wedding,"

The idea had just never occurred to David. He made a bad mistake. He laughed.

"Come on," he said, "it's not like this is Linda's first wedding. This is, what number three?"

"I don't care," shouted Andi, "it's a family wedding and you should be there with me. What's more important, my family or some stupid meeting?"

David wisely didn't say a word, but his expression told Andi everything.

"You selfish son of a bitch!" she yelled, throwing her coffee cup at him.

He got out of the apartment as fast as he could.

As he eased himself into his black Corvette in the basement garage, he glanced at the clock on the leather dashboard.

"Nearly eight o'clock. I'm going to be really late," he thought.

It had snowed during the night, and it was one of those very cold blue sky days in Chicago that frequently follow a storm. The temperature hovered around zero, and an eerie mist hung over the lake as David wove his way through rush hour traffic southbound on Lake Shore Drive towards International Medical Center.

David hardly noticed the spectacular view, as he went over the angry words that had spilled from Andi.

For several months he had been aware of Andi's growing dissatisfaction with their relationship, but he was really shocked by the depth of her anger. He was comfortable with her, but never really thought of their relationship as the most important thing in his life. He had kind of assumed that Andi felt the same way about him. He never saw the cop behind him until it was too late. The next minute he was pulled over. The cop's name badge read Maloney. He was fat, sweating and had an attitude.

He stood impatiently as David fumbled for his wallet and license.

"You know you were doing forty eight miles an hour in a thirty zone?"

David nodded, "I'm sorry, officer. I'm a doctor at International, and I've patients waiting there for me."

"Never hurts to play the M.D. card," thought David.

Maloney was clearly not impressed.

"That's the trouble with you big shot Jew doctors, you think that it's all about you, don't you?"

David just wasn't ready to suck it up.

"At least I'm not a fat Irish ass-hole," he muttered, loud enough for Maloney to hear.

"Get out of the car," yelled Maloney.

"Shit," thought David, *"this is not what I need today."*

He climbed warily out of the car.

"Think you can get away with that?" said Maloney, as he pushed David none too gently up against the squad car.

It was only the arrival of a second cop car that defused the situation. Maloney had a certain reputation in the Chicago Police Department , and it was no coincidence that his sergeant just happened to be in the vicinity.

Cooler heads prevailed and after some negotiation David was free to go, but he still had a ticket for speeding.

Maloney had the last word, however. As his sergeant took off, he looked balefully at David.

"I know who you are, Stern, and where you live. I'll be looking for you. No-one calls me an ass-hole."

David wisely said nothing.

By nine thirty on this bright January morning David had a coffee cup thrown at his head, and collected a speeding ticket.

David was very angry. He was also very late.

Chap 4

As he hurried into the Outpatient Oncology clinic on a Monday morning in January, David Stern was pissed. He was royally pissed.

David was usually very even tempered. The nurses in the clinic really liked working with him. They had the usual complement of arrogant medical assholes at International Medical Center in downtown Chicago. All of the nurses could tell you about the doctors who truly and sincerely believed that their shit smelled like Chanel. There were plenty of doctors who thought that the magic letters M.D. allowed them to treat all those they regarded as inferior with barely concealed contempt.

Everyone agreed that David was different.

David Stern ran the lymphoma program at International, but did so in a quiet way. Although at thirty-four he was already recognized to be one of the best cancer doctors in the USA, he remained friendly and unfailingly polite to everyone. Most of the nurses at International were crazy about him. Of course it didn't hurt that he was unmarried and almost film star handsome, at six two and one eighty pounds.

Unlike so many doctors who were interested in *diseases* and turned off by the *people* who suffered from those diseases, David Stern never lost sight of what it was all about, the patient. Many doctors could turn on the compassion when they needed to. They followed the script, but with David it was the real thing. He genuinely cared for his patients.

Beth Caprio, the Nurse Supervisor greeted David at the nursing station of the Lymphoma Clinic. Beth was a five-foot dynamo who ran a tight operation. She had worked with David Stern for years. They had an easy relationship.

"Good morning, David" she said cheerfully. "You've got a full morning, and I've got some bad news, we're really short staffed today. I've got four out sick and Karen's not coming in. Sounds like her little one has the flu. She had a temp of 102 and vomiting all night."

Karen Folsom was David's nurse, who helped him with all of his patients and set up all of his patients for chemotherapy.

"Shit! That's just marvelous", said David dropping his briefcase.

Beth was shocked. She had never seen David upset before, no matter what the pressure.

"I'll just see them all myself," he said muttering darkly. He shook his head, "What a start to the week!"

Without another word he stalked off to his consulting room.

That morning David had ten patients, including two new patients and a bone marrow biopsy. By twelve thirty he was running over an hour late. He hated to keep patients waiting, and so his bad humor of the morning had deepened.

To make matters worse one of his younger patients had a serious allergic reaction to one of the chemo drugs. Easy to recognize and treat, but by the time he'd calmed down the patient and her husband he'd lost another forty minutes out of a really shitty day.

At one thirty he finally heaved a sigh of relief, *finished at last*. Now he had to rush over to his office, grab his notes and make it to his one o'clock lecture. He had already called to warn the students that he was running real late.

"David, what about Winnie Brown? Did you forget her?" asked Beth, newly returned from lunch.

No such break for David today.

"Today's her last chemo, we've got a cake for her."

This was a tradition in the clinic. When a patient finished their final course of chemo the nurses always got them a cake. No matter that the last thing most of them wanted after chemotherapy was to eat cake! Cake and a group photograph, that was the tradition.

"Oh shit!" said David. "I forgot all about her. Where the hell is she?"

"Treatment room one, Doctor" said Beth frostily. *"He really is in a piss poor mood today,"* she thought.

"I've set up the I.V. in her port, normal saline. It's running fine with good blood return. She's had all her premeds. Her labs are fine. All the chemo's in there, I.V. and Omaya. Same doses as last time. If you need some help, Laurie will be back from lunch in fifteen minutes."

"No, no I can't wait. I'll do it myself," muttered David.

He grabbed her medical chart and headed for the room.

"Hi, Winnie," said David as he knocked and entered, "I'm really sorry to keep you waiting so long. It's been a bad Monday morning. How are you doing, big day today, huh?"

Winnie was already lying on the treatment table. She smiled brightly. She was always happy to see Doctor Stern.

"That's O.K. Doctor. I feel fine, I'll be glad when this over, though."

"Sure," said David. "Listen I'm kind of short of time today. We've done this before, so you know the routine. I'm just going to go ahead and get started. You've already had your pre-meds."

These were medications to relax Winnie and reduce the nausea and vomiting which would otherwise overwhelm her after the chemotherapy.

Winnie's treatment had always included both chemotherapy given by mouth and into her veins, and injected directly into the fluid around the brain. At the start of her chemotherapy in August, Winnie had a device called an Omaya reservoir placed by a surgeon in the skull bone. The Omaya was a small plastic tube that led directly into the ventricle of the brain, allowing easy injection of chemotherapy into the brain fluid.

For the past five months, Winnie had received chemotherapy every three weeks in the International Oncology clinic. First the injection into the Omaya, then through the Portacath in her chest wall, right into one of the major veins.

Winnie would usually rest up for a few hours after the chemo injections and then go home.

David quickly scanned her chart. Her vital signs, which included temperature, pulse and blood pressure were all normal. Her lab tests were also fine.

"Everything looks fine," he said, slipping on a pair of sterile gloves. "So I'm going to give you the Omaya stuff first, and then the I.V. chemo through your Port, okay?"

Winnie nodded, "Fine." She felt very confident with her doctor.

David had done this hundreds of times before. He deftly swabbed the scalp with iodine then alcohol, and inserted the needle. He felt the slight resistance as the needle entered the Omaya.

"O.K. Winnie, here goes. Tell me if you feel anything unusual".

There were four different chemo drugs in front of David on the stainless steel treatment table., each one clearly labeled by the pharmacy. ARA-C for the Omaya, and Adriamycin, Vincristine and Cytoxan for the Portacath.

Adriamycin was easily identified by its bright red color. Cytoxan was drawn up in a small I.V. bag. The other two were clear liquids in 10 ml. syringes.

David withdrew a small sample of brain fluid from the Omaya and placed it in a tube for the lab. It would be tested for protein and sugar content, and the presence of lymphoma cells. David was confident that the results would be fine. Since the third treatment all of Winnie's tests had shown her to be cancer free, in complete remission, heading towards cure.

He picked up the syringe with the ARA-C, connected it to the Omaya line and smoothly injected the drug.

Chap 5

Later, when he went over the whole day in his mind, David admitted to himself that he felt just a moment's doubt as he started the injection. He didn't remember what distracted him and allowed him to continue.

Was he still thinking of his argument with Andi or the ass-hole cop Maloney? Was he rushing to finish to get to his students?

Whatever the reason, David committed an error. A fatal error.

As David finished injecting the drug into the Omaya, Winnie let out a shriek. "My head!"

She never spoke again.

"Shit!" said David. He looked at the syringe still in his hand, "Vincristine! Oh my....."

He had injected 2 milligrams of Vincristine directly into the cerebro-spinal fluid, right into the lateral ventricle of Winnie Brown's brain.

Things happened fast.

Winnie grunted as her limbs went totally rigid. She lost consciousness and started twitching violently. As the deadly poison attacked her delicate brain cells she had one seizure after another. She became deeply cyanotic, a sign that her blood oxygen level was critically low.

David frantically hit the emergency button on the wall. Within seconds the nurse responded.

"Can I help you doctor?" the intercom squawked.

"Call a code blue" yelled David.

Within a few minutes the room was crowded with medical and nursing personnel. Anesthesia quickly inserted a breathing tube to preserve Winnie's airway. With pure oxygen entering her lungs her color quickly improved. Despite I.V. Valium her body was wracked by massive seizures, her tongue torn and bleeding.

"I'm going to paralyze her now" said Bill Rollyson, the Anesthesia chief resident, "we've got to stop these seizures, OK?"

David nodded numbly. He stood to one side as the resuscitation team smoothly took over. This is what they did best.

All he could say was "I killed her, I killed her" over and over again.

Beth Caprio took him by the shoulder.

"Come on David, let's get out of here. Leave it to the team."

She escorted him from the treatment room. They were followed by curious stares from many of those present.

Within twenty minutes, Winnie was stable enough to be moved to the ICU. She lay on the cart deeply unconscious, surrounded by doctors and nurses. Oxygen was being pumped into her lungs, her blood pressure maintained by I.V. drugs. Her EKG monitor showed an erratic heart rhythm. She was completely paralyzed to prevent any more seizures. Ominously her pupils were dilated and fixed.

She was brain dead.

While all of this was going on, David sat in Beth's office, his head in his hands.

"I killed her Beth," he kept saying, "I killed her. How could I have been so stupid." He shuddered, "Vincristine....can you believe I did that... straight into the brain. No way anyone can survive that. Poor Winnie."

Beth just sat and listened as David shook his head.

"I had the ARA-C there. I just picked up the wrong stuff."

They sat there for about fifteen minutes.

"I should really go and see what's going on," said David.

Just then the door of Beth's office opened and Phil O'Rourke, the head of hospital security came in. O'Rourke was a thirty year veteran of the Chicago Police department. He was a big man, six four and two hundred fifty pounds, most of it still hard muscle despite his sixty years. He had an Irish face and a full head of snow-white hair. He smiled easily and often, but his blue eyes were serious now.

"Tell me what happened, Doctor" he said.

David told him the whole story. O'Rourke listened without interruption, his face expressionless. When David finished, O'Rourke asked just one question.

"What are her chances?"

David shook his head, "Vincristine is fatal one hundred percent of the time when it's injected into the brain or spinal fluid."

O'Rourke nodded. "O.K. Go home Doctor. Take the day off. Don't talk to anybody about this."

He turned to Beth, "The treatment room is sealed, no-one goes in there until you get the word from me, understand? I don't want to hear that any of your staff have been talking about this, O.K.?"

Beth nodded. *"Fat chance of that,"* she thought.

Without another word O'Rourke left the room.

"I've got to talk to Winnie's family," said David to Beth after O'Rourke had left the room.

"David, I don't think that's a good idea," said Beth. "Why don't you go home?"

He shook his head," I did this, I have to tell Robert," he insisted, "I'm going to the I.C.U."

David left the room and headed for the elevators. All of the intensive care units, medical, surgical and neurosurgical, were located on the fifth floor. As soon as David got out of the elevator there, he saw a group of people standing at the I.C.U. reception desk. Anne Harvey, the I.C.U. supervisor was listening intently to Gerald Piper, the Director of the hospital. Piper was flanked by Joanne La Rue, the head of Risk Management, O'Rourke and several other security people.

The group turned as David approached.

Piper spoke first. "Dr. Stern, you have been advised to leave the hospital and go home," he said.

"I have to see my patient and talk to her family," replied David.

Piper shook his head in disagreement. "I assume, Doctor that you are referring to Ms. Brown," he said. "She is currently not your patient. She has been admitted to Dr. Keating's service. He is the Attending Physician of record for this admission."

Stuart Keating was the head of the Oncology department.

"But I've looked after her for the past six months," said David.

Piper shook his head. He was adamant.

"I understand, Doctor," he said firmly, "but until you feel better it is more appropriate for Dr. Keating to look after her."

There was no way that David Stern was going into the I.C.U..

O'Rourke turned to one of the security guards, "Joe, please help Dr. Stern get a cab home."

David allowed himself to be guided back to the elevators and out of the hospital.

He never saw Winnie Brown again.

Chap 6

David barely slept Monday night. The image of his patient's vicious seizures would not leave him. He called the I.C.U. at three in the morning. No change in Winnie's condition, still on the ventilator with pupils fixed and dilated. No response to even painful stimuli. Brain dead.

He tried to explain to Andi what he had done. "I killed her, Andi. It's as simple as that."

David sat on the couch with his head in his hands. "That poor woman," he shuddered, "if you had heard her scream."

Andi tried to comfort him, "Maybe it's not as bad as you think, David. Maybe she'll be O.K.."

David shook his head. "No way. Her brain's gone. When they take her off the ventilator, she's dead. I can't even be there for her. They won't let me into the I.C.U."

Andi put an arm around him. "Come on David, you're a great doctor. Everyone says so. You couldn't have injected the wrong medicine."

He shook his head violently. "That's exactly what I did, Andi."

The telephone rang at seven on Tuesday morning. It was O'Rourke from the hospital.

"Dr. Stern, I have a message from Mr. Piper. He wants you to take the week off. Medical leave. You are not to come to the hospital or contact any of your patients, do you understand?"

David didn't respond as O'Rourke continued, "If you need anything from your office for research or writing, please contact my office."

David said, "O.K." He was too numb to say any more.

O'Rourke continued," And Doctor, no contact with Winnie Brown or her family. Dr. Keating is the Attending. He'll take care of the patient."

David listened in silence.

"Do you understand, Dr. Stern?"

O'Rourke was polite but the message was clear. For the moment at least International didn't want David Stern around.

At five o'clock that afternoon David got the news he had dreaded. One of the I.C.U. nurses who had worked in Oncology for years telephoned.

"Dr. Stern it's Chrissie Walker from Neuro I.C.U. I wanted to let you know that your patient Winnie Brown just expired. She was brain dead, and we took her off the ventilator ten minutes ago."

David sighed heavily, but said nothing.

Chrissie went on, "We were told not to talk to you, but I know how much you cared about your patients when I worked with you on Oncology. Take care, I hope you feel O.K."

"Thanks Chrissie," said David quietly. He was close to tears.

He walked slowly into the living room. The view over the frozen lake was stunning but David saw nothing. All he could see was Winnie's face.

The week dragged slowly by. For all of his adult life David had been ruled by the clock. He always had somewhere to be, people to see and things to do. He never had enough time. Now time lay heavily on his hands. He sat around his apartment for hours. He was too upset to concentrate on anything, to read or write. His stomach rebelled at the thought of food. David had never been a drinker but for three days vodka was the only thing that numbed his pain.

Andi couldn't get through to him. Finally on Friday evening she couldn't control herself any more.

"David you have to pull yourself together," she said. "Whatever happened, it's over. You've got your whole life ahead of you."

David didn't answer. He had been drinking heavily all day. He hadn't eaten, bathed or shaved for three days. He lay on the couch, staring at the ceiling. Suddenly he pulled himself off the couch and went to the door.

"Where are you going?" Andi asked.

"Winnie Brown's visitation is tonight," mumbled David, "I'm going."

Chap 7

The cab dropped him off in East Rogers Park. The McMillan Funeral Home on Howard Street was close to Winnie's home in Evanston. David hesitated for a moment, then pushed open the door and went in. The foyer was dimly lit. David was unaware of low organ music in the background.

"Can I help you?"

There stood an older black man, impeccably dressed in dark suit, white shirt and dark blue tie. His black wing tips gleamed. He wore a discreet name badge that read *Rev. John Roosevelt.*

"I'm looking for the Brown party," mumbled David.

Roosevelt looked at David curiously. "That would be room one, straight ahead."

The room was full. Robert Brown sat with Winnie's mother and the twins, surrounded by friends and family. Winnie lay in an open white casket, lined with satin. In her hands she held a single red rose. She was dressed in a plain white dress. She appeared to be sleeping.

David approached Robert.

"Mister Brown," he said, tears streaming down his face, "I'm so sorry for your loss."

Robert looked at him without expression.

David felt that he had to say something else. "This was all my fault. I'll do anything I can to put this right."

Robert looked puzzled. "What do you mean, your fault?" he said, "the hospital told me that Winnie died of seizures. I thought you were out sick."

David shook his head. "No, no. I was there," he said.

He grasped Robert's hand. "I screwed up. I injected the wrong drug."

Robert said nothing, but looked shocked. There was a low murmur throughout the room.

"He's drunk," someone said.

"Throw him out," said another, "he's got no right to be here, disrespecting Winnie."

David felt a firm hand on his elbow, as he was quickly led from the room. It was the man who had greeted him at the door.

A quiet voice spoke in his ear, "Doctor, I don't know what you're trying to do here, but you should leave right now."

David found himself standing on the sidewalk. The Brown family was now grieving *and* confused. David's attempt to apologize had failed miserably.

Chap 8

The weekend dragged by. Friday night's experience had made David feel even worse. Seeing Winnie Brown's body surrounded by her loved ones, especially the twins, had made him feel even more guilty than before. He lay in bed all weekend. He refused to talk to Andi, hardly ate a thing. Several friends called on the telephone. He would not speak with them. He drank steadily throughout the weekend.

Finally by Sunday evening, Andi could take no more.

"David, You've got to snap out of this," she said.

He didn't answer, but lay on the couch in the living room, staring into space.

She came out of the bedroom holding an overnight bag.

"David I'm going to stay with Toni," she said, "I've tried to help but you won't let me."

She walked to the door and turned to face him, "Call me when you're ready to talk."

The door slammed behind her. Now David was truly alone. David thought it couldn't get any worse, but he was wrong.

At seven thirty on Monday morning David answered the phone. It was O'Rourke.

"Good morning, Dr. Stern. Mr. Piper would like you to come to his office at eleven this morning to discuss the Winnie Brown case."

At nine o'clock David dragged himself out of bed. It was now a week since the fatal injection. During that time he had hardly slept. He showered and shaved. As he looked at himself in his bathroom mirror he was shocked by his appearance. He had lost eleven pounds. David was never heavy, now he looked almost skeletal. He had dark circles under his eyes, which were bloodshot.

"Jesus, I really look like shit," he thought, *"Andi's right, I've got to snap out of this."*

As he drove downtown David thought about the upcoming meeting. He was hopeful that the meeting would offer him a solution.

"Maybe when I explain to Piper exactly what happened, International will agree to pay compensation to the Browns," he thought.

It didn't take long for David to realize that wasn't going to happen. When he entered Piper's office promptly at eleven, the middle-aged hospital director was not alone. Sitting around the heavy oak conference table in the large office were several people.

O'Rourke was there, together with Keating the head of Oncology. David also recognized Cheryl Rubin the head of the Department of Psychiatry. Also seated at the table were Frank Crandall, the head of Pathology and another man who he did not recognize.

"Ah, Doctor Stern, please come in," said Piper. "We're just getting started. I think you know everyone here, except for Herb."

Piper gestured to the seat, next to him. "Come and take a seat. Help yourself to coffee and a sweet roll, if you want."

David said "Good morning" to all of his colleagues, and shook hands with the visitor who Piper introduced as Herb Walton.

Walton was about sixty years old, stood five eight and weighed just over two hundred pounds. He was impeccably dressed in a dark blue double-breasted Armani suit whose tailoring hid his bulk. White shirt with a heavily starched collar, French cuffs held in place by heavy gold cuff links, a yellow power tie and a gold Rolex completed the look.

"Mister Walton is Special Counsel to International," explained Piper. "He wanted to review with us the circumstances surrounding the tragic death of Ms. Brown."

"Nice to meet you, Doctor" said Herb.

Herb Walton was a major player. Despite his title of Special Counsel, he was not a corporate lawyer. He was in fact one of the top medical malpractice attorneys in the country. He specialized in defending hospitals and physicians, and over the past twenty years had one of the best batting averages in the US in defense cases. He was consulted by many of the major hospitals and insurance companies, and was on a permanent retainer with Frank Houston the CEO of International.

Despite his urbane manners and smooth talking, he was a street fighter. David would soon find out how tough he was.

Piper started the meeting.

"Dr. Keating, you were the patient's attending physician during her terminal admission, why don't you summarize for us the events leading up to her death?"

David listened in silence as Keating described how Winnie was brought to the I.C.U. unresponsive and paralyzed.

"We had to keep her paralyzed to prevent more seizures," explained Keating.

He then described the decision making process that led to her being taken off the ventilator.

"We knew that her seizures were due to lymphoma in her central nervous system."

David shook his head in disagreement and was about to speak, but Piper interrupted him.

"Doctor Stern," said Piper, "let's hold off with any discussion until we've heard the full report."

Keating continued smoothly, "She was clinically brain dead, according to the Harvard criteria, and when we informed the husband that her chances of recovery were zero, it was agreed to discontinue life support. She died soon after we took her off the ventilator."

"Thank you Doctor Keating," said Piper. "Doctor Crandall, you performed the autopsy. Could you please summarize for us your findings."

"Certainly, Mr. Piper."

Crandall was an arrogant son of a bitch. He was born and raised in Cleveland. International had hired him from Mass General Hospital in Boston, and he never failed to remind everyone of his Harvard background. A spell at the Hammersmith Hospital in London had left him with an affected British accent.

Crandall referred to his notes.

"I conducted the autopsy approximately six hours after the patient expired. The only evidence of lymphoma that I could find was in the central nervous system. There was extensive leptomeningeal involvement with lymphoma. That means in the tissues around the brain," he explained.

"There were also multiple small deposits of lymphoma cells throughout the brain tissue itself, in a distribution very typical of large cell lymphoma. There was also extensive necrosis of brain tissue due to anoxic damage from her uncontrolled seizures."

Crandall looked around the table. "In lay terms she had extensive lymphoma in her brain which caused multiple seizures. She suffered severe brain damage and died."

David stood up. "Wait a minute" he said, "that's impossible. That can't be true."

Piper interrupted him, "Doctor Stern, please sit down. You'll have a chance to speak soon enough. First let's hear from Mr. O'Rourke."

The head of security looked directly at David, as he spoke.

"As you all know, whenever there is a cardiac arrest or code called in the hospital, Security responds as part of the code team. When my people got to the Lymphoma Clinic, responding to the code they observed Doctor Stern acting in a distressed manner. So they paged me."

O'Rourke continued calmly, "Because Dr. Stern claimed that he had injected the wrong drug, I had the treatment room sealed as soon as the patient was transferred from there to the I.C.U.."

David nodded. This was what he remembered from the nightmare.

O'Rourke continued, "We subsequently had the uninjected chemotherapy drugs and the spinal fluid sample tested."

He turned to David, "I've got good news Doctor. You did nothing wrong. The pharmacy confirmed that it was the ARA-C that you correctly injected into the Omaya, not the Vincristine. The Vincristine was still there, with the Cytoxan and Adriamycin. They were never injected."

"If I may interrupt for one second," said Crandall smoothly, "In my report I should have mentioned that we did test the fluid that Doctor Stern removed from the Omaya before injecting the ARA-C, and that fluid was full of lymphoma cells."

He turned to David, "I'll be happy to let you see the slides any time."

David felt the room spinning.

"Can this be true?" he thought.

All eyes in the room were fixed on David.

"Do you want to say something Doctor Stern?" asked Piper.

David stood up. He looked around the table.

"Listen," he said, "I was there. I know what I did. I know what I saw. I saw Winnie Brown nearly every week for almost six months. I took brain fluid from her every three weeks. She had CAT scans, MRIs, the works. I know she was cancer free, and I know what I did that day."

In frustration he struck the table. "I don't know what shit you're all trying to pull here, but I know what happened. I injected Vincristine into the Omaya. I killed her."

There was silence in the room.

Chap 9

Herb Walton stood up and buttoned his coat, as if he were ready to address a jury. He turned to David, his face sympathetic.

"Doctor Stern," he said, "please listen to me carefully. I understand that you are upset by the death of your patient."

He shook his head. "A young woman cut down by a dreadful disease, very sad. I can certainly understand why you may feel guilty about her death. You wanted to save her life and failed. Only another doctor could really understand your feelings."

He paused, frowning. "However, feelings are not important here. I am an attorney and I have to make you understand the potential seriousness of the situation for International and for you personally."

He struck a serious pose. "If you continue to claim that your patient died because of an error on your part, then you will cause grave legal problems for your employer and for yourself."

David started to reply, but Herb waved him silent.

"Hear me out. If the Brown family gets wind of what you claim happened, then they will sue you, and they will sue International. I have no doubt that they would lose the case, but the publicity would be very unwelcome, especially at a time when we are working hard to establish International as the center of excellence for cancer care in Chicago."

All heads around the table nodded in agreement as Walton continued.

"You have all heard today that the facts in the case do not support the idea of an accidental injection. This poor woman died of lymphoma."

More nodding of heads.

Piper interrupted, "David, we all feel for you, but you have to look at your current situation. There is no evidence to support an allegation of wrongdoing on your part. The autopsy results certainly vindicate you. Mr. O'Rourke has told us all that a careful investigation by International showed no evidence of error on your part."

He continued, "You have many colleagues who are on your side. International is on your side. I understand that things happened very suddenly in the clinic, and you are probably confused as to what exactly happened."

Herb nodded his agreement and picked up again.

"I understand that Ms. Brown was cremated on Saturday."

David looked shocked, as Walton continued smoothly.

"The death certificate has been signed. Cause of death is uncontrolled seizures due to cerebral lymphoma. Let that be the end of an unfortunate episode, and we'll all move on."

There was silence. Everyone looked expectantly at David. He looked around the room.

"Please listen to me," he pleaded, "I know what I did. I injected Vincristine into her brain. I killed her."

He turned to Keating, "Stuart, please explain to them what that means. No-none survives that."

Keating did not reply, he simply stared straight ahead stone-faced.

David turned to Walton, "Maybe I am naive. I'm not a lawyer, but isn't there some way that International can do something for the Brown family."

Walton shook his head, "Doctor, you don't understand how these things work. How much do you think this Brown guy earns? He's a truck driver. So fifty, maybe fifty five thousand a year. We're a multibillion-dollar company. Get that in front of an all black jury at Daley Center, and what do you think will happen?"

Walton continued, "An unscrupulous plaintiff's attorney would have a field day with you if you continue to make intemperate remarks."

David started to speak but Walton brushed him aside. "Now listen to me Doctor, It's time for a reality check. Time for you to realize that you're not a boy scout any more. You are International's employee. If you know what's good for you, you will do and say exactly what you are told."

David shook his head, and Walton's tone hardened.

"I don't give a shit what you feel, Doctor. You work for International. I am telling you that the International position is that this woman died of cerebral lymphoma. Do you understand? That is the official line and you damn well better toe that line. If you have a problem with it, now is the time to tell me."

There was a long uncomfortable silence. David looked straight at Walton.

"That's just not true, Mr. Walton."

Walton sighed, "You just don't get it, do you?"

The smooth facade was gone now. "Listen you little prick, who the fuck cares what the truth is? Understand this, I don't want to hear you tell me what happened. I am telling you what happened. If you ever want to work in this city, if you ever want to work in this *country* again, you'd better get this right."

His face was now red with anger as Walton continued, "You can do whatever it takes you to feel good about yourself. Go light a bunch of candles, wear a fucking hair shirt. I don't give a shit. But the word from here to everybody is, this woman died of lymphoma. If I hear one word from you that contradicts that I will personally ruin you. I guarantee it."

"Well it's too late," mumbled David.

"What do you mean?" said Walton.

David explained, "I saw Robert Brown Friday night at the visitation, and told him what happened."

"You stupid asshole!" exclaimed Walton, "What exactly did you say?"

David told him. Walton listened in silence, his face grim.

"O.K. you were drunk, when you said it, no harm as long as you continue to deny it now."

David shook his head, "I can't. I won't do that."

Walton shook his head in amazement, "You just won't listen, will you. You're all the same, you medical fuck-ups, you all think you're so much smarter than everyone else."

He slammed his fist on the table. "International will never admit you did anything wrong. If you keep running off at the mouth and the Browns sue, you'll have to find your own lawyer. Legal fees will easily cost you a quarter of a million dollars. That's your expense, not International's."

Walton was really incensed now. "As soon as we fire you, and *we will fire you*, you will be totally on your own. Who the hell is going to hire you after this?"

Walton opened his mouth to speak again, but Piper interrupted..

"I think, Herb that we've taken this as far as we can for the moment. Dr. Stern is still on medical leave. Let's agree that there is no more that we can do just now. Let's plan to meet again next Monday, same time."

To David he added, "Continue to rest up at home, Dr. Stern. No work for now."

Piper stood to signal the end of the meeting, and looked around the table. "Thank you all for coming. Let's not discuss this issue outside of this room."

No one met David's eye as they left the room.

Chap 10

In the hallway David felt pressure on his arm. It was Cheryl Rubin, the head of Psychiatry.

"David, can you give me a few minutes of your time?" she asked.

He nodded, "Sure, Cheryl. When do you want to get together?"

She smiled, "How about right now?"

David nodded. Together they took the elevator to Cheryl's tenth floor office.

David really did not know Cheryl Rubin well. She was an expert in Alzheimer's disease which had no relevance to Oncology, so their paths did not cross often. They knew each other well enough to say *"Hi"* in the hallway, but no more than that. David was unsure what Cheryl wanted to talk about.

Her office was large, decorated in soft pastels.

"Great for tormented souls," thought David darkly.

They settled in comfortable armchairs.

"It's like this, David," said Cheryl. "I need some help in writing a grant for Pysch. Oncology. It's a study to help people cope with the grieving process."

"Well, that's certainly topical," thought David sourly.

"You know that's really not my area of expertise at all," he said.

Cheryl appeared anxious. "But I really need some input from Oncology," she said.

David thought for a minute. "Why not speak to the Hospice folks? They would be the logical choice."

Cheryl clutched David's arm. "Problem is I'm really up against time constraints. I would appreciate some help this week."

David shrugged, "O.K. It may help get my mind off this other business. I can't do anything else right now anyway. They don't want me seeing patients."

"Great," said Cheryl.

She quickly retrieved her appointment calendar from her desk, and penciled David in for ten till eleven Tuesday through Friday of that week.

"Thanks, David. I really appreciate your help."

As they walked out of the room, Cheryl stopped in front of her secretary's desk. She laid her hand on David's arm.

"Please, please call me at any time, if you need to. Remember, David you're not alone. I'm here to help you."

Cheryl's secretary gave David a curious look. David walked out, confused.

"What was that all about?"

Chap 11

The week dragged slowly by. David was alone and deeply depressed. He heard nothing from Andi. He had not been close with his parents for years, and he ignored the phone calls from his friends. He did not go to his office.

His only contact was with Cheryl Rubin. He dragged himself out of bed each day to go to the hospital for his ten o'clock appointments with Cheryl. His meetings with the psychiatrist were strange. They really did not do very much. By the end of the week, although they had spent nearly five hours together the grant proposal remained unwritten. Despite their apparent lack of progress, Cheryl insisted that they continue to meet.

"I feel we're really making progress, David," she said grasping his hand as she escorted him to her outside office.

Her secretary rolled her eyes at this exchange, very unusual for their boss, who was not the touchy feely type.

If David had not been so traumatized by Winnie's death he might have questioned Cheryl more closely regarding their strange meetings. However he was so apathetic that he just went along with the arrangement. He did not know what Cheryl's agenda was, and frankly he really didn't care. He was barely hanging on.

When he went to the hospital to meet with Cheryl, he hardly acknowledged the greetings of others in the hallway. He looked like a ghost. People were shocked by his appearance, and were embarrassed by the suffering that was so obvious in his face.

The second meeting with Piper and Walton was no better than the first. David was again the last to arrive. The same cast attended as the previous week.

The atmosphere was strained from the outset. Piper ran the show.

"Doctor Stern," he began, "Have you given any thought to our discussions of last week?"

"Have I thought of anything else?" wondered David.

Piper spoke formally. "International needs an assurance from you that there will be no more statements from you that you caused the death of this young woman. Can you give us such an assurance?"

David shook his head. Walton snorted in disgust.

Piper continued. "In that case, I have to inform you that your contract with International is suspended, effective immediately."

Piper read from typed notes. David's response had obviously been anticipated.

"The grounds for your suspension are your mental health. It is clear that the evidence in the Brown case clearly establishes the cause of death as cerebral lymphoma. Without intruding on patient doctor confidentiality, we have evidence that you are suffering from delusions regarding your responsibility for the death of your patient."

David remained silent although he was puzzled. *"What evidence?"* Walton took over.

"International has a responsibility to its patients and shareholders to remove any physician whose physical or mental health prevents them from providing adequate medical care to our patients. Our commitment to patient safety mandates this," he said sanctimoniously.

Piper again, "This is all spelled out in the medical staff documents that you signed when you were hired, Doctor. Suspension becomes permanent termination if you are not reinstated within twelve calendar months."

"Doctor Stern, your office has been emptied and its contents will be delivered to your home at seven thirty this evening. Please give Mr. O'Rourke your hospital ID, office keys and parking card. All of your patients have been re-assigned to other physicians."

Piper was all business.

"Your contract provides for disability pay at full salary for twelve months. Your health insurance will also continue for twelve months. Your retirement fund will continue to accrue interest, but International will make no further contributions to it. You may submit evidence of clinical recovery to International at any time. However, the decision to rescind the suspension is at the sole discretion of International."

"Do you have any questions, Doctor?"

David shook his head silently. He stood up to leave the room.

Walton had one parting shot.

"Oh by the way Dr. Stern, International will be sending a report of these proceedings to the department of Professional Regulation of the State of Illinois."

He smirked, "We do need to ensure that patients are protected from mentally unbalanced physicians."

As David left the room, escorted by O'Rourke, he passed Cheryl Rubin's chair. Now he understood the purpose of their meetings of the past week.

"Good luck with the grant, Cheryl" he said.

Cheryl Rubin blushed. She did not meet his eyes.

Chap 12

As David left the room, Herb Walton slowly shook his head. "Stupid little prick just committed professional suicide."

He fixed everyone in the room with a baleful look. "I want you all to listen carefully to me. Listen as if your professional lives depend on it. Because, believe me, they do."

He struck the table. "That little shit will never work in any hospital again in this country."

"He doesn't know who he's dealing with here. I'm going to destroy him. But we've got do more than that. Because if Robert Brown gets wind of what Stern is saying, he'll find himself some blood-sucking lawyer quicker than you can shit."

"So we are going to do several things," he mused. "First I'm going to try to get this stopped before it goes any further."

He thought for a moment, and a sly grin crossed his face. "And I know just how to do that."

"Second, we must totally discredit Stern, so that even if Robert Brown does go ahead with a lawsuit, there's no way he'll win. That's why we've got to discredit Stern. So that no jury will believe him if he claims to have injected the wrong stuff."

He turned to Cheryl Rubin. "You did a good job getting him in your office every day last week."

Cheryl blushed with pleasure at his praise.

"Write up some notes for those visits that make him sound as crazy as a loon. I don't care what you say."

She nodded eagerly, "How about alcoholism. Could we use that visit to the funeral home when he was drunk, and build a story round that?"

Walton thought briefly then shook his head. "No. With alcohol there's usually a trail, D.U.I.s or something like that. He hasn't got a police record. I've already checked."

Keating said quietly, "How about porn, something really sleazy like violent porn or kiddie porn?"

He explained to the others, "Remember, we've got his office computer. We can put whatever we want in there."

Walton nodded vigorously. "I like it. I have a computer guy who could fix it so it would look like Stern's been visiting kiddie porn websites for years."

Piper shook his head, "People wouldn't believe it. We've got really tough filters here. Everyone knows you can't get into porn websites from any medical center computer."

Walton was disappointed. "O.K. maybe not porn, but I want you to be creative like this. Keep thinking."

Keating, the head of Oncology looked thoughtful. "How about drugs? We could have one of the Chemical Dependency docs produce a file showing that he's been using cocaine or something like that."

Walton sneered. "Right. And International knew it, but let him keep treating patients? Don't be ridiculous, that wouldn't help us one bit."

Keating flushed at this.

"Come on," said Walton, "you're all meant to be such brilliant doctors . Can't you do better than that?"

They all sat quietly for a minute or two, thinking hard.

Walton asked, "What about his family. Is he married?"

Keating shook his head. "He's got a live-in girl-friend. She came to our Departmental party with him at Christmas."

Walton nodded, "O.K."

To Cheryl Rubin he said, "Why don't you get in touch with her. Tell her you're worried about him. Can you meet her and talk. See if you can get any dirt we can use."

Cheryl nodded eagerly, "Fine."

Walton was leading them into battle. And their enemy was David Stern.

Chap 13

That evening David hit rock bottom. His career was over. He was alone in the world. Worst of all he still felt tremendous guilt for Winnie's death.

He lay on his couch, drinking neat vodka. He yearned for oblivion, but even the vodka didn't help. David saw no way out. He knew that he could never practice medicine again. His life was over. He had always been positive and optimistic by nature, but that was all in the past.

"What's the point?" he asked himself. *"I might as well be dead."*

Never in his life had he ever thought of suicide, but now he lay in the darkening room thinking how he could end his life. His thoughts were interrupted by the doorbell ringing.

"Andi?" he thought rising to his feet.

When he opened the door, it was not Andi. An old man stood there, wearing the unmistakable garb of a Chassidic Jew, long black coat and black hat. The face was familiar to David. The visitor smiled at David.

"Good evening Dr. Stern." The voice was warm and deep.

"Yes," said David, "can I help you?"

Although David was Jewish he had spent very little time in a synagogue and even less time around orthodox Jews. Like most modern Jews he felt uncomfortable in the presence of those who proclaimed their religion so openly.

"May I come in for a few minutes?" asked the man politely.

David hesitated for a moment.

Sensing this his visitor smiled, "I'll only take a few minutes of your time."

"O.K. then," said David stepping aside and opening the door wide.

He felt more uncomfortable when his visitor entered the living room. Nearly two weeks of trash littered the room.

"I'm sorry for the mess," said David in a low voice as he swept newspapers off the couch, "I've been sick."

"Don't give it another thought," said his visitor. "I apologize for coming round unannounced but I have telephoned you several times and was unable to get through."

He continued, "You clearly don't remember me, but then you see so many faces in a year. My name is Sholom Shuster. You treated my dear wife Rivka, you knew her as Rebecca, five years ago. You were very kind to us all."

David suddenly remembered the face.

"Of course I remember now, Rabbi Shuster. Your wife was a lovely woman. She had colon cancer into the liver, right?"

Rabbi Shuster smiled gently, "You have a good memory Doctor."

"I also have a good memory, Doctor Stern." he continued, "You were very kind to us at a very difficult time. Our whole family thinks of you often with great affection."

These were the first kind words David had heard since Winnie's death. His eyes filled with tears.

"And that's why I'm here, "continued the rabbi quickly, "I have some contacts at the hospital, and I have heard of your recent difficulties. You have many admirers there who are distressed by these recent events."

"I hope you don't feel that I'm intruding, but I would like to help you in any way that I can. I have heard of your problems today with the hospital administration. I am sure that you are very distressed by the suspension."

David nodded. "Rabbi Shuster, I don't know what to do," he said.

"They've put enormous pressure on me to go along with a story that's just not true. The truth is that I'm responsible for that poor woman's death. I don't want to see my career go up in flames, but I couldn't live with myself if I let them sweep the whole affair under the rug."

David poured out the whole story. The rabbi listened in silence, his face grave.

"Well now I understand why the handsome young Doctor Stern looks like warmed over spaghetti!" he said with a smile when David had finished.

"Listen to me please, David," he said earnestly, "I'm not a doctor or a lawyer but I do know what Truth is. You are right to stick to the truth. It will be harder in the short term."

"It is already," thought David.

The rabbi continued, "But we all have a responsibility to speak and live the truth, and in the end it will be better for you, I have no doubt."

He leaned forward in his chair, his voice earnest.

"Also please remember, especially when things seem very bad, you are not alone. You have many friends who wish you only well. Speaking practically now, you need a lawyer."

He smiled briefly, "And I have a very good lawyer for you."

He handed David a business card with an address in the Loop and a downtown telephone number.

"Tomorrow please call this number. Go see Alex Goldberg. Alex is probably the best attorney in Chicago for you right now," he said with a smile.

The rabbi rose to leave, "Please call Alex tomorrow, and try to get some sleep."

The fact that he was not totally alone, that he had established human contact with someone who obviously respected and cared for him cheered David greatly. For the first time in three weeks he slept soundly.

Tomorrow he'd meet Alex Goldberg.

Chap 14

Three hundred North La Salle was an impressive forty-floor tower in the middle of the financial and legal district, close to the Daley Center. Its proximity to the Cook County Court in the Daley Center made it an ideal location for dozens of lawyers.

David felt the weight of anxiety sitting on his chest as he scanned the roster of names in the entrance hall. His only involvement with the legal profession up till now had been a couple of depositions regarding patients of his who had legal cases. The attorneys questioning him had been low key and respectful. The process had been kind of interesting and caused him no distress. He knew this time would be different.

How different he didn't yet understand.

Alex Goldberg's office was located in suite 2700. *Alex Goldberg Attorney at Law,* read the sign. David took the elevator to the twenty-seventh floor and entered the office.

The room was small, but light and airy. The waiting area contained four comfortable looking leather armchairs grouped around a coffee table. On the table were the expected copies of Time, Newsweek, Crain's Chicago Business and, surprisingly People magazine.

Instead of the usual receptionist's office behind a glass partition, there was instead a low rosewood desk, with matching chair. On the table there was an IBM computer and printer.

At the keyboard sat a young woman. She looked to David to be in her early thirties. She was dressed casually, in blue jeans and a Chicago Bulls tee shirt. No jewelry. Standing to her right was an older woman, about forty-five. She was about five foot four, weighing about 180 pounds, David guessed. Her blond hair was worn short. She was dressed in a dark blue suit of conservative style. Her only jewelry was a wedding ring and pearls.

Both women were studying the computer screen as David entered the office. The older of the two looked up at him and smiled a welcome.

"Good morning, ladies" said David. "My name is Dr. Stern. I have a ten o'clock appointment with Mr. Goldberg."

The older of the two grimaced. "Oh!" she said.

The younger woman looked up at David and smiled sweetly.

"Doctor Stern," she said in a voice that seemed to be dipped in saccharine, "I'll be happy to tell Mr. Goldberg that you're here. Why don't you hang your penis and testicles over there?"

She pointed to a coat hanger in the corner.

More saccharine, "I'm sure you're very tired from carrying that heavy stuff around all day long."

David stared at her. He would have been no more shocked by her response if she had punched him in the mouth.

"Alex!" said the older woman, "That's enough."

"Doctor Stern," she continued quickly, not giving her boss another second to speak, "I'm Cindy Bolton, I'm Ms.Goldberg's administrative assistant. Alex, please."

These last words were addressed in a pleading tone to the young woman who continued to smile innocently at David.

David would soon learn what that smile meant.

Alex ignored Cindy. "Excuse me Doctor," she asked politely, "isn't there some muscle that would help you close your lower jaw? I'm sure you know about things like that, you being a doctor and all."

Cindy tried to interrupt again. "Doctor Stern, I'm sorry about the confusion. Ms. Goldberg and I are almost finished here. Please take a seat for a few minutes."

Alex turned to Cindy. "Why are you apologizing Cindy? You're not the one who's confused. It's the *doctor* whose foot is up his ass."

Alex put heavy emphasis on the title.

David continued to stare at the two women, as he sat down heavily in the nearest chair. After a brief whispered conversation, during which Cindy appeared to be lecturing her boss, while casting several concerned looks at David, Alex retired into the inner office.

A moment later, David was escorted in by a visibly nervous Cindy. The heavy door closed behind Cindy, who left with a last warning look at Alex.

Alex and David looked at each other in silence. She regarded him coolly. He looked and felt uncomfortable.

The office they sat in was furnished in a similar style to the outer office. It contained a rosewood desk and credenza, the latter overflowing with papers. The highly polished wood floor was covered with a large oriental rug, in shades of orange and brown. The walls were pale, either cream or off-white. There were no plaques or diplomas on display. Alex apparently did not favor the vanity walls, which so many professionals seemed to find an essential part of office interior design. On the walls hung several prints that David recognized, including several Calders and a Miro. The drapes were drawn against the early morning sun.

Alex Goldberg was thirty-two years old. She was the only child of Morris and Leah Goldberg, whose brother, Rabbi Shuster had suggested this meeting. She was five nine inches tall and weighed one hundred and thirty five pounds. Her hair was jet black, heavy and straight. Alex wore it long, down to her shoulders. Her hair framed a face that was classic in its beauty. Her cheekbones were high, her lips full and sensuous. Her most striking feature were her blue eyes, which were intelligent and full of expression. Despite his predicament, David could not help noticing her full breasts which strained against her tee shirt.

Like her Orthodox brother, Leah Goldberg had valued education. She was an English teacher in a high school in Lincolnwood, in suburban Chicago for many years. She was thirty-eight years old, and she and her accountant husband had reconciled themselves to a childless marriage, when quite unexpectedly she became pregnant.

The result was Alex. The little girl was a precocious child. Her doting parents were often exhausted by her energy, but were charmed by her beauty and her obvious intelligence. They took her everywhere with them, and involved her in everything they did.

The combination of her parents' encouragement and Alex's own considerable intelligence and drive were unbeatable. After gathering top academic honors in high school, she went to Harvard, undergraduate and law school.

During her last year at Harvard law school two events occurred which would affect her entire professional life.

In October of that year her best friend Marsha Slater died of breast cancer at the age of 25. Alex and Marsha first met when they were three years old. They met in playgroup, and had been inseparable ever since. Theirs was that special kind of friendship where the chemistry was just right. No effort needed. Even when Alex went to college in Boston they spoke at least twice a week.

After Marsha died, Alex got hold of her medical records. It was really very simple. Three years before she died Marsha consulted her family doctor because of a small lump in her left breast.

Doctor Moscowitz had known Marsha since she was in first grade. He laughed when Marsha told him her concern.

"Marsha dear," he said, patting her hand, "twenty-two year old women don't get breast cancer. It's just a little fibro-cyst. It may get bigger for a while, but it'll go away. It's nothing to worry about."

He was wrong.

Marsha knew nothing of medicine, and didn't worry even when the lump doubled in size. Two years later when the cancer spread to her spine, and she became paralyzed from the waist down, Dr. Moscowitz and his wife had already moved to their retirement home in Arizona.

When she died Marsha weighed 85 pounds. Mercifully the morphine needed to control her pain made her quite unaware of her surroundings. Had she been awake, Marsha would have died knowing that Alex Goldberg did not leave her bedside for the last three days and nights of her life.

Marsha's parents were so broken by her death that they were not interested in pursuing a malpractice case. Alex was. She talked to a few of Marsha's doctors. Several were initially amused that a young law student was investigating their treatment of her friend. That amusement quickly evaporated under Alex's questioning.

From the earliest age Alex expected and received honest answers from her parents to her every question. She was therefore at first surprised, and then disgusted by the evasion and outright dishonesty which she encountered from the doctors she spoke with. Worst of all in her opinion were those doctors who were personally responsible for Marsha's welfare. They just did not share her outrage at what was clearly a grievous error in judgment.

Alex's review of Marsh Slater's medical history left her contemptuous of a profession which was so protective of its incompetent members, and so apparently uncaring of human suffering.

The second seminal event occurred six months after Marsha died.

An 81year old woman driving a fifteen-year old Buick struck Alex's parents as they were walking near their Lincolnwood home. They were killed instantly.

The police report documented the accident at 9.30 p.m. The pavement was dry and the streetlights were working fine. The driver was diabetic and had cataracts. Her glasses were 12 years old. Her vision was subsequently found to be 20/200. Her driver's license had been renewed one year previously, with a letter from her family doctor stating that she had no disability. He claimed to have examined her eyes. His records did not show this. The patient could not remember.

The State of Illinois censured the doctor. It didn't bring Alex's parents back. Other than her uncle and his family, and two second cousins in Phoenix Arizona, Alex was alone in the World. She was twenty six years old.

Her parents' death only reinforced Alex's contempt for the world of medicine. Her mind was made up. She would become a plaintiff's attorney, specializing in medical malpractice cases. She buried her grief in her work.

Graduating third in her class, she had the pick of virtually any law firm in the country. She chose a small firm of plaintiff attorneys in Chicago. Davis, Miller & Suskind had eight partners. Alex became the fourth associate in the firm. During the interview process she made it clear that salary and prospects for partnership were not important to her.

She had one request only and this was non-negotiable, she would be involved with medical cases only. There was one critical moment during her interview.

"Ms. Goldberg," asked Jim Davis the interviewing senior partner. "I am somewhat confused. You've made the conditions of your joining us clear. What I don't understand is the difference between a non-negotiable request and a demand. Please explain that to me."

Alex didn't miss a beat. The remarkable blue eyes looked straight at the courtly sixty year old who for many years had been the distinguished President of the Illinois Bar Association.

"Why Mr. Davis," said Alex with a straight face, "I would be happy to clarify this for you. In any negotiation *we* make non-negotiable requests. The other side makes demands."

Jim Davis nodded and smiled. She got what she asked for.

Jim took a special interest in his talented young acquisition. His special skill was as a trial lawyer. He taught her all he knew. She was an outstanding pupil. Her work ethic, meticulous preparation and attention to detail were outstanding. Alex's quick mind, ability to think on her feet, and the considerable presence that she exhibited at an early stage of her career quickly made her an excellent litigator.

After four years with Davis, Miller & Suskind, Alex established herself as one of the top medical malpractice attorneys in Chicago. It was time to move on. When she opened her own practice, she set the ground rules.

She would only take those cases where there was clear evidence of medical malpractice, with serious consequences to the patient. She would not take a case from any attorney who did not share her ethical standards. She was offered enough cases to keep half a dozen associates working full-time, but once she agreed to take a case, she would personally see the case through to the very end. She felt strongly that each and every client deserved her personal attention. For this reason she hired no other attorney. She wasn't interested in empire building.

This was the person who sat facing David Stern. Alex Goldberg looked like a model and cursed like a trucker. She was a brilliant lawyer, who was an implacable enemy of those doctors she considered incompetent and uncaring. Her passionate concern for their victims made her an abrasive attorney who regularly bruised the egos of people who got in her way.

Marsha Slater and her own parents were rarely out of her mind.

Chap 15

David was unaware of Alex's history. He knew nothing of Alex Goldberg as a person. He was very confused. His personal and professional life were in total disarray. His employers had fired him, and their lawyer was threatening him.

An older man, a distinguished rabbi had told him that Alex Goldberg would help him. He had come for help. Now he sat opposite an angry young woman who was looking at him with unconcealed contempt.

"Look," he said. "I'm very sorry. Rabbi Shuster never told me you were a woman."

She interrupted him. "Doctor...."

"Why does she make 'Doctor' sound like 'piece of shit'?" he wondered.

"Doctor," she said acidly, "in my work it's often useful to establish an advantage over an opponent early on. It's not usually as easy as you just made it."

This was said with no trace of a smile.

"Jesus," he thought, *"She's not joking. Why does she call me opponent? Isn't she meant to help me!"*

Maybe this old rabbi just didn't understand, or maybe he had only recommended her because he knew how desperate David was.

She interrupted his thoughts.

"Before we discuss why you are here, I want you to understand three things. First, I understand from Rabbi Shuster that you fucked up."

David winced.

"That can't be what the rabbi said," he thought, *"can it?"*

She continued to speak in a voice devoid of emotion.

"I understand that he feels a certain obligation to you, and as a favor to him I have agreed to listen to your story. However I am not, and will not act as your attorney. The rules of attorney client privilege therefore do not apply to this conversation."

She continued in the same hard flat voice. "You may be asked under oath about any conversation with a third party regarding the matter which we are about to discuss. Please understand, that if you do report this conversation, then I could be forced by subpoena to testify regarding the contents of our conversation. You may find it expedient to lie, and simply *'forget'* this meeting ever took place."

She smiled coldly, "In my experience doctors have no problem with selective memory lapses that suit their case. If I am called to testify under those circumstances, be assured I will not lie."

"I would like to record this conversation. When I have no further use for the tape and any notes that I may make, I will give them to you. I will retain no other permanent record of this conversation. Based on what you tell me, I may or may not be able to offer you some advice. I do not plan to bill you for my time. Do you understand all this?"

David nodded.

"Fine," she said, pulling out a tape recorder, legal pad and gold Mont Blanc from her desk.

"Why do I feel she'd like to stick that pen in my eye?" wondered David.

Alex looked at David coldly, "I want you tell me the entire story, from the first time you met your patient until today. Please leave nothing out. In my experience doctors usually omit details that are unflattering to them. Don't do that. My opinion of you will not be changed by what you tell me."

"I'll bet," thought David.

She switched on the tape recorder. David told her. He spoke without pause for over two hours. He left out nothing. She interrupted occasionally to ask a question or to clarify a detail. She wrote a few words on her legal pad. Most of the time however she simply listened, her eyes never leaving David's face.

Most of the questions she asked related to David's contract, the autopsy findings, and the meetings in Piper's office. She was particularly interested in what International's counsel, Herb Walton had said.

When David finished, he sat back, drained. She sat in silence for several minutes then shook her head.

"What a mess," she said.

For the first time since meeting her, David felt anger.

"Well, thank you for that insight, Ms. Goldberg," he said, "I do see things much more clearly now. Thank you for your time. I'll give the rabbi your regards."

He started to get out of the chair. Her only response was a slightly arched left eyebrow.

"Sit down Doctor," she said. "It is a mess," she mused, "but an interesting one from a legal perspective. Of course from one point of view it's a tragedy, young mother dead, and all. But you guys are used to that. The good news for you, Doctor, is that, in my opinion you are off the hook."

David looked puzzled.

"Look," she said, noticing his response. "It's like this. You screwed up by injecting the wrong drug. She died as a direct cause of your action. No question about that, but I couldn't prove it in a court of law."

"Why not?" asked David, "What's so complicated about it?"

She smiled cynically. "Let me play the defense game here for you," she said.

"What the hell are you talking about?" David raised his voice, "I killed a young woman, and you're talking about *games*?"

For the first time Alex's face showed confusion.

"Doctor, exactly what do you want out of all this?" she asked.

David thought for a few minutes, then spoke softly, "Winnie's dead, and I can't bring her back. I have to live with that. The only thing that I can do for her family is admit my guilt, and do everything that I can to make sure that the system compensates them."

"Even if it means professional ruin?"

David looked at her, "Yes."

She looked puzzled for a moment, then smiled cynically.

"Doctor, you wouldn't be bullshitting me, would you?"

For the second time, David started to get angry..

"Is it so hard for you to believe that a doctor can be ethical?" he asked angrily.

"In my experience," she said coolly, "ethical doctors are as rare as condoms in the Vatican."

"Actually probably rarer," she added with a thin smile.

"Look," she said, "Let me spell out your options very clearly for you. You have three options."

She ticked them off on the elegant fingers of one hand.

"Option number one, you can stand up and say 'I screwed up and killed her,' and hope that International says 'O.K. Doctor we admire your honesty. It's very refreshing in an age of cynicism. We are very happy to pay five or six million dollars to this nice family so you can feel better.'"

"The second option is for you is, in a sense to negotiate with International on behalf of the family. Say to them ' Look, I want you to pay compensation to the family. If you don't, I'll tell everyone what I did. The family will sue. You'll get a lot of bad publicity and you'll still have to pay them compensation.'"

"Option number three is very simple."

She shrugged, "Play ball with International. All you have to do is go along with the defense position that Herb Walton and

International have already decided on. You heard it at the meetings. You deny doing anything wrong. The patient simply died of uncontrolled seizures caused by lymphoma in her brain."

She looked intently at David, "If you testify that you committed no error, that you properly injected ARA-C, and not the Vincristine, well there's no way the family could prove malpractice. No plaintiff's attorney would touch it."

She shrugged, "Body's been cremated. All the evidence is gone."

David started to speak.

Alex lifted one finger. "Wait one minute," she said, "only you can decide what you want to do. But you have to understand the full implications of your decision. Remember you are not the major defendant here. You were acting as a full-time employee of International here. You were acting as their agent. If you are responsible for this woman's death, so is International, as your employer. Any attorney going after you will also go after International.'

She paused briefly, "That's a fifteen *billion* dollar company. Most of the plaintiff guys I know would have wet dreams just thinking about going after them."

She smiled thinly, "You have to understand, your little *mea culpa* could cost International millions, and give them a lot of lousy publicity. Do you think that they will still want to write your pay check every month after that?"

She smiled sardonically, "You know, you may not make employee of the month."

David started to respond but she held up a hand.

"Wait, there's more. If you and International are not together on this, they'll try to void your malpractice insurance. Now I'm not saying that they can do it. But if they can, then you could be personally responsible for every dollar awarded to the plaintiffs for your malpractice."

She pointed to his wrist. "That's a nice watch you're wearing, do you want to send it to the Browns now? Are you ready to sell your house and go back to live with your parents?"

David tried to interrupt but she stilled him again with a raised hand.

"Hear me out. You are really quite insignificant in all this. Frank Houston, the CEO of International is one ambitious son of a bitch. He's invested hundreds of millions in International Chicago. Shit, he has invested *himself* in Chicago. He wants to be Mr. Health Care in the U.S. And then I wouldn't be surprised if he used that position to run for the Senate or even higher office. He wouldn't be the first multi-millionaire with the bucks and the ego to do it. Remember Ross Perot and what's his name, Forbes?"

Alex stood and paced around her office. She turned and gave David a questioning look.

"Did you ever wonder why Houston got into International Chicago in the first place? He already has a multi billion dollar insurance company and a major share of the market in community hospitals across the country."

She paused, "Now he's going after the rest of the market by developing a system of major hospitals that are centers of excellence. Why do you think he hired all you whiz kids, and pays you the big bucks? You've heard him say it. International Chicago is the first of these super hospitals."

She turned to face a silent David.

"Did you know that the Mayo Clinic has fought and won every malpractice case brought against it? Do you think every guy up there walks on water? I'll tell you why. *Image.* Remember that stupid Minolta ad with the bald hairy tennis player, what's his face?"

"*Image is everything*, to the Mayo Clinic and to International. Do you think all those rich hypochondriacs would keep going to

Minnesota in February in twenty below weather, if a few docs up there admitted, *'Yes, here at the Mayo Brothers we also have the occasional fuck-up. Gee, we're only human!'* "

She continued relentlessly, "So how do you think Frank Houston will react to your plan to spill your guts on Channel 2? Do you think that one of the young stars of his first center of excellence publicly admitting that a young woman needlessly died because of gross negligence on his part fits with Frank's plans for International and Frank's plans for Frank?"

"When did you last here any politician or wannabe admit that he or any of his underlings screwed up?"

She stopped pacing and sat down, looking directly at David.

She shrugged, "That's my quick analysis of your situation, Doctor Stern,"

David sat pale and silent, as Alex spoke more softly.

"My uncle said you're a decent man and I have no reason to disbelieve him. However, like the virgin in Attila the Hun's camp, your options are fairly limited."

David thought for a while and then spoke slowly.

"If your analysis is correct, and I don't doubt you, then the practical solution is clear. I must play ball with International. Winnie died of seizures caused by the cancer. Sad, but happens all the time. The scenario is certainly clinically valid. She did have brain involvement when we started treating her. There's no evidence that the wrong drug was injected. Security sealed the treatment room immediately after we moved her to ICU. The body was cremated so there's no way anyone can come back at us."

Alex's face hardened as David continued thoughtfully, "My outburst at the scene can be easily explained as the natural reaction of someone overwhelmed by a totally unexpected seizure, which occurred out of the blue at the worst possible moment."

He nodded, "This way I keep my job, I don't lose every dime I've worked for over the years. There is no adverse publicity for the hospital. I'm seen as a team player at International. No downside, right?"

Alex said nothing, but her expression was now stony.

"Well, Doctor," she said icily, "I'm pleased that things have worked out well for you. I'm sure my uncle will also be pleased."

She rose to dismiss him.

"And all of your predictions and prejudices about doctors are confirmed," thought David.

"Ms. Goldberg," he said as politely as he could, "to borrow a phrase from your play-book, if you think I would go for that option, then you are truly out of your fucking mind."

Chap 16

Alex looked at David for a long moment. She picked up the phone. "Cindy, get your ass in here," she said.

David winced. Alex looked at his expression with mild surprise. An apprehensive Cindy came into the room.

"Cindy, could you get a couple of sandwiches and Cokes. The doctor is staying for lunch."

"No longer 'Doctor pile of shit', more like 'Doctor rotting meat.' She's warming to me," thought David.

Cindy looked like she'd been hit by a two by four. "Sure, Alex." She turned to David and smiled, "Doctor, anything special you'd like in your sandwich?"

"Tuna salad would be fine, thank you," said David.

"Unless they have some nice boiled children, they're every doctor's favorite, right Alex?"

The thought made him want to laugh, an impulse that he somehow turned into a snorting cough. Alex looked at him suspiciously.

"Doctor," she said in that sugar sweet voice that always heralded trouble.

"Just listening to that voice is going to give me diabetes, I know it," thought David and snorted again.

"Doctor, I know it's probably different in that temple of healing where you perform miracles every day, but we mere mortals generally don't start exercising our facial muscles until the food actually arrives," said Alex.

"She's definitely mellowing," thought David," *She'll probably be asking me for recipes soon."*

Lunch was eaten in a strained silence. Thankfully Cindy joined them. Although no words were spoken, her mere presence helped.

"That woman's got a future with U.N. Peacekeepers in Bosnia or the Middle East. One look at her resume and she's in," thought David and snorted again.

"Excellent, jaw exercises to help the digestion, just what the doctor ordered." from Ms. Diabetes.

The remains of lunch were cleared from the desk. Alex instructed Cindy to open a new file.

"I said earlier that this case was interesting from the legal perspective. It's pretty unique I think," she said thoughtfully.

"In most cases of medical screw-up, the plaintiff says, *'You did wrong, and I got hurt as a result.'* The defendant or defendants say either, *'I did nothing wrong,'* or *'Well, even if I did screw up, that didn't cause any harm to you. It was going to happen anyway, for whatever reason.'"*

"You then have experts who look at the facts in the case, and offer completely opposite opinions based on the same facts. The plaintiff needs at least one doctor who is willing to stand up and say: *' My esteemed professional colleague was a tad negligent in ignoring that itsy little lump in the patient's breast. Leaving it in there undiagnosed and untreated for two years is the reason that the patient is now unable to feel or move anything south of her navel. Bad as that may be, it's only for a little while. Because, in my opinion she will die within six months, fifty years before her time should have been up.'"*

(Marsha again).

Alex continued, "Generally the defense has an equally eminent expert who's reviewed the same medical facts, and has come to the astounding conclusion that the plaintiff's expert is full of shit. His opinion is that the defendant is the medical equivalent of Michael Jordan and that the plaintiff's case is as valid as Jeffrey Dahmer claiming he's a vegetarian."

Alex was pacing again. She apparently thought better while on her feet.

"Winnie Brown's case is different. Here the defendant physician does not deny that he screwed up royally, and that his error killed the patient. If this will be your testimony, no matter what pressure is brought to bear on you."

This was said with a questioning look at David, who nodded slightly.

Alex continued, "Then you present a great problem for your co-defendant, International. You see, they can hardly claim that your testimony is screwy and that you were always an untrustworthy person and a liar, because they hired you. Not only that, they presented you for years as Super Doc, a medical ubermensch."

More pacing.

"Likewise they can't really introduce a lymphoma hot-shot as an expert at the time of trial to contradict you, because you've been their lymphoma hot-shot for more than five years, right?"

Alex spoke thoughtfully, "No-one can argue the science here. Everyone knows that you don't inject rat poison into the brain. Even the idiots on the O.J. Simpson jury would agree that any doctor who did that committed malpractice. So they have to produce evidence that you did not do what you say you did."

She paused and gave David a piercing look.

"And, just as important, they have to come up with a valid explanation for the jury why a supposedly rational doctor would claim to have done something terribly wrong, when the 'facts' of the case don't support that claim."

She continued pacing.

"We know that they can, and already have manipulated the autopsy evidence to show that Winnie died of lymphoma, not of Stern's fuck-up."

David shuddered at her words. She did not seem to notice his reaction as she continued to pace.

"They will also manipulate other evidence to support that position. Securing the scene as quickly as they did, getting rid of the unused chemotherapy was part of the same process."

She stopped pacing. "They have one big problem." She paused, "That problem is David Stern."

She looked at David directly, "As long as you continue to say, 'I screwed up,' then they can lose this case. They have to convince the jury that you are somehow damaged goods, that you cannot be believed. At the same time they have to be able to say, 'Look, he was a good guy. He wasn't always a screw up. We were not negligent in hiring him and letting him treat patients.'"

She nodded to herself, "That's how they have to play it."

She addressed David, "I know Herb Walton well. He will have any number of people say shitty things about you, and I mean really shitty things."

David started to protest but Alex waved him quiet.

"I know, she said, "you don't want to believe that they could turn on you. Believe me they will, with a vengeance."

David shook his head as if to say, "No way!" and Alex raised her voice.

"Listen if they could claim that you killed her deliberately then they would, because then it wouldn't be malpractice, just murder and they would be off the hook. The problem with that is that no jury would accept murder without a motive. Generally physicians don't go around deliberately knocking off their patients. After all Doctor, no patients no fees, right?"

Alex continued thoughtfully," No. International needs you on their side, agreeing with their story, or else they have to convince the jury that you are so unreliable that they can't believe what you say."

She looked at David. "They'll know more about you than you know yourself. If there is anything, and I mean *anything* that's not kosher in your past, you can bet the farm that that's just the stuff that Herb Walton will drag out. Even if you are as pure as the girl of your dreams, then they'll invent whatever they need."

David still looked skeptical.

"Listen asshole," snarled Alex.

Cindy moaned quietly.

"You've never been involved in anything like this before. Just because you're sitting here now feeling real noble like some young Doctor Schweitzer, don't underestimate these people for one minute. Have you been listening to me? You could cost them millions, and screw up Frank Houston's plans for his future. Do you think he wouldn't pay a couple of hundred thousand bucks to cover you in shit? I guarantee, you will not come out of this smelling like a rose."

David still looked skeptical and Alex continued, "What does International pay its nurses, fifty five, sixty thousand a year? They'll have them lining up to bad mouth you."

She looked at David's expression. "I know you don't believe me. You've worked with these people for years. You don't believe they'll turn on you. Trust me, they will."

"International controls almost everything in this case," she said, "You did it in their fucking hospital! They control the physical evidence. They control every potential witness in the hospital. They control the attorneys."

Alex was pacing again. She turned and pointed at David.

"The only element they don't control yet is you. To win this case International has to destroy you. My bet is they'll claim that you are suffering from some psychiatric illness precipitated by the death of your patient. And they'll have evidence to prove it."

"*Cheryl Rubin,*" thought David.

There was a long silence. Alex continued in a softer tone.

"Perhaps you didn't realize how rough this is going to be. Maybe you should reconsider your decision for a day or two."

David shook his head.

Alex shrugged, "O.K. young Doctor Schweitzer. You're over twenty-one, and I'm not your fucking mother."

David shuddered at the mental image.

Alex had one last observation, "Just remember, Doctor Stern there's one characteristic that identifies every martyr throughout history."

David looked at her questioningly.

"They all ended up dead," she explained.

Chap 17

Alex looked at her notes and addressed Cindy," First thing I have to do is contact Robert Brown and become the attorney of record for the plaintiff, and we have to file. Until then we're simply blowing smoke."

David interrupted her, "Do you want me to call him?"

Alex looked at him as if he'd just slithered out from a dark place.

"You know," she said in her most contemptuous voice, "International 's right. You are out of your mind. You killed his wife and now you want to help! Sure, it would make you feel better to hug him and say I'm sorry. What about his feelings? Don't you realize that his skin must crawl every time he thinks of you?"

David said nothing, but looked stricken.

Cindy broke the silence. "Alex, you have to remember that Doctor Stern has had no previous experience with any of this."

Alex sighed and fixed David with a very intense look. "O.K. let me spell it out for you in big letters, nice and slow. If I become the Brown's attorney my job will be to nail your ass, and the big fat corporate ass of your employer to the wall. As my more refined colleagues would put it, ours will be an adversarial relationship."

She held up one finger to stop David's interruption. "I know, this is an unusual case. I've already said that. First you are not denying the facts of the case. You will not fight settlement. Indeed you probably want a settlement more than anyone. But your wishes are not relevant. That reminds me Cindy, we have to get Dr. Stern an attorney."

When David looked puzzled, Alex sighed wearily. "This is becoming tedious. Look Doctor, if I become attorney for the plaintiff I cannot represent your interests. Equally if you do not agree to the defense that Herb Walton will formulate for you and International, then he can't represent you."

She smiled thinly, "I suspect that he's going to be too busy trying to prove that you're damaged goods, that you're a crazy son of a bitch. So you need your own attorney."

"Where was I? Oh, yes, Robert Brown."

She looked at her notes. "What was the name of the guy you met at the funeral home, John Roosevelt."

Alex and Cindy exchanged a look.

Alex smiled, "Well that shouldn't be a problem, right Cindy?"

She continued, "Remember the Whitley case a couple of years ago, that ass-hole O.B. guy. What was his name, Fletcher?"

David recognized the name of the head of Obstetrics of one of the major Chicago medical schools. Alex and Cindy shared a wicked grin.

Cindy explained to David, "Jennie Whitley was a client of ours. Her pastor was Reverend Roosevelt. He's now a good friend."

Alex smiled, "Well, if it's the same John Roosevelt we should have no problem getting on board."

Alex stopped pacing and sat down behind her desk. "Cindy, why don't you take a five minute break. I need to make a few calls."

Cindy tactfully escorted David from the room. He felt like he was coming apart at the seams. It must have shown in his face, because Cindy gave him an encouraging smile.

"This whole thing must be very hard on you, Doctor Stern."

Apart from Rabbi Shuster, these were the first kind words that David had heard since the disaster. He suddenly felt close to tears.

"Don't worry about Alex," said Cindy, "I know she sometimes runs off at the mouth a little, but she is very passionate about what she thinks is right. She will fight tooth and nail for you if she believes in you. I can tell she respects you."

"Nail my ass to the wall was the exact expression" thought David, *"I hate to think what she says to people she doesn't respect."*

"Thank you, Cindy" was all he could say.

Cindy went back into Alex's office. The door closed behind her. David was left outside. The five minutes stretched to forty five, then one hour.

"What was it she had said? Your wishes are not relevant."

This was a new experience for David. He was a professional man, used to having attentive patients and family members hang on his every word. In the cancer world he was someone of importance. When he spoke at conferences, people listened. David had never before considered himself to have a big ego. He suddenly realized that he didn't like being on the outside while important issues affecting him were being discussed.

The anxiety sat on his chest like a four hundred pound weight. He had the sudden thought that this was exactly how many of his patients must have felt as he discussed their case with his colleagues. He didn't like being in the situation where decisions about his future were being made by others. Frightened and out of control, David sat and stared at the wall.

The door opened. Cindy gestured him back in. Alex was reading a long FAX. Her concentration was total. Finally she looked up.

"Progress, Doctor. I have an appointment tonight with Mr. Robert Brown's pastor Reverend John Roosevelt."

A pause, "I also have some good news for you."

"What's that," thought David, "The earth has agreed to swallow me up?"

She indicated the FAX in her hand," I have here a copy of International's standard physician employment contract."

"How the hell did she get that," he wondered, *"Did she fly over on her broomstick?"*

"If your contract is similar, and there's no reason to think it would be different, you are not bound to use International's attorney."

Alex read from the FAX, *"In the event of any claim for medical negligence resulting from your actions as an International employee, you are entitled to obtain the services of a personal attorney of your choice. International agrees to pay the reasonable costs of same."*

She smiled, "Wait till Herb Walton sees they let that through. I bet some poor corporate counsel loses his job, or worse, over that."

"You have a copy of your contract?" she asked.

David nodded.

"Just to be sure, get it to your attorney as soon as you can. He'll certainly want to see it."

"Based on this," she said indicating the FAX," I feel very comfortable recommending John Rowland to you. I wanted to be sure that he would get paid."

Only Alex knew that when John Rowland's wife left him, and took her three hundred dollar a day cocaine habit to Los Angeles, she had left him with nearly six figures of debt and two little kids, one of whom had cerebral palsy. John's practice was small, and he was a kind and patient man.

"Fine", she thought, *"He'll have plenty of time to support this young doctor, who is already hurting badly, through all the shit that lies ahead. And if Frank Houston has to pay John three hundred bucks an hour to do it, well so much the better."*

Alex smiled to herself.

Maybe something good could be salvaged from this mess after all.

Chap 18

It was only three thirty but the winter sun was already fading. David felt worn out. If he had been more familiar with the syndrome, he would have recognized the symptoms of severe stress.

In contrast Alex looked and felt energized. With more insight, she would have recognized that she always felt better when she was actively pursuing the thousand and one details of a case.

That's when the rage for her parents, for Marsha and her fellow victims, was tolerable. The rage never left her. It was as much a part of her as her skin. Life without it was unthinkable it was always there.

When her brain was not exercised, when her intellect did not control her emotions, the rage threatened to overwhelm her. Her slash and burn take no prisoners style, her biting humor, her florid cursing, her weary cynicism, all were the furious attempts of a sensitive woman to protect her very essence from the traumatic experiences of imperfect reality.

The choice of medical malpractice as her life work, forced on her by the death of her parents and best friend, was in a sense a disaster. It continually exposed Alex to frequent and ever increasing episodes of psychic trauma. Each of these episodes made her even more desperate to overcome the cruel Fates that had so punished her parents and dearest friend.

But no matter how hard she fought, no matter how successful she was, she could never win. No amount of money or vindication for the victim and no amount of humiliation for the defendants could remove the suffering from Alex's soul. This was the tragedy of her life. The rage burned on.

Alex was quite oblivious to all of this.

She leaned back in her chair.

"Doctor," she said, "I'm sure you're tired, but I need another few minutes of your time. There are some important rules that we have to follow, and you have to know what they are. Please listen carefully."

David was shocked.

Did she say 'please'? This intellectual Alex was certainly easier to deal with than her evil, emotional twin.

"First, given the fact that I may well soon be filing a lawsuit on behalf of Mr. Brown in which you will be named as a defendant, I cannot give you any further advice in this matter. That's why I have recommended John Rowland to you. I strongly recommend that you see him as soon as possible. Be as honest and forthcoming with him as you have been with me."

"Honest and forthcoming? Is this the same person?" thought David, *"whatever happened to 'Doctor pile of shit'?"*

Alex continued, "If Mr. Brown does indeed retain me as his attorney, and I proceed against International on his behalf, it would not be appropriate for you and I to meet or discuss the case under any circumstances, except when all other parties either are present, or have been given the opportunity to be present."

"The court has very strict rules concerning this. If we violate those rules, the other defendants could legitimately claim that we participated in a conspiracy against them. This could lead to criminal charges. It would certainly cause me to lose my law license. I'm sure you can appreciate this."

Alex continued, "I always want to win for my clients, but I want to win honestly. At the moment International does not know for sure where they are with you. I know Herb Walton. He's almost certainly playing it both ways to be safe. He'll try very hard to keep you on his team, because if he does, he wins."

"At the same time he'll be working very hard to smear you, should you refuse to cooperate with him. Until you make it clear that you're out, you may be part of their discussions, and hear things that might be to my advantage to know. Please understand, I don't want to hear anything from you regarding their plans or approach to the case. You must not act as a spy on my behalf."

Alex's face grew serious. "Finally, I want to warn you again of the considerable danger that you are in. I mean professional, but also personal. I sense you are an honorable and sensitive man."

David turned to look at Cindy.

"Was she as shocked by the change as he was?"

She was smiling and nodding her head encouragingly.

"What was happening here?"

David felt like he had gone out on a date with Ms. Attila the Hun, who halfway through the evening turned into Mother Teresa.

Alex was still speaking in calm and measured tones.

"What! no wide eyed raving, no spittle on her chin?"

"You don't think that your colleagues will act against you, because you yourself would not act dishonorably. You are mistaken. Please be very careful. I know this sounds paranoid."

"This from Ms. Piranha."

"Until this case is over, because of your central position in it, and especially because of their need to totally discredit you, you need to be very careful."

Alex gave David a serious look, "Please examine everything that you do and say, every personal and professional interaction, every event in your daily life, even the most trivial in the light, of *'how can this hurt me, how can this prevent me from doing what I am committed to do.'* "

Alex stood and graciously extended her hand, "Doctor Stern, it was a pleasure to meet you. Cindy will give you John Rowland's number as you leave. Please call him soon."

David grasped her hand.

"It feels human," he thought, *"but these aliens really are clever. Never underestimate them."*

Despite his confusion regarding the sudden change from Evil Alex to the Fairy Queen, David was aware of a jolt of electricity that passed between them as he held her hand. From the change in Alex's expression, she felt it too.

Thoughtfully he walked to the door. Despite the terrible events of recent weeks, despite the weight of guilt that he felt, despite the threat to his career, despite his dreadful weariness, despite his traumatic introduction to Alex and her biting comments, despite or perhaps because of her almost maniacal change in mood, speech and yes, even appearance, he knew that he had just met a very special person.

His own reaction to her was a sign of this. Yesterday he was thinking of suicide. Today he giggled through lunch at the mental images she produced in him.

Alex Goldberg was a very interesting person. Probably crazy as a loon, but certainly interesting. Of that there was no doubt.

He said goodbye to Cindy (no electricity this time, more like walnut, solid and dependable), and casually remarked, "Interesting job you have Cindy, been here long?"

Cindy replied somewhat defensively, he thought, "I have been with Ms. Goldberg for nearly five years."

"Does she get her dose of medications checked regularly?" he asked casually.

"Ms. Goldberg is in excellent health, Doctor," Cindy said stiffly as she shut the door.

David sighed. *"Back to Doctor pile of shit."*

Chap 19

At seven that evening, Alex took a cab from her condo on Dearborn Street to Reverend Roosevelt's church in Evanston, just north of the city. She hated to drive in the city, an unconscious legacy of her parents' death. As her condominium was within walking distance of her office, the Daley center where the Cook County Court was located, and most of the major spots in downtown Chicago, she rarely missed not owning a car.

Hebron Baptist Church was a simple one storey building on the corner of Oakton and Dodge in south Evanston. The cab driver gave Alex a strange look as she paid the fare. This was not a good neighborhood.

Two young African American men wearing matching jackets and baseball hats were standing casually on either side of the church door. They looked her over carefully as she approached.

"You Alex Goldberg?" the bigger of the two asked.

"That's me," nodded Alex.

The younger held the door open for her.

"Go right in then," he said with a smile, "The Reverend says that you're O.K."

Alex smiled in return, "Thank you. He's O.K. too."

As always the Reverend John Roosevelt was dressed impeccably, in a dark blue suit with crisp white shirt and a wine red tie. His black shoes gleamed with a high polish. He leaped to his feet and embraced Alex warmly as she entered his office.

"Well, you're a sight for sore eyes. How are you?"

His voice was deep and resonating. When he used it to full effect during his Sunday sermons you could hear a pin drop in the church.

"I'm fine John, thank you," replied Alex, "I don't need to ask how you are, you look great!"

John smiled, "Thank you, Alex."

Unlike many of his colleagues, the seventy year old was a dedicated clergyman who actually ministered to his flock. Although he was a charismatic man with spellbinding oratorical skills, he had no interest in the brand of social activism and very public relations embraced by so many of his colleagues.

He had turned down more offers from wealthy churches, and radio and TV stations than he could remember. His place was with his people in the working class and lower middle class homes of black Evanston.

Alex hugged him, "How are Sarah, William and the kids?"

John Roosevelt was a widower of many years standing. Sarah, his only child was a Professor of Humanities at Georgetown University, married to an environmental lawyer in Washington D.C.

John nodded towards a picture of a smiling family group on his cluttered desk.

"They're all well. She's working on number five, now. They're moving into a bigger house in Fairfax next month. I'll be going out to see them in a few weeks."

Alex smiled, "Give her my love, please."

They sat down on an old comfortable sofa in the office. The Reverend looked at Alex curiously. "So, what's this all about Alex? You were quite mysterious on the phone today?"

Alex briefly told him the story. He looked shocked. After a few minutes thought, he nodded slowly.

"Now I understand. It seemed so strange, how suddenly she was gone. I knew that Winnie was very sick in the beginning, but she seemed to be doing well. And then, dying so suddenly."

He nodded thoughtfully, "And that explains why the doctor was so distressed."

He looked at Alex, "Did you know he came to the funeral home, to the viewing? He was as drunk as a skunk."

Alex shook her head, "He told me that he came to the visitation. That's how I knew about you. But I didn't know he had been drinking. He didn't tell me that."

Roosevelt smiled sadly, "I'm not surprised he didn't tell you. He looked terrible. Now I understand why."

He mused, "Poor guy, he must be eaten up with guilt. What a terrible load to carry, knowing that you are directly responsible for another person's death."

He shook himself. "Well, Alex, knowing you as I do, you're working on some solutions to this mess, how can I help you?"

Alex took a deep breath. "David Stern is a decent person, I'm sure of that. He has admitted his error, and wants to make amends."

She paused, "You're right of course, it's a terrible loss for the family. And you can never really make amends for something like that."

She shrugged, "But he came to me because he wants to see the family properly compensated."

She paused and looked John directly in the eye.

"That's where it starts to get messy. The hospital, International, is denying the whole story. They say she died of lymphoma in the brain causing seizures. They are putting enormous pressure on Dr. Stern to go along with that story."

She stood up and started walking up and down the cluttered office. She turned to the older man.

"Can you believe, they've suspended Dr. Stern, and are threatening to fire him unless he backs up their story!"

John was outraged. "That's shameful!"

Then he added thoughtfully, "But that's a lot of pressure for a young man to withstand."

Alex smiled, "You know me well, Reverend. I generally don't have a very high opinion of the medical profession, but I don't think that this doctor will go along with their story."

Roosevelt nodded, "And that's where I come in."

"Exactly," said Alex, "If I am to help Robert Brown, I have to represent him, and sue Dr. Stern and his employer for medical negligence in the death of his wife."

Roosevelt stared thoughtfully at the lamp on his desk.

"Let me tell you a little about the Browns. They are, or rather they were a very fine family. He's ex- military, as straight as they come. She was a very gentle soul, devoted to the twins. I baptized them here, in this very church," he added softly.

Alex saw a tear glisten in his eye as he looked directly at her.

"The best way for you to impress Robert Brown is don't talk about money."

He shook his head, "He won't be interested in that. Best thing is to appeal to his sense of fairness and honesty."

Alex nodded, "Fair enough."

John Roosevelt stood and put on his raincoat..

"Let's go see him right now. We can walk, they live three blocks from here."

Chap 20

They soon reached the front door of a small Cape Cod house with green shutters. Roosevelt rang the doorbell. An older woman smiled broadly when she opened the door.

"Well Reverend, this is a pleasure, please come in."

Agnes Brown was Robert's mother. She carried her seventy-three years very well. Her smile faded somewhat when she saw Alex, but she nodded coolly and held out her hand when John introduced Alex.

"Well, it's just raining white folk in here tonight!" she said, "Come in and join the crowd."

Alex and John looked at each other, puzzled. They followed Agnes into the small dining room. Robert Brown was sitting at the table with three visitors. One was an African American woman age about thirty. The other two were white. One was a man about forty, the other a woman who appeared in her early thirties. All had the unmistakable look of corporate America.

As Alex and John entered the white woman was talking earnestly to Robert, who was holding a single sheet of paper. She grimaced when she saw Alex who smiled brightly at her.

"Go ahead, Jodi, please don't let us interrupt a thing," said Alex.

Robert stood when he saw John Roosevelt. He looked relieved by the interruption.

"Reverend, thank you for coming."

He looked at Alex curiously.

Roosevelt made the introduction. "Robert, this is Alex Goldberg. I want you to listen very carefully to this young lady. Don't be fooled by her sweet smile, she's one of the smartest people I have ever met. If I'm ever in a tough spot she is the one person I would want in my corner more than anyone else."

He continued, "She's also one of the most honest and honorable people that I have ever met. She is a good friend of mine and she has a story to tell you."

He turned to Robert's other visitors. "I don't know what your business is with these other folks...."

Alex put a hand on his arm. "Reverend, I apologize for interrupting you."

She turned to Robert. "Mr. Brown, have you signed any document that *Attorney* Miller has given you?"

The emphasis was unmistakable. Robert looked surprised. He turned to Jodi Miller.

"Attorney! You told me you were with the Hospice and Bereavement Program at the hospital!"

Jodi Miller gave Alex a look of pure poison.

Her African American colleague spoke in a soothing tone. "Mr. Brown, Robert, it's true that Jodi is an attorney, but we all work for International."

She turned to Alex and John Roosevelt, and stretched out her hand.

"Hi, my name is Elaine Butters. I'm the Director of Bereavement Aftercare at the hospital."

She nodded to the third member of the group.

"And Tim Johnston is the Director of our Hospice Program."

"And the purpose of your visit tonight?" asked John Roosevelt politely.

"That's confidential," said Jodi Miller.

John Roosevelt didn't answer her. He simply looked over at Robert Brown who was following the entire conversation with a bemused expression.

"It's like this, Reverend." Robert explained, "They've got this new program at the hospital for folks like us. Somebody came up with some money to help pay funeral costs. If I understood this lady right, they want to pay me ten thousand dollars. That'll cover all the costs for Winnie's funeral and cremation. Did I get that right?"

The last question was directed to Jodi Miller.

"No strings attached right, Jodi?" asked Alex sardonically.

She gently retrieved the one page document from Robert Brown's hand.

"May I take a look at this, please?"

Robert looked to John Roosevelt who nodded. Alex quickly read the document, shaking her head. She read from the document aloud.

"In consideration of the payment of ten thousand dollars described above, Mr. Robert Brown acting as executor for his late wife and on behalf of his minor children, agrees to hold harmless International Medical Center Chicago, International Health Care, and all its agents and employees for any acts of omission or commission which may have potentially or actually caused harm to Robert Brown or Winnie Brown or their minor children during the past twelve months."

John Roosevelt nodded, his face hardening as Alex continued reading.

"Furthermore Robert Brown accepts the payment of ten thousand dollars as full payment for any potential or actual damages which may be alleged to have occurred as a result of the actions or failure to act of any agent, employee or independent contractor of International Medical Center Chicago and International Health Care. Mr. Brown further agrees that he will not seek any further compensation from International."

Alex shook her head. "You know, Jodi, your sleazy boss never fails to surprise me. Whenever I think he has excelled himself in slime he comes up with another one, like this."

She indicated the paper she had just read and shook her head again.

"I'm kind of surprised at you, though. You must know that failing to inform Mr. Brown that you are an attorney working on behalf of International while trying to have him sign this," she once again referred to the document, "This little charade here tonight could well get you disbarred."

Jodi Miller flushed beneath her perfect makeup but remained silent. Alex turned to Robert Brown and John Roosevelt.

"Reverend, I suggest that someone ask these three clowns to leave now. We need to speak to Robert alone."

She returned the document to Robert. "My strong advice to you, Mr. Brown is that you hear me out before you sign this. After you've heard what I have to say," she shrugged, "well, then you can make whatever decision you wish. No pressure from me."

Alex saw Robert Brown smile for the first time that night.

"Please call me Robert," he said, "every time I hear *Mr. Brown* I'm looking around for my Papa."

He stood and looked over to the three representatives of International. "Thank you for coming."

Jodi Miller reached for the paper she was so keen to have Robert sign a few minutes before, but Alex was too quick for her. She pulled it away from Jodi's outstretched hand.

"I'm sure Mr. Brown will want to study this some more before he signs it, Jodi," she said sweetly.

As three disappointed people left the room, John Roosevelt laughed out loud.

"Alex, I've missed you," he chuckled, "It's been too long since we last kicked ass like this."

Chap 21

As the three disappointed representatives from International left, Agnes Brown let out a long breath.

"I don't understand what all is going on here, but I didn't know what all the hurry to sign that paper was, Robert," she said.

She turned to John Roosevelt, "Reverend, would you and the young lady like to join us in a cup of tea? I know I need one."

John smiled, "That would be very nice, thank you Agnes."

Pretty soon the four were seated comfortably with their tea and a plate of Agnes' chocolate chip cookies.

John spoke, "Agnes, I've known you all for what, more than twenty years? I wasn't exaggerating when I spoke about Alex before. She's a good friend who has helped several families in our community. She came to me tonight with a remarkable story about Winnie's death. I want you to hear it from her own lips."

Robert and his mother nodded solemnly. All eyes in the room were turned to Alex. She spoke softly, her eyes never leaving Robert's face.

"First," she said, "let me express my deepest sympathy to you all. I know that nothing will ever completely heal the dreadful pain you must feel."

Robert nodded soundlessly, while Agnes raised a white lace handkerchief to her eyes.

Alex continued, "Robert, I learned of your wife's death earlier today." She paused, "I learned of it from David Stern."

Robert looked like he was about to speak, and Alex raised a hand.

"Please, if I may suggest, let me tell you the whole story as it was told to me, and then I'll be more than happy to answer all your questions."

Robert and Agnes nodded, and Alex continued, "First, I am an attorney."

She turned to Agnes, "I guess you were right, it is raining attorneys tonight!"

Everyone smiled, and Alex continued, "About six years ago my late aunt was treated for cancer by Dr. Stern. My uncle was very impressed by his kindness during a very difficult time. As you will hear, since your late wife's death, certain events have occurred at the hospital. These have caused big problems for Dr. Stern. Because of these problems, my uncle suggested that David Stern come to see me for advice, which is how I met him today and learned of your loss."

"I should point out," she continued, "Doctor Stern is not my client, because if he were my client I couldn't tell you anything of my conversation with him and also," she said with a little half-smile at John Roosevelt, "I couldn't possibly give you any advice about what you should do."

Alex continued, "After listening to what Dr. Stern had to say, I knew that I had to speak to you."

She turned and smiled at John," Reverend Roosevelt and I go back some years. I learned from Dr. Stern that he was probably your pastor, and I gave him a call. He graciously offered to bring us together, and so here we are."

She hesitated, "There really is no easy way to say this, Robert, Winnie did not die from her lymphoma. She died because of a terrible mistake that Dr. Stern made. He injected the wrong chemotherapy drug into her brain."

She gestured to her own head.

"You know, the Omaya reservoir, that your wife had. Well Dr. Stern injected Vincristine into the Omaya instead of ARA-C."

Alex continued in a quiet voice. Robert Brown had to hear and understand it all.

"That's what caused the seizures, and that's what caused the fatal brain damage."

She shook her head, "You can't inject Vincristine into the brain. It's a deadly poison if you do that. It was a terrible mistake that Dr. Stern made."

Agnes Brown gave a strangled cry, and pressed her handkerchief to her breast.

Robert looked mystified. "How that can be? I wasn't with Winnie that day she went for the chemo. I had to take a load to Memphis. But my boss flew me back that night, and I met the other oncologist, what's his name? Doctor Keating."

"Wait a minute."

He stood up and went out of the room, returning a minute later with a piece of paper.

"Look at this," he said, "This is the death certificate. Keating signed it. He told us. He said the day Winnie passed that the lymphoma had come back in her brain, and that there was such severe brain damage that there was no hope for recovery. That's why I took her off the breathing machine. The death certificate says she had lymphoma in her brain."

He paused and looked to John Roosevelt for support.

"You were there, Reverend when she passed. Don't you remember hearing the same thing I'm saying now?"

Roosevelt stretched out and touched Robert's arm, nodding in agreement.

"You're right, John. That's what we were told at the time."

Robert shook his head as if to clear his thoughts.

He addressed Alex, "This is just too much to believe. They did an autopsy, and told me it confirmed Dr. Keating's diagnosis. They told me that Dr. Stern was out sick, and now you're telling me that he was there and gave her chemotherapy in the clinic that Monday?"

Alex nodded, "That's right. He was there. He gave the chemo himself. After Winnie collapsed, the hospital wouldn't let Dr. Stern see her anymore, and that's when Dr. Keating took over. That was a hospital decision."

Robert Brown shook his head again. "What you're telling me Alex, is that everyone I dealt with at the hospital that night I flew in and afterwards, they all *lied* to me? You're saying this death certificate isn't true?"

Agnes Brown had sat silently listening, but now she spoke, "The problem with you, Robert Brown is that you are an honest man, just like your father, rest his soul. I wouldn't have it any other way, and I love you for it."

She leaned forward and grasped his hand. "You're so honest that you can't imagine anyone else would act in such a lying, devious way. But that's the way of this world. True, Reverend?"

Roosevelt nodded silently.

Alex said softly, "Your mother's right, Robert. It's hard to believe, perhaps. But if Dr. Stern is telling the truth, and there's really no reason for him to make up a story like this. If Dr. Stern told me the truth, then Dr. Keating certainly lied to you, and that piece of paper," she nodded at the death certificate that Robert still held, "is a fabrication."

"Let me qualify that last remark," she added, "It's true that Winnie died of severe brain damage, but that brain damage was not caused by lymphoma. It was caused by Dr. Stern's error, injecting the wrong drug."

Robert Brown raised his hands helplessly. "But why would the hospital lie about such a thing?"

Agnes shook her head and snorted in disgust. She turned to Alex. "Spell it out for him, please."

Alex nodded. She addressed Robert once again.

"First of all, Robert it's likely that the junior doctors and the nurses who were treating Winnie were perfectly honest with you. They were only repeating what Dr. Keating had told them. That Winnie had lymphoma in her brain."

"I suspect they didn't know all of the details about the accident. Once irreversible brain damage has occurred, whatever the cause, patients look pretty much the same. I suspect some other senior people at the hospital were also involved in the cover up, but not the doctors and nurses who were caring for Winnie in the I.C.U."

She reached out and took Agnes' hand, but continued to direct her words at Robert.

"Robert, I'm not a doctor, but I sincerely believe you did the right thing taking her off the ventilator. There is no doubt that during the last day of her life Winnie had every sign of irreversible severe brain damage. As soon as the wrong drug was injected into Winnie's Omaya there was no chance of recovery."

Roosevelt was very impressed by Alex's sensitivity.

Alex shrugged, "As for why the hospital would try to cover up Dr. Stern's error, there are several reasons why. First, you have to understand there is tremendous competition among the big Chicago teaching hospitals."

She ticked them off on the fingers of one hand.

"You've got the University of Chicago, Northwestern, Rush, Loyola. And now there's International added to the mix. No hospital wants to admit publicly that a serious error was made by one or more of its staff, especially when that error has such tragic consequences."

She shook her head, "You wouldn't believe how important it is for these hospitals to be seen as the best, for a lot of different reasons. They're constantly comparing their performance with their competitors, and they advertise their ranking compared with the others. In the final analysis it all comes down to dollars. The best hospitals are able to attract more patients and negotiate better rates of payment from the insurance companies."

Agnes was watching Alex closely. She spoke to her fiercely, "Go ahead, Alex tell him the rest. He may not want to hear it, but those little children back there."

She gestured towards the back of the house where the twins slept, "They've lost their mama. You tell him the rest now."

Alex nodded. Again she addressed her remarks to Robert.

"The last thing I want to do is cheapen Winnie's memory with talk of money. But you have to understand Robert, that when a young person is killed by a doctor's negligence like this, it generally results in a multimillion dollar legal case against the doctor and the hospital. Dr. Stern worked for International. They're on the line if he makes an error, as he did here."

She shrugged, "That's a very simple reason why International would lie to you."

Robert shook his head violently, "No. I don't want to hear this. I'm not interested in suing."

His voice broke, "Winnie suffered enough. I don't want her good name dragged through any more."

John Roosevelt had been listening silently up till now. He leaned forward as he spoke.

"Robert, you haven't heard it all yet. Let Alex finish the story."

Alex shot John a look of gratitude.

"Robert, I absolutely understand where you're coming from. I know how badly you're hurting. I've never been married, but I hope that if I ever do, I'm lucky enough to have the kind of marriage that Reverend Roosevelt described to me. That you and your late wife shared in this home."

Her voice broke, "I also think I understand the pain and rage that you feel. I lost both of my parents in an accident because of an incompetent doctor. Different circumstances, but believe me, I have lived through something like you're experiencing now."

Agnes gripped Alex's hand tightly as the young lawyer fixed Robert with an intense look.

"Of course, right now you are grieving, and the idea of even thinking about money, it seems like an insult to Winnie and her memory."

Her emotional energy propelled her from her chair and she starting pacing up and down the room.

"But Robert you need to understand, this is what I do every day of my life. This kind of thing happens too often. Good people, like Winnie are terribly harmed by a doctor or hospital."

She turned and gave all three a fierce stare, "And what happens? The doctors close ranks to protect their incompetent colleagues. The hospitals and insurance companies have millions of dollars, so they pay teams of lawyers to delay justice or try to confuse juries. All to save them having to pay innocent victims what is rightfully theirs!"

Agnes seized her son's arm and shook it, "Why do you think those three cream puffs came here tonight? Do you think they really cared about the funeral expenses?"

She turned to Alex, "That's right, isn't it, Ms. Goldberg?"

Alex nodded, "One of the oldest tricks in the book. Get a potential plaintiff to sign an agreement for a nominal amount while they're still numb with grief."

She indicated the document lying on the table, "If you had signed Robert," she smiled briefly, "And it looks like they had you going when John and I came in. If you had signed this, then you would have relinquished any and all future claims against International."

Alex smiled sourly, "As I said, oldest trick in book. Although that was a new low, coming in pretending to be bereavement specialists."

She shook her head in wonder, "I don't know how some people can look at themselves in the mirror in the morning."

There was a long silence. Alex sat down, and spoke quietly.

"What else can I do, Robert? None of us has a time machine. I can't go back and undo the terrible harm that has been done to fine decent people."

She sighed, "People come to see me all the time because their doctor screwed up. I could tell you horror stories. The arrogant fool who simply reassured a young woman with a breast lump when anyone who reads Ladies Home Journal would be saying *'biopsy it, you stupid asshole?'* I can't take them back three years to make it all right."

She looked over to John Roosevelt, "Sorry, Reverend."

John smiled a waved a hand, as if to say, *"It's nothing."*

Alex continued in the same soft tone, "Or the patient who died because some doctor was too lazy to check the correct dose of a new prescription, and the idiot pharmacist just went along with a dose that was a *hundred* times too high!"

She shrugged, "All I can do is seek compensation for the victims. Fight the doctors and Big Medicine. That's all the system allows me to do."

Agnes stood and hugged Alex, "You are carrying a very heavy load on those shoulders, sister."

John Roosevelt responded, "Amen to that."

There was a long silence. Then Robert turned to Alex.

"The Reverend said there was more."

Chap 22

Alex sighed, "Yes, Robert. Much more."

She quickly summarized the events of the two weeks since Winnie's death.

Robert was shocked. "You mean they actually had a meeting to plan how they were going to lie about all this!"

Alex nodded, "Yes, two meetings, actually. Two meetings that I know of, that Dr. Stern attended. There were probably others."

"And because Dr. Stern wouldn't go along with this story, they fired him?"

Again Alex nodded in the affirmative. "Suspended, actually, but if he doesn't go along with their story he'll never work there again."

It was Robert's turn to pace. "Listen, I don't have a whole lot of sympathy for Doctor Stern right now. You say he killed my wife!"

He continued pacing, his fists clenched, "But you don't lie to a man about how his wife died! Doctors are meant to look after people, not lie to them!"

"And you don't fire someone for refusing to lie! They taught us in the Corps that your honor is worth more than your life, and I believe that! You don't lie and cover up something like this to save a few dollars."

He sat down again, muttering, "That's just not right."

Alex leaned forward, "What you saw tonight was just a glimpse of how they operate."

She regarded the paper on the table scornfully, "*Bereavement Specialists.* Please!"

Robert looked at John, "O.K. you've convinced me, what do we do now?"

Beside him Agnes looked up and gave a silent prayer of thanks.

John waved a hand towards Alex and said, "This is her show, Robert."

Alex nodded, "Let me explain the process to you, Robert. The only recourse you have against Dr. Stern and his employer, which is International Medical Center, Chicago, is to sue them for medical negligence."

She paused, "This is a wrongful death case, meaning we have to prove that if Dr. Stern had acted with proper care, Winnie would not have died. I believe we can do that, especially if Dr. Stern will testify honestly about what he did."

She picked up the paper from the table.

"First, my strong advice to you for now is that you don't sign any piece of paper that International may send or give to you."

John looked surprised, "Alex, do you really think they'd try again?"

She shrugged, "I wouldn't be surprised. What have they got to lose? You don't know their main guy Herb Walton. He's good, but let's just say he probably flunked legal ethics in law school!"

She smiled at a passing thought. "He and I have had a few battles in the past. It's probably true to say he's not my biggest fan!"

Agnes was impatient, "I understand everything that you've said, I think. So what's the next step, you're going to sue them? How much will that cost?"

Alex shook her head and smiled at Agnes. "Slow down for a minute. You have to understand that right now I have no legal standing in this matter."

She turned to Robert, "Do you have a lawyer?"

He shook his head, "Never had the need."

"O.K." said Alex, "you need to obtain the services of a lawyer. I will be happy to provide you with some names."

Agnes interrupted her, "We want you. Right, Reverend?"

Alex smiled and shook her head. "Thank you Agnes for your vote of confidence, but this is not your decision. In the law, Robert is the surviving spouse. Any lawsuit would be filed on his behalf, and the children. You understand, Robert?"

He nodded, "I understand, and I want you as my lawyer."

His mother snorted, "Alex you have to understand, in this family it's the women who make the decisions. We tell the men-folk what to do!"

John Roosevelt smiled, "Let me say, John that you just made a very smart choice."

He patted Alex's hand affectionately, "This young lady is the best there is."

Alex smiled gratefully, "Thank you John."

She turned to Agnes, "You were asking about how much it would cost you if you do go ahead and sue the doctor and hospital here. Let me explain to you both, it won't cost you anything."

She explained, "The way it works in most personal injury cases like this is that when a client signs up with an attorney, it's on what's called a contingency basis. That way the attorney pays all of the costs associated with filing the case, court costs, paying expert witnesses and so on. In exchange the client agrees to pay a percentage of any damages awarded to the attorney."

She smiled, "And if the plaintiff, that would be you, Robert, loses the case and there are no damages paid, then the attorney gets nothing for her troubles."

John Roosevelt nodded in agreement.

He addressed Robert, "Either way you don't pay a penny out of your own pocket. The attorney assumes all the risk. And that can be a fair amount of change, right Alex?"

Alex nodded, "Yes, on average the costs of taking a case like this all the way to trial and appeal are probably about a hundred thousand dollars. More, if lots of medical experts are involved."

Agnes was shocked, "That's a lot of money!"

Alex agreed, "Yes, but you have to understand that the size of awards in many of these cases can easily exceed a million dollars. And the attorney's share of those awards is usually forty percent. That percentage has been set by the Illinois Supreme Court."

Robert nodded, "I get the picture. Let's do it."

Alex looked at her watch. It was nearly eleven o'clock.

"I apologize, I know it's late, there's a few more things that you have to hear."

She addressed Robert, "Before you make a final decision I want you to understand this is a slow process. The legal system moves very slowly. If I file a lawsuit on your behalf tomorrow it could take years before we would ever see a trial."

"Second, this is not a pleasant process, it becomes a dogfight. The other side have the right to pry into your personal life, and finances, Robert."

She waved a hand, "You got a glimpse tonight of what can happen. Unfortunately there are many unethical layers out there who don't mind bending the rules or the truth if it helps them win a big case."

"And, this is a big case. The stakes are high," she mused, "I know the people involved quite well. They won't go down without a fight."

For the first time that evening Robert Brown smiled, "I'm not afraid of a fight, Alex. After what I saw in ten years in the Marines Corps, I think I can handle a bunch of Chicago lawyers."

Alex nodded, "I'm sure you can Robert. And you too, Agnes."

She stood up, "O.K. Thank you all for your time."

She handed Robert her business card, "Can you come in to my office tomorrow, anytime after nine? You have to sign a standard agreement form. Then I'll file a lawsuit against the doctor and International. Once I'm the attorney of record, I get to see all the medical records and anything else that they've got."

Robert took the card, shaking his head, "I never thought I'd ever be doing something like this."

Agnes scolded him as she hugged Alex good night. Her goodbye to Alex was warmer than her greeting.

"Hush! You stop your complaining, Robert. This nice young lady is going to help you, and you just be nice to her!"

Alex and John Roosevelt said their goodnights and left. As they were walking back to the church, John complimented Alex on her presentation.

"You did real well back there. You pitched it just right. You can see they're fine people, and poor Robert is hurting badly. Agnes sees it for what it is, but if you had gone on about money you would never have gotten him to agree."

Alex nodded, "Thank you. I agree they're very special. Thank goodness we got there when we did."

She laughed, "Did you see Jodi Miller's face when she saw us?"

John nodded, "Saw you, you mean. She probably thought I'm just another dumb ass black man she could fool! She saw you and she knew that she was out of luck!"

Alex stopped and looked shrewdly at her friend, "John, *no-one* and I mean *no-one* underestimates you!"

John smiled broadly, "We do make a good team, don't we?"

Alex nodded and they walked on together. They reached the church door.

As John reached for his keys, he said, "Come in and I'll call a cab for you."

They stood in the vestibule, waiting for the cab and John asked Alex, "So what about Dr. Stern. How's he doing in all this?"

Alex frowned and shook her head, "Not well. I didn't talk about it a lot to Robert for obvious reasons, but I sense Stern's really hurting badly."

John nodded, "I'm sure he is. Can you do anything to help?"

Alex shrugged, "Not really, you know how it is. As soon as I sue him, and I have to sue him to get at International, as soon as the legal process starts, I can't have any contact or discussions with him without all parties present. And I can't give him any advice. He becomes the enemy."

John nodded, "He must be a remarkable young man if he refuses to go along with the International cover-up story. To the extent of getting fired!"

Alex nodded in agreement, "I agree. The very best solution would be if International would admit culpability and settle."

She shook her head, "But that's not going to happen."

She added, "The one good thing I was able to accomplish was set Dr. Stern up with a good personal attorney, a friend of mine John Rowland. He'll look after him."

At that moment the cab arrived. Alex kissed John lightly on the cheek, "John, once again, as always a million thanks.

She hugged him tightly. "I'll keep you up to date on developments, as we move along."

John stood in the doorway and waved goodbye as the cab took Alex back downtown.

Chap 23

Next morning Robert Brown came to Alex's office and signed up. Alex wasted no time. That afternoon she filed a wrongful death lawsuit against David Stern and his employer, International Medical Center of Chicago and the parent company International Health Care U.S.A. When Cindy returned from the Cook County courthouse in the Daley Center with the papers, Alex called John Rowland on the telephone.

"Alex, what a surprise! Nice to hear your voice."

John Rowland smiled across the desk at his new client, as he spoke to Alex on the phone. Alex quickly got down to business.

"John, I gave your name to a Doctor David Stern yesterday. I advised him to contact you. If he does I hope you'll be able to help him."

John Rowland sat in the modest office he rented a few blocks from the Daley Center.

He smiled again. "Actually Doctor Stern is here right now. Thanks for referring him to me. He's been filling me in on the story."

He blew out his breath, "Quite a story, huh? Sounds like Herb Walton's going to play hardball on this, don't you think?"

Alex laughed, "Oh yes! That's why I wanted Doctor Stern to see you. He really needs someone in his corner."

She hesitated for a minute. "I checked what I was told is a standard International employment contract for doctors. The way I read it, if Doctor Stern's contract is the same, then he certainly can have his own personal attorney, and International have to pay your fees. I asked him to bring you his personal contract. If that's how it reads, I think you should go for it!"

John nodded and looked at the paper on his desk.

"I have his contract here and that's how it looks to me. Thanks again for thinking of me."

He smiled again at a pale and tense looking David Stern.

Alex continued, "Actually this is really a courtesy call. I wanted to let you know. I represent Robert Brown and his kids, and the estate of Winnie Brown. I just filed a wrongful death claim against your new client and International. You'll be getting the papers tomorrow."

She hesitated for a minute." You understand, I really have no choice. Stern screwed up very badly and she died. He's a full time employee of International. You understand that I have to include him in the suit."

John nodded gravely," I understand completely, and we appreciate the heads up."

"O.K. then," said Alex, "I'm sure we'll be talking soon."

She hesitated, "You know, I'm not famous for having a high regard for the medical profession..."

John interrupted her with a laugh, "Really?"

Alex laughed too, "Really. But I do think David Stern sincerely wants to make whatever restitution he can. So hopefully you and I can work something out."

John nodded, "I hear you."

She paused again," I do think that Herb is going to make him the focus of the case. So, John you're going to have to work hard to support him. We both know what an asshole Herb can be."

John nodded again, "That we do. O.K. Alex, thanks again for letting us know. Are you calling Herb also?"

Alex laughed again," No. If I had my way I'd have the papers delivered to him at three in the morning!"

John laughed, "Now that sounds more like the Alex Goldberg we all know."

She added, "Let me tell you a cute story."

She quickly told him about her visit to the Browns.

John was amused. *"Bereavement Specialists*. Well that's a new one! One thing you've got to say for Herb, he may be an unethical bastard, but he is creative!"

They both laughed. John hung up and turned back to his client.

"Well, as you probably gathered that was Alex Goldberg."

David nodded.

John rubbed his chin thoughtfully as he explained, "It was a courtesy call. She wanted to let us know that she has just filed a wrongful death lawsuit against you and your employer, on behalf of Robert Brown."

David winced at the words *'wrongful death'*.

John noticed his reaction.

"I know the language sounds very harsh. But that really is what this case is about."

He looked down at his notes. He and David had spent nearly three hours together, reviewing the events of the past few weeks.

"Let me summarize for you," said John, stretching his six foot three frame.

"Please correct me if I'm wrong, but as I see it, number one you freely admit you made a serious mistake, and you want to see the Brown family compensated for their loss."

David nodded, "That's most important, for sure."

John ticked off on the fingers of his left hand.

"And number two, you want, if possible to be re-instated by International, and resume your job."

"That's right," said David anxiously, "If I can."

John nodded, "Fair enough."

He leaned back in his chair, which creaked ominously. He looked closely at David.

"Well, I agree with Alex we're in for a dog fight. Goal number two depends entirely on achieving goal number one. I'll explain in a minute why I say that."

David nodded, "Alex said she thinks that International are going to make the case all about me."

John nodded his agreement.

"In a perfect world, they would simply say *'We agree that our guy committed a serious error which we deeply regret.'* Then they would negotiate a financial settlement with Alex on behalf of her client. Your name would be reported to the National Medical Data Base. There would be no serious recriminations from them. It was an honest mistake, albeit with tragic consequences."

He shrugged, "But these things happen unfortunately, and you freely admit your error. Appropriate compensation is paid, and you move on."

He looked keenly at David. "I'm not trying for a second to minimize how badly you must feel. I'm sure you feel just awful."

He shook his head, "I don't know how you guys do it all the time. I mean dealing with cancer patients every day, that's very heavy stuff."

David choked up. He said quietly, "I feel so guilty. She shouldn't have died like that."

John looked at him sympathetically. "But you're doing everything you can to make amends. You're only human."

He continued, "Anyway that would be the best scenario." He sighed, "But it sounds like they've chosen a different tack. It sure looks like they're going to fight it all the way, starting with the death certificate."

David nodded glumly. "Even if I insist that I screwed up?"

John nodded, "You don't know their attorney, Herb Walton."

He shook his head, "He's an arrogant son of a bitch. He's very successful. He wins most of his cases, although I must tell you Alex has beaten him a few times."

He smiled half to himself. "Beat him very badly, too."

He stretched again. "Trouble with Herb is, he's an unethical bastard. Doesn't care how he wins. Whatever it takes, that's what he'll do."

He smiled. "Their strategy is easy to predict. If you stick to your story...."

David was insistent. "It's not a story. It's the truth. I couldn't live with myself, knowing that I'm responsible for Winnie's death and then lying about it."

"I'm sorry," said John, "if you stick to your version of the facts, then they have no choice. If they insist on fighting the case, they have to discredit you. They have to convince a judge and jury that you cannot be believed. They'll have their other doctors claim that she died of the cancer, like the death certificate says. And they'll have to somehow paint you as unreliable, try to make the jury think you somehow imagined it all."

He shook his head, "That's not going to be easy, though. I think you'll make a great witness."

He nodded thoughtfully, "Alex is right. This case will be all about you. It won't be pretty."

"As for goal number two, getting you re-instated, that's going to have to wait until the jury returns with a verdict that you did indeed cause the injury. Then we'll file a suit against International for wrongful dismissal. They haven't a shred of evidence to justify terminating or suspending you on grounds of ill health, physical or mental."

He went on, "There are federal whistle blowing laws that protect an employee from being terminated or punished for refusing to conceal wrongdoing in the organization. No federal judge would rule for them if we can show that you were terminated because you insisted on telling the truth about this incident."

He looked at his watch.

"It's nearly four thirty, I have to go, David. I've got to pick up my little guy from day care. We'll speak very soon. In the meantime, I don't want you speaking to anyone about the case. If you receive any communication, written or verbal, from anyone, you don't respond. You say nothing, you write nothing, you sign nothing. Just let me know O.K. David?"

David nodded as he rose. "John, just one thing. If International somehow convinces a jury that I imagined it all, that she actually died of lymphoma, what would that do to my chances of getting my job back?"

John's confident smile faded. "That would be a problem."

David spoke thoughtfully as they left the office.

"So what you're saying is that we want Alex to win her case against me, to prove that I screwed up, and that I'm telling the truth?"

John nodded, "That's about it, David."

"O.K." said David, "Well, I hope she's as good as everybody says."

John clapped David reassuringly on the shoulder as they walked out of the office.

Chap 24

"Thank you so much for coming in," said Cheryl Rubin.

Andi Kaplan sat opposite her, in the very chair that David had occupied a few months earlier. She smiled nervously.

"You said on the phone that you wanted to talk to me about David?"

Rubin nodded, "That's right."

She studied Andi carefully. She saw a young woman in her late twenties, casually dressed in jeans and a grey wool sweater. She wore expensive red cowboy boots.

Cheryl Rubin was into shoes, she always noticed them.

Andi was the cute cheer-leader type, with honey blonde hair cut short. Rubin was on the wrong side of fifty, losing a life-long battle with her weight. She disliked Andi on sight.

"May I call you Andi?'

Andi nodded and Rubin continued. "Let me explain, Andi. I am David's psychiatrist."

Andi's mouth dropped, "He never told me he was seeing a psychiatrist!"

Rubin shrugged, "I'm not surprised. Many patients feel uncomfortable about admitting that they're having emotional difficulties. Especially men."

Andi nodded and Rubin continued, "Anyway Andi, I've been seeing David for several years."

If you include seeing him at lunch in the doctor's dining room that was true!

"As you can imagine I'm very concerned about the difficulties he's been having recently. And that's why I asked you to come in. David talked about you often."

Hardly. Cheryl Rubin had actually only learned of Andi's existence at the meeting with Herb Walton in Piper's office.

She smiled encouragingly at Andi, "I know you two were very close, Andi. Any information that you can give me about David might be very helpful."

These were almost the first true words that Rubin had uttered. Helpful, maybe, but not helpful to David Stern.

Andi began to cry and Rubin gestured to the strategically placed box of Kleenex.

"Please Andi, help yourself,"

Andi wiped her eyes, smearing her mascara.

She sniffed, "It's like this Doctor Rubin...."

Rubin leaned forward and grasped the younger woman's hand in what was meant to be a reassuring gesture.

"Please call me Cheryl."

"O.K. Cheryl. It's like this. I've known David for about three years. We've lived together for nearly two years."

She shook her head, "I don't know, he can be very difficult at times. It's not been so good recently."

Cheryl Rubin nodded. Andi didn't need any encouragement. The floodgates had opened.

"He just doesn't seem that interested in spending time with me. The problem is he works so hard! I hardly ever see him, and when I do, half the time I don't think he's listening to me. He spends so much time at the hospital. I swear he cares for his patients more than he cares about me."

Andi told of her grievances over Cousin Linda's wedding and David's lack of interest in her parents. How she wanted commitment, and felt rejected or at best ignored.

"Ask the spouse of any type A professional and you'd hear the same complaints. Grow up lady." thought Rubin.

Her right foot tapped impatiently. If this were a real patient or family interview she would never allow herself to show such impatience, but this young woman was not giving her what she needed,

Andi spoke softly, "I do feel guilty about that day."

Rubin raised an eyebrow. *Was this something she could use?*

"Why do you say that?"

Andi told of their argument on the fateful day.

Rubin could scarcely control her impatience. The foot started tapping again.

The crap that she had to listen to!

"Andi," said Rubin, "everything you've shared with me is very interesting. But let me ask you a few more direct questions regarding your relationship."

Rubin fixed Andi with the most empathetic look she could muster.

"I don't mean to embarrass you, and please remember everything you tell me is in strictest confidence. Has David ever been sexually or physically abusive to you?"

Andi shook her head, "No.

"Has he ever abused alcohol, or any kind of drug use?"

Andi shook her head again, "No."

Nothing there that they could use.

"Tell me about David's relationships with other people. How about friends?"

Andi shrugged, "His best friend is a guy called Joe Malone. He's also a doctor at the hospital. They trained together, I think."

She shrugged again, "He's a nice enough guy, I suppose. They go to ball games together, the Cubs and the Bulls."

She pouted a little, "I don't go. I don't like sports."

Rubin knew Malone, one of the other hot shots that Houston had hired. She had no dealings with him but she'd heard on the hospital grapevine that the little shit was causing trouble, stirring up some of the medical staff on Stern's behalf.

"How about other friends?"

There's a guy he goes skiing with every winter.

She shrugged, "He lives in Los Angeles. He and David went to high school together. I don't really know him. "

"How about David's family?"

Andi looked at Rubin strangely.

"Hasn't he spoken to you about his family?"

Oops!

"Well, of course," said Rubin, "But I'm interested in how you see his relationship with his family."

Careful!

Andi shrugged again.

"David was never really that close to his parents," she said, "I don't know why. We hardly ever saw them. We saw much more of my folks."

Rubin made a mental note to follow up on this.

"How about his childhood?"

"He never spoke about his childhood."

"What about other relatives? Does he have siblings?"

Andi shook her head, "I can't believe that you don't know about his family after two years of therapy!"

Rubin made a vague non-committal gesture.

She had to be very careful here.

"He had a sister but she died young. He never talked to me about her."

Andi started to cry again, "He never talked to me about anything important!"

Rubin looked at her watch. *Time to wrap this up.*

She rose and led Andi to the door.

"This has been very helpful, Andi. You've given me a lot to work with. I'm very grateful to you for coming in. I just want to emphasize one thing. Please don't tell David about this meeting. I could get into serious trouble if he knew we had spoken about him without his knowledge and permission."

That part was certainly true!

Andi gave Cheryl Rubin another strange look.

"Didn't he tell you that we've split up?"

"Oh...I thought you were still talking," stammered Rubin.

She quickly escorted Andi to the outer office.

*"Conspiracy was not easy "*thought Rubin, *"But maybe, just maybe, she'd got some stuff that Walton could use."*

Chap 25

The case of Brown versus Stern and International made its way slowly through the crowded court system. Herb Walton represented International. The early legal skirmishes made it clear that there would be no talk of settlement.

Walton blandly stated that all of the medical facts supported the position that Winnie Brown had tragically died of uncontrolled seizures caused by malignant lymphoma involving her brain. At the preliminary hearings Walton ignored David's outburst in the Oncology clinic, and David's continued insistence that he had injected the wrong drug.

David was represented by John Rowland. Alex's recommendation of Rowland was right on target. He was a good lawyer. More importantly he was a kind man whose own personal problems had sensitized him to David's situation. David needed his support.

Several months after his initial meeting with John Rowland, David received formal notification of his discovery deposition. A week before the appointed date he met with John Rowland to prepare for the deposition. He found John sitting in his office, surrounded by boxes of paper.

John waved a hand at the mess, "Welcome to legal hell! Do you want a cup of coffee?"

David shook his head as John cleared some space for him to sit.

"I don't know why in the computer age, we still kill so many trees," he grumbled, "It's like you can't have a law suit without all this paper."

He looked at David closely," Anyway, enough of that, how are you doing?" David gave a non-committal gesture, "So, so I guess."

John nodded sympathetically, "I'm sure it can't be easy."

David shrugged, and John pulled out a blank legal pad from the drawer of his battered desk.

"O.K. Let's talk about next week, have you ever been deposed before?"

David nodded, "A couple of times. I had one patient who sued another doctor for missing their Hodgkin's disease for a year or so, and another lymphoma patient who was killed by a drunk driver. They wanted my opinion about how long he would have lived without the accident."

John nodded, "O.K. so you're at least familiar with the process."

David nodded, "I think so."

"Let me explain. Contrary to what the general public thinks and the way it is on T.V., trials are not marvels of legal performance where attorneys think like lightning on their feet. In fact everything is pretty well scripted. The other side has a right to know everything that you are going to say at trial, and has a right to see everything that we may wish to show the jury."

"That's what next week's deposition is all about. It provides an opportunity for the other side to elicit all of your testimony in advance. You testify under oath. A court reporter writes down everything you say and produces a transcript of your testimony."

David nodded, "I understand."

John continued, "We call this whole process *discovery*. Your deposition next week is a discovery deposition. So when it comes to the actual trial, the attorneys all have a copy of your deposition transcript there. If your trial testimony is different from what you said at the deposition, the other lawyers will try and use any inconsistency to make out that you're either unreliable or confused or whatever. We call that process *impeachment*. The idea is to make the jury less likely to believe the witness."

David once again nodded his understanding.

"Actually," said John, "in this case I keep saying other side, but as you know there are really two other sides in this case. You are a defendant, and in most cases the defendant has to beware of the plaintiff's lawyer most. That's Alex Goldberg, of course."

John smiled thinly, "Here we have to be more concerned about your co-defendant, International. You've already seen how Herb Walton operates."

David nodded.

John drank some of his coffee and grimaced. "When I finally get paid by International, first thing I'm going to do is buy a decent coffee maker. Sure you don't want some?"

David smiled and shook his head. "My stomach hurts enough without any more abuse, thanks."

John nodded, "O.K I think we're pretty clear about the process. All of the lawyers get a chance to ask you questions. I expect most of the questions will relate to the actual day of the incident, although they're not limited in any way to what they can ask."

David shuddered inwardly at the thought of reliving that fateful day, and John noticed his reaction. He gave David a sympathetic look.

"I'm sorry that you have to go through this, but it really can't be avoided."

David said, "That's O.K. I'll be fine. I understand that this has to be done."

John nodded his agreement. "I have great confidence in you. Remember, the lawyers are just reading from a script, you're the medical expert."

"Some expert," said David darkly.

"I do want to mention a couple of other things," said John hastily.

"First, lawyers have different ways of approaching discovery depositions, but they all want the same thing. They want you to talk."

He paused, "Don't be fooled, the International attorneys are the enemy. You don't have to worry about Alex. All she needs is for you to commit to your version of the facts on the record. She has no interest in attacking you. On the contrary, the more credible you are the better for her case."

He shook his head, "I'm more concerned about the International lawyers. Remember they have to discredit you and your version of events. If you say anything that they can use at trial to paint you in a bad light, I guarantee they'll use it. Although they're going to ask you questions, they aren't really interested in your version of the facts."

David started to speak, but John raised a hand.

"Let me finish. What they really want is for you to say something on the record that they can use against you."

He smiled grimly, "I've seen lawyers use every trick in the book to get a witness talking. Some come over real friendly, make out that it's just a friendly chat."

He shook his head, "No way. Remember every word you say is being recorded."

"Other lawyers pretend to get impatient or angry, so the witness unconsciously tries to please them by volunteering more information. I've seen women lawyers flutter their eyelashes."

He smiled, "And a whole lot more."

John pointed a finger at David for emphasis.

"Cardinal rule of discovery, never volunteer anything. Answer the question, then stop talking. Got it?"

David started to speak, but John interrupted.

"I'm sorry David. I know it sounds like I'm going on about this too much, but I can't emphasize it enough. If you want to learn how to behave at a discovery deposition, listen to the tape of Clinton being deposed at his Monica Lewinsky depo."

"Everyone knows how Clinton likes to talk, but listen to him at his depo. He was very, very careful with his words. He would answer each question and then stop talking. Nothing volunteered, nothing spontaneous. He's a lawyer, he knows how these things go."

David listened with growing anxiety as John prepped him.

"I'll be there with you," said John, "although I can't answer for you. I can only make legal objections, that are based on points of law. But if I think they're beating up on you too much, I'll intercede."

"Oh, one other thing, they have no right to ask about any discussions we have had. All lawyer client communications are privileged. You have the same thing with patients, right?"

David nodded his agreement as John added with a smile, "They're not going to ask you directly what we may talked about, they know I'd object to that. Just be sure you don't volunteer anything, O.K.?"

Again David indicated that he understood.

They spent the better part of two hours reviewing all of the medical records.

John reminded David, "All of the records will be available to you at the deposition. Don't guess. *I don't remember*, or *I don't know* are perfectly acceptable answers."

Finally John was satisfied. "O.K. I think we're done."

He looked at his watch, "Oops, I've got to run," he said apologetically, "Childcare run again!"

They parted company at the office door. David watched him hurry away. Alex had told David nothing about John's family troubles. At that moment David envied John his family. He was obviously busy and very committed. In contrast, David's life seemed very cold and empty.

Chap 26

The following Monday morning, the first Monday in July, David met John in his office at eight thirty. In deference to the day, David wore a suit and tie. The once elegant dark grey Paul Stewart suit now hung loosely on David's frame.

"He must have lost about twenty pounds in the past six months," thought John.

He made no comment.

"We've got a few minutes," said John, "any questions or thoughts before we head over there?"

David shook his head and John nodded, "O.K."

"Just one thing I want to mention. With big firms like Herb's, discovery depositions like this are often taken by fairly junior attorneys."

He raised a warning finger. "But with key witnesses, the big guy usually does it himself."

He paused, "I expect Herb Walton will be there today, and depose you himself. You O.K. with that?"

David shrugged, "I'm a big boy. I'll be O.K."

He smiled, "Can I tell him to go screw himself?"

John shook his head vigorously, "Absolutely not! At least not on the record! We always try to maintain an appearance of professionalism at depositions. The judge gets to read the transcript, and they don't like that kind of thing. Also, remember anything you say today can be read to the jury at the time of trial."

David laid his hand on John's arm gently, "Relax, John. I was only joking."

John visibly relaxed. He smiled as he said, "O.K. If anyone tells Herb to go screw himself today, my money would be on Alex."

David laughed.

"I may be tempted, but I'll behave. I promise."

Together they walked the few blocks to Herb's office. It promised to be a hot day.

They entered the enormous marble lobby of Sixty-two Dearborn, and took the elevator to the thirtieth floor. The double glass doors of the offices of Reilly, Walton and Coopersmith revealed a reception area that could easily accommodate thirty people. A blond receptionist sat behind an elegant Chippendale style desk. Whether the desk was genuine or reproduction David couldn't tell.

The blond was definitely not genuine.

John announced their arrival to the receptionist who haughtily asked them to take a seat for a few minutes.

Two people sat in the reception area. John introduced David to Alex Goldberg, for appearances sake. The other person sitting waiting was the court reporter, an elderly man who sat reading a copy of Crain's Chicago Business.

Theodore Stevenson was one of the grand old men of the Cook County Court system. He had been a court reporter for over forty-five years. Many of the younger lawyers thought he was old fashioned, not as up on the newer computerized systems as the younger court reporters.

John greeted him warmly, "Hi Ted, how are you doing?"

Ted smiled, "I'm fine, John. Trying to keep out of trouble. How're the kids?"

"Fine , thank you."

John knew that the main reason Ted Stevenson kept working long after his seventieth birthday was to keep busy. He had lost his beloved Peggy after nearly fifty years of marriage. Alex always booked him for her depositions.

Alex wore a pair of jeans and a Disneyland tee shirt. She didn't appear to be overawed by the fancy surroundings. The only incongruous note was struck by her expensive leather brief case. She smiled at David as they shook hands.

"How are you doing?" she asked quietly.

Privately she was shocked by his appearance.

"I'm O.K." he answered, "By the way, I want to thank you for recommending John."

He gestured towards John Rowland. "He's a good guy."

Alex smiled as she nodded," He is a good guy. I'm glad he's with you."

She lowered her voice and leaned close to David.

"Just one thing, you may be in for a hard time today. Not from me, but...."

She gestured around the office, "They're a tough crowd here. I'm going to suggest that you don't volunteer the information that you got John's name from me. They can't ask you how you met him."

She smiled briefly, "So, if you don't mention it, they don't need to know."

She shrugged, "Just don't volunteer any information about it. That's the kind of little thing that they would try to make something of with the judge."

David nodded, "Thanks for the heads up."

Alex gave him a warm smile.

Shortly after, the receptionist invited them all into a palatial conference room. Decorated in walnut and cherry the room was dominated by a massive table which could easily accommodate twenty people. Along one wall was a server with silver coffee urns and a selection of sweet rolls. One entire wall was filled with windows looking out onto the Loop.

Two attorneys from Herb Walton's office rose as they entered the room.

Alex greeted Jodi Miller coolly, "Morning Jodi, how's the bereavement counseling going? I'm *dying* to hear!"

Beneath her heavy make up, Jodi Miller flushed angrily. She was wearing a scarlet halter top and short white skirt that did little to conceal her figure. She ignored Alex and concentrated her attention on David Stern.

"Good morning, Doctor. It's a real pleasure to meet you."

Her voice was low and husky. She held out her hand to David, who took it, somewhat nonplussed.

Alex could not contain herself. She laughed out loud. "All right! I love the hooker look, Jodi. Very becoming."

To John she said in a stage whisper, loud enough to be heard by all.

"I see it's going to be another Penthouse depo, John. Maybe you and I should go and change into skimpier outfits. You know, match the mood here."

Alex was on a roll. She smiled sweetly at Jodi Miller.

"What's the deal here, Jodi? You show Dr. Stern your boobs if he admits he made it all up?"

She shook her head, "That may not work. He's probably seen lots of silicone before. Remember he's a *doctor.*"

She turned to Jodi's colleague. He appeared to be about twenty nine or thirty, with heavily gelled dark hair brushed straight back. He wore dark pinstriped pants with no suit coat. A heavily starched white shirt with a yellow power tie and matching suspenders completed the look.

Alex looked him straight in the face, "Let me guess, you're the bad cop today, right?"

John Rowland smiled quietly as Herb Walton's junior associate, Richard Peterson looked silently to Jodi for help. His colleague gave Alex a look of pure poison. If Alex noticed she gave no sign.

Alex shook her head as the court reporter set up his equipment at one end of the table. *Beating up on opposing counsel was fun, but there was serious work to do here.*

John got himself a couple of sweet rolls and a cup of coffee. David declined the offer of coffee. The court reporter indicated he was ready as more formal introductions were made all round.

Despite John's prediction, Herb Walton was not there.

Alex started the deposition after David was sworn in. Deposition testimony was elicited under oath and a formal record was kept, just like a trial. Alex reminded David of these facts.

Under Alex's skilful questioning David described in detail his education, experience and training before coming to International. Alex then had him describe his relationship with International. Copies of his resume and employment contract with International were entered into the record as exhibits.

After a short break the questioning resumed.

In every case there was a critical moment.

"Here it comes," thought Alex. She took a deep breath.

"Doctor, I'd like to turn now to your treatment of Winnie Brown. I have here a certified copy of all the inpatient and clinic records that relate to her care at International. Certified means that all of the attorneys in the case have agreed that this is an accurate copy of the records. This is not meant to be a test of your memory, so if you feel the need to refer to the records at any time, please feel free to do so. O.K.?"

David nodded, "Fine."

Alex then had David describe in detail his treatment of Winnie Brown from their first meeting late in August of 2000 until the fateful day in January of 2001. She then went through all of the events in the clinic that led to Winnie's collapse, and her subsequent admission to the ICU.

David answered every question frankly and truthfully. When it came time to talk about the fatal injection there was no hesitation on his part. Alex was not surprised. Despite her young age she was a keen judge of human character. She fully expected David to stick with the truth, as he had ever since their first meeting.

He didn't disappoint her.

It took a solid hour of detailed questions and answers, but by the time Alex was finished she had a clear record of the events of that fateful day. Alex suggested a brief break but David declined.

He felt fine. What he was experiencing was the relief of finally being able to do something concrete to make amends to the Brown family.

The questioning was not over, however. To David's surprise Alex spent a considerable length of time questioning him about his experiences at International after Winnie's death. John understood that this was important to her building a complete case against International.

Over the objections of Jodi Miller and Richard Peterson, she had David describe in detail the meetings where Herb Walton had pressured David to accept the International version of events. She made note of all the names David identified as present at the meetings.

"So many people to depose, so little time!" she thought.

John understood that this part of David's testimony would be very inflammatory for any jury who believed it, and would paint International in a very bad light.

To see a young woman needlessly die, and then lie to cover it up!

Alex also had another agenda. She was outraged by Walton's treatment of David. Her game plan was to win the case for Robert Brown, and then provide a basis for John Rowland to sue International for the wrongful dismissal of David Stern. Herb Walton was in her sights.

Her final questions related to David's opinion regarding Winnie Brown's prognosis.

"I may have asked this question already but I want to be sure the record is clear. What is your opinion, Doctor, regarding Winnie Brown's prognosis for cure, had the accidental injection of Vincristine not occurred?"

David took a deep breath, "In my opinion had I not injected the wrong drug, Winnie Brown would be alive and cancer-free today, with every probability of complete cure."

Alex nodded, "And that is an opinion you hold to a reasonable degree of medical probability?"

David nodded, "Yes."

Alex nodded gravely.

"That took guts," she thought.

"Doctor, That's all the questions I have for now. I'm going to look over my notes, but in the meantime I'm going to pass you over to my colleague, Ms. Miller."

Jodi looked at her watch. It was nearly twelve fifteen.

"Why don't we break for lunch, and start again at one o'clock?" she suggested.

Everyone agreed and they rose to leave. As they walked out, Alex touched David lightly on the sleeve.

"That took a lot of courage," she said quietly, "If it helps any, I know that Robert Brown will be grateful you stood up for him and the kids."

She paused, "And I don't *know*, but I *believe* that right now Winnie also feels the same way. Robert says that you were always there for her."

David nodded silently as he left with John Rowland.

This was very tough.

Chap 27

After lunch it was the other attorneys' turn. Jodi Miller was up first. Her style was different from Alex's. She smiled seductively at David, who sat opposite her. As she leaned towards him her heavy perfume filled the room.

"I hope David doesn't get an asthma attack from all that crap," thought Alex. "Doctor Stern, we met this morning. I'm Jodi Miller and I represent your former employer, International Medical Center."

She first asked a few soft-ball questions about his research, and seemed very impressed by the number of scientific papers he had published.

"You've done lot of research," she said, "I'm very impressed!"

Alex silently rolled her eyes.

The mood suddenly changed.

"Doctor, are you currently working as a physician?"

David shook his head, "No."

"And why is that?"

"I decided to wait until this case is resolved before seeking another job," replied David.

"Were you advised by any physician that you should not work, because of health issues?"

Beside David, John Rowland shifted uncomfortably in his chair. Alex sat with no expression on her face.

This was standard Herb Walton sleaze, character assassination by innuendo.

David answered the question.

"No, I have not been advised by any doctor that I shouldn't work."

"And I don't have any health issues," he added.

From the other end of the table, Richard Peterson joined in.

"Doctor, for the record my name is Richard Peterson, and I also represent International."

He paused as if he expected David to be impressed.

"There is a sworn affidavit in this case from a psychiatrist, which will be confirmed shortly by deposition under oath. In this affidavit the doctor states that she strongly advised you not to take care of patients until you complete psychiatric treatment. Do you deny ever receiving such advice?"

David remained cool, "Yes, I do."

On her legal pad Alex made a note.

Get independent psychiatric evaluation.

She would have to discuss it with John and get his O.K. It was all a crock of course, David was as sane as they come, but these were the hoops that Herb and his team would continue to put them through until this was over.

Jodi again. "So your testimony is that you just decided yourself not to work, until this case is resolved?"

David nodded, "That's correct. Yes."

Richard Peterson made a skeptical face but David remained cool.

John was pleased. David was doing very well. Alex smiled to herself. David was more than a match for the pair. Her smile quickly faded, however at the next question, asked abrasively by Richard Peterson.

"When did you first have psychiatric treatment?"

David looked straight at Peterson, "I have never had psychiatric treatment."

Peterson threw a piece of paper across the table at David.

"Let me remind you doctor, you are under oath. And I have just shown you a sworn affidavit......"

"Enough of this," thought John Rowland.

He leaned across the table and picked up the paper that Peterson had thrown in David's direction. John spoke firmly.

"Stop right there, Mr. Peterson. You have not shown Dr. Stern anything. For the record, you just *threw* a piece of paper across the table at him."

Peterson turned on John Rowland.

"No speaking objections! You know the rules, you can make legal objections only!"

John remained calm. "Please don't raise your voice at me or my client, Mr. Peterson. My legal objection is that your question is argumentative. Second you did not show the document to the doctor, you threw it at him. That is unprofessional, and is unacceptable behavior on your part."

John knew the buzz-words. No attorney wanted to be accused on the record of acting in an unprofessional manner. Peterson started to speak, but John cut him off.

"Let me finish my objection. The doctor cannot be expected to comment on a document that he has not read, and *he will not comment* on any document until I have had an opportunity to read it also. Is that clear to you, Mr. Peterson?"

Peterson muttered, "Yes."

John was not done with Peterson. "Furthermore let me state for the record, if there is any more unprofessional behavior from you, I will immediately terminate this deposition, and we'll continue it in front of a judge."

On rare occasions when feuding attorneys could not control themselves or their clients, discovery depositions such as this would be conducted in the presence of a judge. The judge would then act as police officer to keep the proceedings civil.

John knew that the mere statement on the record that an attorney was acting inappropriately, coupled with the threat of taking the deposition to a judge was usually enough to restore order.

For the first time, John raised his voice as he stared hard at Peterson.

"You will not browbeat my client, do you understand?"

Alex sat quietly during this whole exchange.

"John's doing just fine," she thought.

Once again she felt good about recommending him to David.

Ted Stevenson spoke quietly, "I need to change the paper in my machine. Can we take a five minute break?"

Alex smiled to herself. No-one questioned why they had run out of paper so soon after the lunch break. She looked at Ted who calmly fussed with his ancient machine. Ted clearly felt that a break in the proceedings would allow everyone to calm down.

During the break Jodi Miller and Richard Peterson had a quiet but obviously animated conversation in one corner of the room. When they resumed, it was Jodi who directed David's attention to the affidavit.

"Doctor, you've had a chance to read what I've marked as Stern deposition exhibit number six, haven't you?"

David indicated that he had read the affidavit.

"And you agree that in this affidavit, Doctor Cheryl Rubin, a psychiatrist at International Medical Center states under penalty of perjury that you were in fact her patient, isn't that correct?"

Jodi seemed to have abandoned the seductress mode, at least for the moment.

"That's what it says," said David, "but....."

"Thank you, Doctor, you've answered my question."

It was clear that Jodi had cut David's answer off.

John Rowland spoke up, "This is a discovery deposition, and the doctor is entitled to answer the question fully."

He turned to his client, "Doctor, if your answer to the previous question was incomplete, please feel free to finish your answer now."

David nodded calmly. "Thank you, my complete answer to the previous question is yes, the affidavit does state that I was a patient of Dr. Rubin, but that is a false statement. I was never a patient of Dr. Rubin."

He paused and spoke firmly, "I have never received psychiatric care from any physician, including Dr. Rubin."

Richard Peterson broke in, "Are you calling Doctor Rubin a *liar?*"

David refused to be goaded. "I am saying that this affidavit is incorrect."

"So you are calling Dr. Rubin, a well respected psychiatrist in a major Chicago hospital, a doctor you have worked with for years, a *liar?*"

Before David could respond, John interrupted.

"Objection, that question is argumentative. It's also been asked and answered."

He turned to David, "You don't need to answer it again, Doctor."

"Unless you want to Doctor," said Jodi hopefully.

Alex rolled her eyes silently at this, while David merely smiled.

"Let's move on," suggested John.

Jodi looked at her notes. "Doctor, what is a delusion?"

John Rowland sat up.

"Objection. Lack of foundation. Doctor Stern is not a psychiatrist. He is an oncologist."

Jodi then explained to David that he could answer questions after a legal objection. John added that he should only answer if he felt qualified to do so.

David nodded his understanding. "A delusion" he said, "is a fixed irrational belief in an idea that is unsupported by facts. There are two major types of delusions. Primary delusions are the hallmark of schizophrenia, while secondary delusions may be seen in a variety of psychiatric illnesses."

He shrugged, "That's my understanding, based on medical school Psych, about twelve years ago."

Jodi again read from her notes.

"Doctor, you just defined a delusion as a fixed irrational idea, not supported by the facts. Have you ever suffered from delusions?"

David looked very uncomfortable, "Well...."

Jodi looked eager while Richard Peterson leaned forward.

"You have to answer the question, Doctor," he said, "Let me remind you that you are under oath."

David seemed very reluctant to answer. He addressed his attorney. "Do I have to answer, John?"

John nodded in the affirmative. Jodi and Richard held their breath, expensive pens poised above legal pads in eager anticipation. Alex watched all this with a half smile.

David looked down at the table for a few moments.

Finally he spoke, "I'm almost ashamed to admit this."

He looked straight at Jodi, "But I have to tell you the truth. Every year I suffer from the same delusion."

He sighed, "Every April I really believe it's going to be the Cubs' year."

He smiled broadly. "But by May or June at the latest," he said, "I'm usually cured."

John burst out in relieved laughter. Jodi and Richard flushed angrily.

Alex shook her head, smiling. "Always the smart ass!" she muttered.

She looked over at Ted, "That was off the record!"

Ted smiled and lifted his hands off the keys as if to show Alex that he had not recorded her words. Back on the record, David completed his answer.

"Other than that annual delusion, Ms. Miller," he said coolly, "no, I have never suffered from delusions."

They continued to wrangle for another full hour, but David refused to be seduced by Jodi Miller or intimidated by Richard Peterson. Despite their strenuous efforts, he stuck to his version of events, and denied any hint of mental illness.

It was nearly four o'clock by the time they finished. The home team of Miller and Peterson left, barely concealing their ill humor. John rushed off, citing his need to pick up his youngest. Ted packed up and left.

Alex and David were left alone in the cavernous conference room. She closed the door securely and turned to David.

"You did very well," she said.

She shook her head with disgust, "I can't believe that those two clowns actually believe the shit they tried to pull in here!"

David shrugged as Alex mused, "I don't really understand why Walton wasn't here. He certainly understands that you're the most important witness in this entire case."

She shook her head, "It doesn't make a lot of sense for him to send his B team."

She smiled at him, "Anyway, this is probably the only chance we'll get to speak privately. I just wanted to know that you're doing O.K."

David shrugged, "Thanks for your concern. I guess I'm as well as can be expected."

Alex nodded as she looked at the door. "O.K. I'd better go. I don't want any of Walton's crew to see us talking."

As she headed for the door, David spoke, "Alex, you were very funny with Jodi Miller."

He smiled, "Especially the comment about her showing me her boobs if I gave her the answers she wanted."

Alex smiled at the memory.

"I was just thinking Alex," said David innocently, "I answered all your questions, didn't I?"

Alex turned at the door and looked at David for a long time. She gave him a wicked smile as she left the room.

"If you think I'm going to....."

She shook her head, "In your dreams, Stern. In your dreams!"

Chap 28

The months following his deposition dragged by for David with no resolution of the situation. He remained full of guilt over Winnie's death and depressed by the disastrous end of his own career. His testimony at the deposition had made it clear to International that he would not change his version of events. As a result he had no further contact with his former employers.

He had no contact with Andi, other than a session with a moving company who came and took all her stuff from the condo. He was less distressed by this than he would have expected. David spoke with few people other than John Rowland. His parents did not understand his position.

"It's not like you can bring her back. You can't ruin your life over this," said his mother when he tried to explain to them what had happened.

"You worked so hard for so long. Don't throw it all away."

For many years his life had revolved around his work. Patient care and research had filled his days. Now the hours weighed heavily on him. Rowland suggested that David attend the discovery depositions of the other witnesses, thinking that the process might be therapeutic for David. It was not.

The witnesses that International planned to use at trial followed a predictable line. Crandall and Keating described a clinical course and autopsy findings consistent with death due to cerebral lymphoma. According to Crandall there was just no evidence at autopsy to support David's contention that he had caused Winnie's death. O'Rourke described a distraught David in the Oncology clinic immediately after Winnie's seizures.

International obviously planned to paint David as mentally unstable. It was deeply painful for David to listen to a parade of ex-colleagues, all International employees, describe how he would be in the hospital for many hours, day and night looking after sick patients. According to the witnesses this excessive involvement with his patients was evidence of David's neuroses.

Alex was at her acid best during these encounters. When one of the head nurses on the oncology floor stated under oath that David's continued presence at the bedside of one patient had concerned her, Alex could not contain her disbelief.

"So let me be sure I understand what you're saying here Donna," said Alex sweetly in a voice that David knew well.

"You had this man with lymphoma, post bone marrow transplant, no white cells or platelets, bleeding from the nose, rectum and urethra, temperature 104, positive blood cultures and septic shock. Very sick, right? And you were upset because his doctor was there too much, is that what you're telling me?"

Donna Vazquez squirmed, "Well, not exactly. It's just that Doctor Stern always seemed to be too involved with his patients."

Alex nodded sagely, "Of course. I understand. Too involved. You would have preferred if he'd spent more time on the golf course, perhaps?"

Such moments of humor for David were few. The process of preparing for trial was very hard for him. As Alex Goldberg had predicted, a large part of the trial was going to be about David Stern.

International's star witness appeared to be Cheryl Rubin who claimed to be David's psychiatrist. She refused to discuss details of David's illness, citing patient confidentiality. At her deposition however she did paint a picture of a deeply disturbed man.

During these months David's only contact with Alex was at the depositions, when the other attorneys were also present. There was no direct communication between David and Alex at these times other than a *Good Morning*. Their relationship appeared no different from that of any plaintiff's attorney and defendant.

What David didn't know was that Alex had developed a great respect for him. Although she showed no sign of it, she was very moved by his commitment to the truth, and his resistance to the pressure from International. She was upset by his obvious unhappiness.

Because of the restrictions imposed by the legal process there could be no personal contact between Alex and David. One morning, late in January of 2002 all that changed.

David sat in his apartment listlessly watching an old movie when his phone rang. Outside it was bitter cold, almost zero degrees.

"David, it's John Rowland, how are you doing?"

"O.K." replied David, "how are you, John?"

"Fine," replied John," listen, I wonder if you'd be free to meet me for lunch today or tomorrow. We have some important things to discuss."

David sighed, "Today's fine. I've got nothing but time, John."

They agreed to meet that day at twelve thirty at Tony's on State, John's favorite Italian restaurant. The pressures of the upcoming trial had no obvious effect on John's appetite. He finished a large bowl of pasta with obvious enjoyment while David listlessly pushed some salad around his plate. David's stomach hurt and he had little appetite.

Finally John pushed his empty plate away.

"Let's talk about our options here, David. Usually the defense likes to delay any trial as long as possible, but as you know, Herb

Walton has been pushing for an early trial here and I'm certainly in agreement."

David nodded and John continued, "No question the quicker this whole business is wrapped up the better for you."

He gave David a keen look. "This limbo existence you're in must be just awful."

No response from David. None was needed. His face told it all.

John pulled out his notes. "You know, this case is a little unusual as far as medical malpractice cases are concerned. Neither side is using outside medical experts, so discovery has already been pretty much completed. There's just a couple of minor witnesses still to depose, and you don't have to worry about them."

"We already have a trial judge, name of Reagen. He's a good guy. No bullshitting him. Used to be a federal prosecutor, not one of the political hacks that we're blessed with here in Cook County."

"We've got a trial date in just under three months, due to start April 8, and the pre-trial conference is coming up in six weeks."

John shook his head. "Alex and I agree, there's no way International's going to settle. I want to talk to you about our position. You know of course that you have the option of settling with Robert Brown and his family if you wish."

David started to speak, but John held up his hand.

"David, wait a minute, let me give you the whole picture first. You certainly can settle before trial, and that would save you some of the stress of a trial. It would also allow you to make amends as best you can to Winnie's family. I know that's important for you."

David nodded eagerly, "That's exactly what I want."

John nodded. "I know. But David, you have to understand what the risk is for you. You acted throughout this affair as an employee of International. As such they are responsible for you. Whatever you agree to pay, International has to pay to the limits of your personal policy, which is one million dollars for a single case. They are self-insured so of all the financial responsibility falls on them rather than another insurance company."

John smiled, "I wouldn't worry about them, they have deep pockets. They can sure afford it."

His face became more serious as he continued, "The problem is if we settle with Robert Brown for, let's say a million dollars and Alex loses her case against International. If that were to happen, then they would certainly come after you for their million."

David looked puzzled and John explained, "Let me lay it out for you. Assume for a moment that hypothetically you agree to pay Robert Brown one million dollars, O.K?"

David nodded O.K. and John continued. "But then after the conclusion of the trial the jury says, *'we agree with International, this patient died of lymphoma, natural causes. David Stern did nothing wrong.'*"

John looked David straight in the eye, "That's a possibility we have to consider."

David nodded reluctantly.

Coffee arrived for John. David declined. John took a sip, added two packets of sugar and continued, "Under those circumstances International would certainly bring a motion before the trial judge, arguing that they should not be held liable just because you had independently agreed to pay the Brown family a million dollars."

He paused, "It would be a very strong argument, especially if the facts of the case established by a jury trial exonerated you, and by extension them also. In my opinion, in those circumstances the trial judge would have to support that position."

He shrugged, "Pretty much a slam dunk, in fact."

David was silent.

"It's kind of bizarre," continued John, "because we certainly should settle. You have no intention of denying your responsibility now. Not only that, you have already admitted your error on the record at your deposition. So the only real arguments that we can make at trial would be to find some mitigating circumstances to reduce your financial liability."

David shook his head. "No way I'm going to wrangle with Robert Brown over money. Not after what I did to Winnie!"

John nodded, "Well, that's right. I know that's your position, and it's an honorable one, but my main concern is to protect you personally in the event that Alex loses her case against International."

John frowned, "I have discussed this with Alex. She understands the situation we're in. I suggested to her that you settle with the Browns, and pay a token settlement of one dollar."

He smiled at David, "I won't quote you her exact reply to that suggestion. Let's just say it was colorful."

He looked around the crowded restaurant, "I can't repeat her exact words. I'd like to come back here some time."

John declined a second cup of coffee and asked for the check.

"What she is demanding is the maximum allowed by your individual coverage with International. That's one million dollars."

David looked kind of sick when he heard the sum *one million.*

John noted David's reaction and quickly continued, "It's actually very reasonable in a case like this, where there's the wrongful death of a young woman with children. Alex would have been perfectly justified in asking for a whole lot more. She's making her big case against International. They're the ones with the deep pockets."

He shrugged, "In fairness to Alex, she's got to do what's right for her client. I know she feels a great deal of sympathy for you, but if she loses against International she has to get the maximum she can for Robert Brown."

He shrugged again, "So no token settlement with David Stern."

David nodded glumly.

John added, "She did make one concession though, She agreed that she wouldn't look for any payment from you until after the trial."

"Well that's something at least."

John agreed, "Yes and remember, if she wins her case against International, they'll have to pay the million for you, and you're completely off the hook."

David looked up from his salad plate, "What do you recommend John?"

"I want to protect you as much as I can, and I don't just mean financially. You're going to get hammered at trial. Alex will not try to destroy you. She's already told me that, and I believe her. You saw how she handled you at your deposition. It's actually in her interest to make you look as good as possible. She wants you to appear competent, professional and above all, credible. You're an outstanding young doctor who made one terrible error which you freely admit."

He waved a hand for emphasis. "It's International you have to worry about. Herb Walton has to convince the members of the jury that they can't believe anything you say. They're going to do their best to make you appear crazy, that you're deluded in thinking you killed her. Simple as that. You got a taste of that in your discovery deposition, and you heard what your ex-colleagues have said about you during discovery."

David nodded bitterly, "Alex warned me the day I first met her that this case would be all about me."

Then he relaxed a little, "Don't worry about the trial, John. I'm just going to tell the truth, and hope the jury believes me. And as far as the settlement with the Browns is concerned, there's no way I can have you fight in court for me against the Browns. Please try and settle this with Alex.'

He made a sour face. "The equity in my condo is probably worth at least half a million, now."

He smiled wanly, "I suppose I could always go back and live with my parents."

John smiled and shook his head, "Let's hope it doesn't comes to that. O.K. David. For what it's worth, I think that it's the right decision for you, tactically and emotionally. Please understand that you will be on the line for one million dollars if International wins at trial."

He shrugged, "I can't imagine that even Herb Walton would look for punitive damages or legal costs from you."

"I certainly don't have a million dollars in cash, and my employment prospects are pretty poor at present, so I guess Alex had better win."

John smiled, "I'll call her this afternoon. If we agree, and it's virtually a done deal, one thing will change."

"What's that?" asked David.

"Well, as soon as you settle with the Browns, she will no longer be suing you. In fact you'll become her star witness. There'll be no reason why you and Alex can't communicate directly. I'm sure that she'll want you to help her prepare for trial. She's already told me that she would greatly welcome your input."

"*Oh,*" thought David, "*Did she actually say that?*"

Chap 29

As expected, John and Alex came to a final agreement without any difficulty. A few days after their lunch date John Rowland telephoned David.

"David, Could you come into my office some time in the next few days? I'd like to go over the settlement papers with you before you sign them."

The next day found David in John's office. The weather matched David's mood. The day was overcast and gray. It was barely thirty degrees and three inches of snow were in the forecast. After John carefully explained the settlement agreement, David signed all six copies.

He noted that Robert Brown had already signed.

David's signature was notarized by a secretary from an adjoining law office. Despite his recent billings from International on the David Stern case, John still couldn't afford his own secretary.

David's hand trembled a little as he signed. According to the documents he was now committed to pay the sum of one million dollars to Robert Brown and his children. For a person who had never been wealthy, who had always depended on a regular paycheck, and who was currently unemployed, the prospect of being in debt to the tune of a million dollars was unsettling, to say the least.

John watched David carefully as he signed. When David was finished, John telephoned for a bicycle messenger to send a copy to Herb Walton's office, and to the court.

When he hung up the phone, John put a friendly arm around David's shoulder.

"Welcome to the world of the truly impoverished," he said with a smile.

Despite himself, David had to smile. "It's not that bad, John. I'm not complaining. As you know I've been getting a year's severance pay from International."

As part of the fiction that David was disabled by mental illness, International had committed to pay him a year's salary, as they did for all physicians who could not work due to real disability.

"Although that's due to run out soon," thought David.

"You and Alex had better come up with some kind of miracle here."

As if on cue, the door to John's office opened, and in walked Alex Goldberg.

"Well it's the young Doctor Schweitzer," she observed archly.

She smiled at John as she took off her coat, revealing a dark blue pant suit with black patent boots. She shook out her thick glossy hair as she took off her woolen hat, which she had worn in deference to the winter weather outside.

Despite the fact that she had just cost him one million dollars on paper, David was very glad to see her. He thought she looked like, well, a million bucks.

No way he was going to tell her, though.

He rolled his eyes, and turned to John.

"How do you lawyers do it?" he asked. "Honestly, you're like sharks. They can smell blood in the water at ten miles, and you lawyers can smell a million dollar settlement at what, a hundred miles?"

John laughed and shook his head.

David turned to Alex, "How did you get here so fast? Where were you when I signed it," he looked at his watch, "let's see ten minutes ago, Wisconsin?"

"She probably came on her broomstick," he said to John who couldn't keep a straight face.

Alex regarded him archly," Listen Buster." She waved the copy of the agreement that John had just given her, "you'd better be nice to me. I've got you by the you know whats! "

David smiled, "In your dreams, Goldberg in your dreams!"

John looked mystified at the exchange, while Alex grinned wickedly.

The arrival of the bicycle messenger interrupted them. John gave him copies of the agreement to be delivered to the court and also to Herb Walton's office.

"Please make sure that you get signed receipts," he asked the messenger.

"Sure, Sport," nodded the messenger.

He was dressed in fluorescent orange Spandex. John couldn't take his eyes off the large safety pin which adorned his left eyebrow. He counted at least eight earrings.

As the messenger left the office, John shuddered. He turned to David.

"I know it's not real P.C. of me to say this, but if you were to tell me that my kids would look like that one day, I think I just might kill myself."

Alex laughed, "Come on *Sport*, it's just a look. I'm sure he's a real nice kid."

"Right," said John, "a million dollar agreement, and we give the papers to someone who looks like a refugee from a hardware store."

John shook his head as if to dispel the image. He looked at David and Alex.

"I don't quite know what you two were talking about a minute ago."

He paused as David and Alex smiled at one another.

"And I'm not sure I want to know anyway."

John looked at his watch. It was four thirty.

"I've got to go. Will you two be O.K. alone. No blood on the floor, promise? Or should I just call the cops now?"

Alex arched an elegant eyebrow.

"John, I cannot speak for the doctor. However I will conduct myself with all the dignity and composure that one expects from an officer of the court."

She grinned wickedly, "Of course, if he does act up, then I may have to kick him in the balls!"

"Purely in self defense," she added.

David shook his head, "I'm no psychiatrist, but Alex, I really think you may have a serious genital fixation."

Before Alex could respond David nodded his head, "I know, I know. *In your dreams Stern!*"

Alex nodded her agreement, "Darn right!"

John looked at his watch again. "Oops, time for me to go. I'll talk to you both tomorrow. Just close the door behind you as you leave."

To Alex he said, "You'll work things out here?"

She nodded and John was out the door, waving goodbye as he left.

Chap 30

David looked at Alex, curious. "What's he talking about, work things out? "

Alex looked at her watch. *Nearly five o'clock.*

"You hungry?" she asked.

David shrugged. Truth was, his stomach hurt. He had never been what anyone would call a big eater, but over the last few months he had lost his appetite, big time. Still if he could spend some time with Alex.......

He nodded, "Sure."

"What do you fancy?" she asked him.

"Whatever you want," he said.

Alex thought for a moment, "I'm in the mood for Chinese, that O.K. with you?"

David hated Chinese food.

"Fine," he said.

They hopped a cab to a small place on Clark and Halsted. It was early and they had the place to themselves. They sat in a booth at the back. David didn't look at the menu. Alex inspected it carefully.

"You sure you don't want to see the menu, David. They have a great chicken with dumplings. Sweet and sour chicken is good, too"

David shuddered inwardly. He shook his head.

"Why don't you order whatever you want, Alex. I'm just going to have some tea."

Alex looked concerned, "Are you O.K.?"

David nodded, "I'm fine, just not hungry. I had a big lunch."

Not technically a lie. He did have a big lunch once, about ten years ago.

They ordered, sweet and sour chicken for Alex, just tea for David.

As they waited for their order, David asked, "How's Cindy?

Alex smiled, "She's fine thanks, she sends her regards."

David raised an eyebrow, "Did she know that you'd be seeing me today?"

Alex looked embarrassed.

"David, I don't want you getting upset with John, but you should know he called and told me that you were coming in today to sign the papers."

She smiled, "Despite your comment about sharks in the water, I really can control myself. I would have been fine having the papers delivered to me. It was actually John who suggested that I come over. He thinks we should talk."

David didn't say anything. He simply made an *O.K. let's talk* gesture.

Alex looked at David very directly.

"She really has the most amazing eyes!" he thought.

"First David, let me thank you for being so co-operative. Frankly, I don't know whether Robert Brown will win his case against International or not. As you know, they've stacked a lot of witnesses against you. And they're all telling the same story. The jury is going to have a clear choice. They're either going to choose to believe you, or they're going to believe the International bullshit."

The food arrived and Alex paused for a minute as the waiter poured tea for them both.

When he left she continued, "What I *do* know is that without your testimony Robert Brown would have no chance of winning. There would never have been a case to pursue with if you hadn't stood up."

She reached across the table and put her hand on his. "I also know that it takes an enormous amount of courage to do what you are doing. I agree with John about that. We both respect you a great deal. I know that you are paying a very high price to do this."

She held onto his hand as she spoke with quiet passion, "And I promise you that after this trial is over, I will do everything that I can to help John rectify your situation. You have been treated very shamefully, and Herb Walton will not get away with it."

David shook his head and said quietly, "It's the right thing to do, Alex. After what I did to Winnie Brown, I couldn't live with myself if I'd gone along with their story."

Alex nodded her understanding. There was a moment's silence as each of them thought about the upcoming trial.

Then David brightened, "When you say you'll make it up to me for my sacrifice, does that mean you will show me your boobs?"

Alex laughed out loud, "You are incorrigible! And you say I'm the one with the genital fixation?"

David laughed too, "I know, *in your dreams*, right?"

Alex just smiled. They ate in a comfortable silence, or rather Alex ate and David drank his tea and watched her.

"Hell, it's almost worth a million bucks just to be with her!" thought David.

"Alex," said David, "I'm curious, why did John think we should talk?"

Alex laid down her fork and pushed her plate away, "That's it, I'm done. I always eat too much before a trial, I guess it's the stress."

She had eaten maybe half of what was on her plate.

David looked at her, surprised, "Stress, really? I'm surprised that you get stressed. You always look so much in control."

Alex smiled, "Don't be fooled by appearances," she said, "trials are very stressful, at least for me."

She sipped her tea. "You have to remember a trial is usually the culmination of years of work. It's also the last chance to get justice for ordinary people, sometimes very poor people, who have been horribly damaged by the system."

She spoke almost to herself, "If I fail them, it's over, plain and simple."

She flashed David a brilliant smile, "So that's why I overeat."

It was David's turn to take her hand in his. "Alex," he said softly," I can't imagine you ever failing anyone."

They looked at each other in silence for a long moment. Finally Alex smiled.

"That's very sweet David, but I'm not showing you my boobs, and I'm not giving you back the million dollars!"

Chap 31

"Ouch," said David, "That hurt! You saw through my plans, get you naked and then get my money back!"

Alex smiled and looked at her watch.

"You know, that reminds me," said David, "What's with John? He's always looking at his watch. It's like Cinderella or something. What happens, he turns into a pumpkin if he's still in the office after four thirty?"

He shook his head, "Don't get me wrong, I'm not complaining, I think he's an excellent attorney and I'm glad you recommended him to me. But he seems to get real antsy after four o'clock."

Alex nodded, "Let me tell you what that's all about, David."

She hesitated, "I may be revealing a confidence, but I think it's only fair that you know. It will make John's behavior easier for you to understand. And maybe you have the right to expect a little more support from your attorney during the next month or so."

"You're right, John does have to leave pretty early, at least by Chicago lawyer standards. Actually that may be one of the reasons he suggested we get together tonight."

David looked puzzled, "Now you've got me really curious, Alex."

Alex took a deep breath, "O.K. Do you remember the day you first came to my office?"

"Sure," nodded David, "*Go hang your penis and testicles up*, I think you said."

"Stop it!" said Alex sternly. But she smiled at the memory.

"Well that's what you did say!" said David.

"I was provoked. Severely I might add," said Alex.

"Whatever," shrugged David.

"Do you want to hear this, or not?" asked Alex.

David gestured, "Go on."

"O.K. seriously now, I recommended John Rowland to you first and foremost because I know from past experience, he's a very fine lawyer. Second, he's not too busy with other clients. So I knew he would have plenty of time to devote to your case. Third, I know he wouldn't be intimidated by any crap from Herb Walton and his minions."

David nodded, "I know all this."

Alex drew a deep breath, "But what you don't know is that John has had a very difficult time of it himself recently."

She leaned back in her chair as the waiter brought a fresh pot of tea and poured for them both.

As he left, Alex leaned forward and lowered her voice. She didn't want to share this information with the whole restaurant. David had to lean forward to hear her. Their heads were inches apart. David caught a whiff of something delicate and very feminine.

"What are you wearing?" He asked suddenly.

Alex was startled, "Oh, you mean perfume. I don't remember, Rive Gauche, I think."

David nodded approvingly, "Very nice, suits you."

Alex lost her train of thought for a moment.

This man was having quite an effect on her.

"Where was I?"

"What I don't know about John," David gently reminded her.

"Oh yes," Said Alex, "What you don't know is that John's wife left him almost a year ago. Her name's Sherri, with an *i*."

She made a face, "He's in the process of getting a divorce, it'll be final in a few months."

David shrugged, "That's no big deal."

Alex shook her head, "No, you have to hear the rest. Sherri's really bad news. She's a coke head and she cleaned out all of their money before she took off, with her dealer, would you believe it! Last John heard they're in L.A. She left him with tens of thousands in credit card debt.

She shook her head, "But the worst part is she abandoned their two kids. Two boys, Joey is nearly seven, and Patrick is almost three."

She was almost in tears.

"Patrick has severe cerebral palsy. The doctors say it's almost certainly due to all the shit she stuffed up her nose when she was pregnant with him."

She looked at David with an expression he'd never seen before.

"He's retarded and almost paraplegic. Urinary catheter, diapers for stool, the whole nine yards. You know more about that than I do, of course."

David nodded silently.

Alex continued quietly, "Several doctors have suggested that Patrick should be institutionalized. But John won't hear of it. He won't separate the kids. He has a retired pediatric nurse take care of Patrick from eight till five, and he takes over from five every evening until eight in the morning. He does everything for Patrick himself, seven days a week."

Alex shook her head, "Every penny John earns goes to pay off Sherri's debts, and for care for Patrick. You've seen his office, you know it's very basic."

She looked at David almost defiantly, "That's one of the reasons I recommended him to you. Apart from the fact that he is an excellent attorney, and won't let that shit Herb Walton run roughshod all over you."

She shrugged, "When I realized that you weren't going to jump on board with International and deny everything, I knew that you needed your own attorney."

She spread her hands wide, "And when your contract confirmed that International had to pay for your attorney, it seemed like a golden opportunity. This way you got the attorney you need, and I could help John at the same time. He's too proud to accept direct help. I know."

David nodded and smiled, "Almost poetic justice isn't it, Herb Walton has to pay for my attorney.

He looked at Alex, "Thanks for telling me this. I certainly didn't feel he was abandoning me, but it explains quite a lot. By the way I certainly won't tell John about this conversation."

He reached across the table and took her hand, "You know Alex, with everything else going on, the fact that you thought of him, and took practical steps to help him, I'm really impressed. You really are a very special person."

There was a long silence.

Finally Alex disengaged her hand, "Listen, it's getting late. I have a busy day tomorrow, but I do want to make one thing clear. Now that you and Robert Brown have settled, you're out of the case as a defendant."

David nodded, "John explained that to me."

Alex continued, "That's why we can meet like this. You're now just another witness in the case, albeit the most important one."

David made a face, "Just another witness! I am the cutest one, don't you think?"

Alex laughed, "Are you *pouting*? O.K. I agree you're the cutest witness in the case."

"*Actually the cutest person I've seen in years,*" she thought.

"But seriously, David, I need your help. Now that we're no longer on opposing sides, will you help me prepare my case against International?"

David nodded vigorously, "Absolutely. Just tell me what you want me to do."

Alex held up her hand, "One minute. Please understand, in a sense the easy part is over. It wasn't hard for John and I to reach a settlement."

"Because you are an honest and honorable person," she thought.

"The hard part," she continued, "is going to be the trial. You've heard how all of the International witnesses have been lying through their teeth about you?"

David nodded grimly.

"Well, that's what we need to prepare for. I want your help, I need your help, but part of me feels very badly, because I know it's going to be very hard for you. You're their target!"

David smiled, "Don't worry about me. I can take care of myself."

Alex looked a little embarrassed. She pulled a business card from her purse.

"O.K. For starters, will you go and see this doctor?"

David read the card, *"Melissa Walters M.D. Consulting Psychiatrist."*

He raised an eyebrow and looked at Alex.

Alex explained, "Remember at your deposition, Jodi Miller, the happy hooker, kept asking you about delusions?"

David nodded.

"Well, it's pretty obvious they're going to claim that you were deluded and remain deluded, in believing that you caused Winnie's death. It struck me at the time that I want expert medical testimony to the effect that you're absolutely sane."

She indicated the card that David still held and added hurriedly, "I mentioned this to John, and he agrees we should definitely do it. "

"Melissa's good," she added, "I've used her as an expert several times. By the way she'll bill me directly, so don't worry about the bill."

David nodded. "No problem," he said easily. "Only one thing," he added with a smile, "I'm not talking about my sexual obsessions. Some things you'll have to find out for yourself."

Alex smiled and stood up, "Now it's definitely time to go. I've told you before, in your dreams, Stern."

David looked at his watch, "It's only seven forty, what's the rush?"

Alex looked a little embarrassed, "I have an appointment, actually it's kind of a standing commitment every Thursday evening."

She put thirty dollars on the table, "That should cover my share. I'll see you tomorrow?'

David nodded and she was gone.

Chap 32

What David didn't know about Alex was that she had a hidden vice.

She was a poker addict. Well maybe not an addict. She preferred to think of herself as an enthusiast.

Every Thursday evening would find her at a high stakes poker game in a private room at the back of Bannion's tavern in New Town. All of the regulars at the game were attorneys, and all were male.

Alex first heard of the game years ago from her boss at the time, Jim Davis. He played almost every week except when he was on trial. In an unguarded moment he once mentioned the game casually to his young associate.

"So you play poker every Thursday night?" asked Alex.

Jim nodded, "There's usually about ten of us. You know most of them from the Daley Center. We have a few drinks and play from eight until eleven. We stop on the stroke of eleven so there's no hard feelings, whoever's winning or losing."

Alex appeared only mildly interested. She didn't tell Jim that her late father, an accountant by training, had played poker for pennies with her every Sunday evening, ever since she was eight years old. Alex's mother didn't approve but father and daughter had a great time.

When she went to Harvard she quickly found a Sunday evening game. She loved to get in the face of the Harvard men. She quickly realized that their inability to accept defeat at the hands of a woman was a weakness that she could exploit. It was a source of pride to her father that she rarely lost.

Since coming to Chicago she hadn't played, except for a couple of brief trips to Vegas, so she was very interested to learn of Jim's game.

Next Thursday evening Alex made a sudden entrance, sweet-talking her way past the burly barman who stood sentinel at the door.

"Please," she said with all the considerable charm she could muster, "I have to deliver this important package to Mr. Davis."

She held up a FedEx package, "I'm from his office."

Well, that was true enough.

"And he'll be very angry if I don't give it to him right now."

Roddy the barman could hardly take his eyes off her breasts.

"Go ahead, but be quick," he said, "they don't like being disturbed."

Most of the room was in semi-darkness, full of cigar smoke and the smell of expensive bourbon. She counted eight men, all in shirtsleeves, sitting around the green baize card table which was brightly illuminated by an incongruous chandelier. She saw a variety of power ties, reds and yellows, all loosened.

"Evening your Honor," she smiled at one startled Cook County jurist.

All heads turned and Jim Davis gave her a concerned look.

"Alex, is everything O.K?"

Alex smiled her sweetest smile, and pulled out a thick wad of hundreds from the FedEx envelope.

"Good evening Jim, got room for another player?"

There was a rumble of dissent from around the table. The consensus appeared to be that women were not welcome, that their presence would spoil the ambience and that only real men played poker.

Alex stilled the dissent by placing ten thousand dollars on the table and inquiring sweetly if they were all scared of competition from a *girl?*"

That was a challenge that eight Chicago attorneys couldn't back down from.

One of the players stuck a fat cigar in her face,

"Do you need one of these?" he leered.

Alex learned later his name was Herb Walton.

"No thanks," she said coolly, "sometimes a cigar's just a cigar. Anyway, it looks like you need it more than me."

There were hoots of laughter from around the table. Herb Walton flushed angrily.

Roddy asked if she'd like a drink, and she demurely accepted a glass of white wine. There were still some muttered protests, which were quickly stilled by Patrick Reilly, a short rotund real estate lawyer who chewed constantly on a fat stogie. He was down nearly three thousand dollars and wanted to get it back.

"Are we here to talk or play poker? She's here." He indicated the pile of cash in front of her, "She's got the price of admission with her. Let her play."

He turned to the only African American at the table, "Deal!"

Bobby Davis, a well known criminal defense attorney flashed Alex a smile.

"No Limit Texas Hold'em nothing wild. Twenty bucks to post, O.K?"

Alex nodded, "O.K."

She was in.

Alex played very conservatively for the first hour. She studied the other players as carefully as she studied her cards. She soon realized that Jim Davis was as conservative in his poker as he was in the office. Patrick Reilly was hopelessly erratic, and Bobby Davis was shrewd.

She looked for *tells*, the subconscious signs that many less than successful poker players exhibit. It didn't take long for her to spot them.

Judge Roberts kept looking at his cards when he had a winning hand. When he was bluffing, he scarcely looked at them. Lou De Angelo stared into space before every raise, except when he held a high pair or better. Then his eyes never left the table.

And Herb Walton? The slightest twitch of his jaw when he bluffed.

Midway through the evening she realized that although the players were older, and the cigars and booze were more expensive, it was just like Sunday evenings at Harvard.

That first night she won nearly four thousand dollars, over half of it from Walton on one epic hand, four of a kind over a full house.

More important than the money was the fact that she won. No way they could turn her away in the future. It would be admitting that she was too good for them. She was in for as long as she wanted.

One concession though, she had to promise that she wouldn't bring any more women to the game. She solemnly promised.

As if she would bring another woman and give up her secret advantage!

She smiled to herself as she shampooed the cigar smoke out of her hair later that night. It took nearly an hour.

Next morning she wrinkled her nose as she smelled the suit she had worn the night before. She realized that whatever she wore to the game would immediately have to go the cleaners. But it was worth it.

Jim Davis regarded his young associate in an entirely different light next day. He solemnly reminded her that all winnings were reportable to the Internal Revenue Service. She solemnly thanked him for the information.

That was nearly five years ago, and she rarely missed a game from then on. She continued to win on a fairly regular basis.

But she could no longer share the thrill with her father.

During the cab-ride from the Chinese restaurant to Bannions she wondered whether Walton would be there tonight, and whether she could resist the temptation to ram his cigar down his throat.

Chap 33

Next day David showed up at Alex's office at nine sharp. It felt good to back on a schedule, if only for a few days.

As he entered the office he remembered his first visit a few months previously. Once again Cindy and Alex were in the front office looking intently at the computer screen.

"Morning Ladies," said David with a brilliant smile, "I know the routine, *genitals on the coat rack,* right Alex?"

Alex rolled her eyes while Cindy smothered a laugh.

"Good morning Doctor Stern," she said, "It's nice to see you again."

"Cindy, I like all the beautiful women in my life to call me David, please?"

Cindy actually simpered at that!

Alex rolled her eyes again, "Are you here to work, or just interfere with my staff?" she asked.

David and Cindy exchanged a conspiratorial smile as he accompanied Alex into her office.

Alex gestured at the boxes of papers, which filled her office.

"It's nuts, the amount of paper that a single case generates. It'll only get worse before trial, but what can you do?" She shrugged, "That's the system."

David nodded, "John says the same thing."

They sat on opposite sides of Alex's desk. Unlike his previous visit, there was no tension. They were comfortable with each other. They were now on the same side of the case. It felt good.

For the next three hours, David brought Alex up to speed on lymphomas and their treatment. She was a fast study. Finally, just after twelve David looked at his watch.

"I've got to watch my time. I've got a one o'clock appointment with my psychiatrist."

He said this with a straight face.

Alex looked a little embarrassed. "I hope you're not mad with me about this. Honestly, I would never have suggested it except for that asshole, Walton. You know where they're coming from. Their whole explanation for your testimony is going to be that you're somehow suffering from delusions. That puts your mental state front and center in the case."

She looked directly at David, "You and I both know it's bullshit, but if we don't address it now," she shrugged, "they'll make a big deal of it at the time of trial."

David smiled, "Please don't give it another thought. I understand completely."

He stretched his lanky frame. "Do you want a quick lunch?"

Alex thought he looked good enough to eat. She shook her head.

"Before a trial like this, I don't break for lunch, I usually just send Cindy out for soup and a salad."

David nodded, "Sounds good, while she's doing that I want to give you a copy of a couple of review articles on lymphoma. They show that even advanced high grade lymphomas like Winnie had, are curable if you get them in complete remission."

Alex nodded, "That's excellent, and you'll testify that these articles are authoritative?"

Authoritative was the key phrase. To have them admitted as exhibits in the trial so that the jury would have access to them, an expert doctor had to testify that they were authoritative.

"Sure," said David.

Cindy brought back tomato soup and tuna salad.

After a few mouthfuls of soup, David made a face, "Too much salt for me."

He looked at his watch, "Oops, I've got to go, my ego's feeling fragile. Got to see my shrink. See you nine o'clock tomorrow?"

Alex nodded goodbye. She was deep into Crandall's deposition. David blew a kiss to Cindy as he exited the outer office.

Later that afternoon Melissa Walters telephoned Alex to report on her interview with David.

"What a hunk! Got any more like him, just send them along!" she said.

Alex smiled, "Is that your clinical opinion, Mel?"

She heard Melissa laugh, "Yes, absolutely!"

Melissa paused for a second and glanced at her notes, "Actually my clinical opinion is that he's as sane as they come. He's well grounded in reality. No evidence whatsoever of abnormal thought processes. If this guy's deluded about anything, I don't see it."

She continued thoughtfully, "He's certainly somewhat depressed at the moment, but that's just a normal reaction to his job situation. Can you believe what they did to him?"

Alex said, "Shameful, isn't it?"

Melissa agreed, "Absolutely. Is there anything you can do about that?"

Alex smiled, "It's on my agenda. Anyway, you feel comfortable testifying as a rebuttal witness?"

Melissa said, "Sure, I'll testify that he he's totally rational. I'm going to see him a couple of more times, although there is no question in my mind that he's healthy. No way he's deluded."

"You know, I really don't need to spend more time with him to tell you that. But I don't want the other side making a big deal on cross examination, '*Well you have all these opinions and you only met with him one time, isn't that true doctor?*' You know how that goes,"

Alex nodded. "Absolutely." *Melissa was great, she was a real pro.*

"Mel, I need you as a rebuttal witness. You'll be rebutting Cheryl Rubin. She's the one testifying for International. Claims she saw Doctor Stern as a patient, says he's real disturbed. I'll send you her discovery deposition."

Melissa Walters was incredulous. "Cheryl Rubin claims she treated Doctor Stern! But that's ridiculous. No way! Everyone calls her *The Alzheimer Queen*. She refuses to see any patient except Alzheimer's. She's notorious for it. Cheryl Rubin treating David Stern, that's too funny for words."

Alex scribbled a note as she listened. "Can you provide any example of when she refused to see a non-Alzheimer's patient, Mel?"

"Let me see what I can come up with, Alex."

"O.K. Mel, hold on for a minute, I'm going to have Cindy pick up. We'll need to disclose you as a witness. They may want to depose you. Give Cindy a couple of dates and times in the next two or three weeks. We'll fit in with your schedule. And thanks again."

"Fine," said Melissa, "Oh there is one thing I can tell you about your Doctor Stern that you should know."

She paused, "I'm not sure that you want use it at trial though."

"What's that?" asked Alex curiously.

"Well, I wouldn't call it an obsession Alex, but he is very interested in you,!"

With that Melissa hung up the phone.

Alex felt a shiver of excitement.

If anything the stakes had just got a little higher.

Chap 34

At the same time as Alex was speaking on the phone to Melissa Walters, Herb Walton sat in his large corner office. Sitting facing him across his enormous desk was an uncomfortable Jodi Miller and an equally uncomfortable Robert Peterson. Herb was immaculate as ever in a charcoal grey Armani suit. Sartorial elegance was not on his agenda today.

He was too busy tearing a strip off his two associates.

"Jodi, I'm real disappointed in you. First you let that Goldberg bitch get to Brown before he signs the waiver."

He shook his head in disgust, "I told you how to get in there! I know these people! All you have to do is wave a check under their noses, and you're halfway home. You just had to follow the script I gave you. But instead you screw up and the next thing we've got Alex Goldberg suing our asses off!"

His baleful gaze shifted to include Peterson.

"And then later, after we're stuck with a lawsuit that was completely avoidable, you two geniuses depose Stern."

He flipped the pages of the deposition transcript that lay on his desk.

"I can't believe that you let that pissant of so easily! He was *laughing* at you."

In his anger Herb started pacing up and down in his office, holding the transcript that so offended him. He turned abruptly and threw the transcript onto his desk. It skidded onto the floor. Neither of his associates dared pick it up.

Herb's tirades were famous in the firm, but this was the mother of all tirades.

"You gave me nothing I can use at trial. Nothing! What are we paying you for? I'm not interested in your ideas. *I* have the ideas. Your job is to do what I tell you, no more and no less! That's all I pay you to do. If you can't do that you're no use to me!"

He took a deep breath, "We've got less than three weeks till trial. That's less than three weeks to find something I can use. There's got to be some dirt on this guy. Find it! I don't care what you have to do. I don't care what it costs, find it!"

He leaned close to the hapless pair. They could smell the sour smell of lunchtime cocktails on his breath.

"I don't need to tell you if we lose this case, you're both history. Now get out of my sight!"

As they left his office, Herb smiled to himself. Like all good trial lawyers he was an actor, and he wasn't just a good trial lawyer, he was a *great* one.

Let the lazy bastards think they'd really screwed up. They'd do anything he demanded the next time.

Despite his performance for Jodi and Robert, Herb felt the case was going just as he'd planned it. He had deliberately sent his incompetent assistants to depose Stern. He knew that the sanctimonious little shit would never accept the International version and that eventually he, Herb would have to discredit him in front of the jury.

It was something he was looking forward to. *Hell, he wasn't going to discredit him, he was going to destroy him.*

After the deposition went as well as it did for Stern, Herb calculated that an over-confident Alex Goldberg would not suspect the trap that he planned for Stern.

He already had just what he needed to take care of the doctor.

But Herb knew that every trial was a battle, and in any battle the original plan never survived more than a few minutes. This was a case that he absolutely could not and would not lose. He needed a back-up plan.

Herb was so successful because he always made meticulous plans. He opened his private safe and took out a slim black notebook.

"Best to make this call from a public phone," he thought.

Chap 35

The seat belt warning light was turned off. David leaned back in his seat as the United 777 turned slowly, climbing up through 20,000 feet. He liked to fly. No matter how often he did it, the experience of leaving O'Hare and landing in a completely different environment a few hours later always filled him with a kind of awe.

The trial was less than three weeks away. David had done everything he could to help Alex prepare. Now the tension sat in David's gut like a lead weight. John Rowland had suggested that David take a week off.

"Maybe it'll help you relax a bit," he suggested. "Why don't you go to Florida? Alex tells me that you've been a great help to her. She says you really nailed down all the medical stuff for her. She says you're a great teacher."

They were speaking in John's office. Outside the temperature was twenty two with a wind chill of close to zero. People were walking down Michigan Avenue with their heads bent against the wind. March in Chicago was always tough, but this was really cold. Winter seemed to have lasted forever.

David agreed that a vacation sounded pretty good right now. But Florida was not his idea of fun. That's why he was now flying to Denver on his way to the Rockies.

Like so many Chicago kids he had first learned to ski in bitter cold on man-made snow on small Wisconsin hills with names like Alpine and Little Norway.

After Wisconsin, his first experience of Western skiing on a real mountain with blue skies and warm sunshine was an eye-opener. He was hooked. He tried to get at least one week a year out

West. His favorite resorts were Vail, Breckenridge, and where he was heading today, Snowmass Colorado.

After a brief layover in the massive new Denver International, he arrived at the small Aspen airport at eleven thirty on a clear Saturday morning. As he disembarked from the United Express jet, he felt his spirits rise.

From the airport, the ski lifts on Tiehack Mountain were clearly visible. Aspen Mountain, Ajax lay a few miles away. But David was headed in the opposite direction.

David disliked the jet set atmosphere and crowded runs of Aspen. He preferred Snowmass, a huge ski area that lay about ten miles west of Aspen. Within an hour of arrival, he had checked into room 118 of the Maroon Bells Lodge, a small luxury hotel that offered direct access to the mountain.

Changing quickly into his ski gear, he grabbed his skis and glasses, bought a seven day ski pass, and headed for the chair lift. It was a perfect day. There wasn't a cloud in the sky, and only a light breeze. The snow was perfect.

David rode all the way up to the top of Big Burn. He was an excellent skier, and could handle all but the most extreme runs without difficulty. But he was skiing alone and had just arrived, so for the first day he contented himself with the wide-open intermediate terrain on Big Burn.

He had no difficulty adjusting to the altitude, because he had been taking Diamox pills for two days before leaving home.

"I'm probably the only person in Chicago who'd trust me with a prescription drug right now," he thought darkly.

Soon all thoughts of Chicago and his problems were dispelled as the mountains began to work their magic on him.

The combination of physical exercise, clean air, sunshine and the physical beauty of the mountains always made him feel good.

Despite the fact that he hadn't skied for a year, he quickly found his rhythm.

Dancing with the mountain is how he thought of skiing, and at times it really seemed as if the mountain welcomed him. He skied with only a short break, to drink some cold Evian and eat an apple. On the chair lift he closed his eyes, took of his sunglasses and enjoyed the warm sun on his face as he rode back up.

By the time they closed the mountain at four o'clock, David was very tired. He skied down non-stop from the top of Big Burn to his hotel, about three thousand feet of vertical. He stored his equipment and got back to his room. The early start from Chicago, the travel, and the effects of the altitude and exercise all conspired to make him ready for a hot bath and bed.

After twenty minutes of soaking in a tub he got into the one of the warm fluffy robes the hotel provided. He ordered onion soup, a grilled cheese sandwich and a Heineken from room service. By eight he was in bed.

For the first time in nearly a year he slept without dreaming of Winnie Brown.

Sunday and Monday he spent in a similar way to Saturday afternoon. By late Sunday morning he felt ready to push himself.

He spent the rest of the day in his favorite area of the mountain, Campground. These were long steep expert runs, with plenty of bumps. They were never crowded. Often David would be the only skier in sight. It was easy for David to imagine that he was truly one with the mountain.

The evenings he spent alone. David had never been a party animal, and did not look for the bar scene. He had brought a laptop computer with him, in case he wanted to do some writing. He had a research paper to write. It had been due for many months, was in fact long overdue.

Somehow he could not bring himself to review any data on lymphoma treatment right now. He contented himself with reading a Dean Koontz paperback he'd picked up at O'Hare.

Tuesday he spent at Aspen Highlands, a real skier's mountain with challenging runs and some of the best views in the area. He was having a good time. Only occasionally would he feel a gnawing pain in the pit of his stomach.

"Stress," he thought, *"I guess Chicago's not that far away."*

Wednesday morning was as perfect as every other day had been. David had signed up with a Mountain Masters group. This program allowed better skiers to spend the entire day with a ski school instructor exploring steep un-groomed terrain outside the usual ski area.

In his group of five David noticed a very attractive woman. She was small, about five foot two, but she moved with a fluidity and grace that was a pleasure to watch. Not that David had a lot of time to watch, most of his time was spent trying to keep up with the fast pace his instructor set.

The woman wore a green one piece ski suit that set off her bright red curls perfectly. David sat beside her in the Snow Cat as they slowly climbed high above the tree line. He introduced himself.

"Nice to meet you," she said. "I'm Chris."

Her voice was low and pleasant. Chris was from San Bernardino, near Los Angeles. She was on her way back to California from a real estate convention in Dallas, and had decided to sneak in a couple of days skiing. She was also staying at the Maroon Bells and, like David was on her own.

They agreed to meet for a drink at six o'clock in the hotel bar. The remainder of the afternoon was spent skiing hard. David didn't get a chance to speak to her again.

After a shower and a brief nap, David dressed in a pair of jeans and a dark blue cashmere turtleneck. He went down to the bar. It was dark, crowded and noisy. Chris waved to him from a corner booth. She also wore jeans, and a pair of cowboy boots in a deep burgundy shade. Her sweater was bright emerald green. Although the bar was dark she wore her sunglasses.

"Hi," she said, as David approached the table, "nice to see you. Sorry about the glasses. I know they make me look like a spy, but I have allergies and my eye doctor says I should wear these all the time."

David smiled, "We'll just tell people you're a film star, who doesn't want to be recognized."

She laughed easily, "That's right, if anyone asks, tell them you're my agent."

Chris was drinking brandy, so David joined her. In truth he was not a big drinker. The most he ever drank was a couple of beers while watching the Bulls or the Bears, or a couple of glasses of wine while dining out.

But he was on vacation, and it was nice to be with an attractive young woman, who neither knew nor cared about his problems in Chicago.

They talked mainly about their ski experiences and her business. She owned a real estate company in the San Fernando Valley, and had made a lot of money in the early nineties. She was now kind of marking time until the California market picked up again. She was divorced, no kids.

The pressure of her thigh on David's leg felt good. He felt definite stirrings in his groin, the first for many months. That felt good too. After one large brandy, David began to feel a buzz, and suggested that they eat.

"I'm not real hungry," she said, "why don't we go up to your room and maybe order something in?"

The messages from his groin were quite loud now. He nodded, "O.K."

Chap 36

On the way to his room, Chris made a quick detour to her room and picked up a bottle of brandy. In David's room she filled two glasses, and they drank. He found himself stumbling over words. His tongue was pleasantly numb. Chris seemed to be able to hold her liquor much better than he could.

"David," she said with a smile, "why don't you call the front desk and tell them to hold any calls. Tell them you're going to bed."

He did as she suggested. They sat on the couch by the fire. The lights in the room were low, and her hair shone like burnished copper in the light cast by the flames. They kissed. Her lips were soft and warm, her tongue was in his mouth and his groin was hard. She felt it and smiled. She poured another drink for him. He found himself getting sleepy.

"Hey, David," she said softly, "don't disappear on me yet. I'm going to my room for my diaphragm. I'll be back in a minute."

He kind of grunted, "O.K."

She returned in a few minutes. As she came in the room she put the *DO NOT DISTURB* sign on the door. She found him lying on the couch, fast asleep.

She smiled to herself. *This would be easy.*

If David had been awake, he would have wondered why she was wearing rubber gloves of the type used by surgeons. She brought with her a small black leather bag, like an old-fashioned doctor's bag. From it she removed a bottle of pills, and a plastic tube. David would have recognized this as the type of tube that doctors and nurses pass through the nose, down the esophagus and into the stomach of patients undergoing stomach surgery.

She took David's glass, filled it with brandy and added about forty pills from the bottle. Her movements were as precise and fluid as on the ski slope. She gently swirled the contents of the glass, to dissolve the pills. Most of the pills dissolved, the rest formed a kind of slurry at the bottom of the glass.

Looking around the room, she saw the computer and smiled. *Better and Better.*

The last time she had used this method, the absence of a suicide note was of some concern to the investigators.

Isn't technology great!

She booted up the computer, and quickly typed.

"I'm sorry. I just can't take it any more. It's my fault she's dead."

She put her brandy glass in her bag. She then took David's limp right hand and made sure his prints were all over the bottle. She did the same with his brandy glass and the bottle of pills to ensure that the only prints present were his.

She did not wear lipstick or perfume so that there would be no residue left on his body. She checked the room thoroughly. There was no other sign that she had ever been there. If the police were to look, and find a few green fibers from a sweater, *well so what?*

This was a hotel room, with people coming and going all the time. She and the sweater would long ago have parted company. With an obvious suicide like this, it was unlikely that there would be a detailed investigation.

Satisfied that everything in the room was O.K., she approached the sleeping David.

"I'm sorry Doc," she whispered, "I know you guys use lubrication when you do this, but for obvious reasons I can't do that."

David offered no resistance as she expertly passed the tube through his nose into the stomach. The doctor that she had discussed this with had warned her that passing the tube might cause a few small hemorrhages in the wall of the stomach or esophagus.

"That would be O.K. though," he had said, "any bleeding would be easily explained as either damage from the alcohol, or caused by retching or vomiting before death."

She scattered a few of the pills on the floor around David. She once again checked that everything was in place. *Good.*

She picked up the glass that was full of the lethal mixture of brandy and barbiturate.

"B&B," she thought, *"What a great cocktail."*

All she had to do now was pour most of the stuff down the tube, make sure it stayed down for at least ten minutes, then pull the tube and get out. With luck he wouldn't be discovered till late tomorrow, and she'd be long gone.

As she bent over the sleeping David, a voice behind her suddenly yelled. "Freeze!"

Straightening up, she dropped the glass and turned towards the voice. She reached behind her and her right hand came up holding a small blue handgun.

Before she could fire there was the sound of two shots fired in rapid succession. The first caught her in the throat, the second in her chest. She died as she hit the floor.

The sounds of the shots brought David around. He saw a tall black man walking towards him with a gun in his hand. The man looked down at him with a grim expression. Through the shock and confusion, David knew he was about to die.

"Just relax, Doctor Stern," said the man, "you're safe now, everything's going to be fine."

He kicked the gun away from her body and checked to make sure that she was dead.

Straightening up, he said to David, "I'm sure that tube isn't comfortable, but I'd like you to leave it in place until the police arrive."

With that he picked up the phone and asked the hotel operator to immediately call the Pritkin County Sheriff and the FBI. He then placed a call to Chicago.

Six hours later, after the police and FBI had completed their investigation, and the body had been removed, David sat with a cup of black coffee, nursing a giant hangover.

The man who had saved his life sat opposite him in his room. The first light of dawn was beginning to show through the drapes, the drapes behind which his guardian angel had been hiding.

His name was Sam McClendon, ex-Chicago cop and now the senior partner in a Chicago security company.

He explained to David, "You've been under pretty close surveillance since you got here. We didn't think she'd try anything on the mountain, but there was one of our men in your ski group today."

He smiled, "You know, it really would have been easier for us if you had gone to Florida like John Rowland suggested."

"We only got really concerned when she made her move on you tonight. You know she put a drug, probably a barbiturate in the brandy you drank in the bar and here in the room. That's why you went out so fast."

"Her name incidentally was Julie Bishop or Tallon. We're not sure which name is the real one. She's from Miami. She's never been arrested, has no record, but she was a professional. No question about that."

"The F.B.I. thinks she's responsible for at least twelve murders for hire in the past, four with the same basic M.O. she used on you. That's why I also called them. They're happy to have her out of the picture."

Sam stretched as he continued. "They're used to having private security people around here, because they have a lot of V.I.P.s, especially at Aspen. Of course we told them ahead of time, and got their O.K. to provide you with an armed guard."

He shook his head, "There's no way to prove who hired her. She was too much of a pro for that, but I'm sure that you have a good idea who wants you out of the picture."

"My instructions are to get you home to Chicago in one piece, and keep you healthy and safe until the trial. I'm afraid your ski vacation is over."

David waved a hand weakly, as if to say, *"That's OK."*

He'd come within an inch of being murdered, and skiing was the last thing on his mind right now.

McClendon smiled, "We've got a private jet waiting at the airport. I've had your things packed. We can go as soon as you're ready."

The stress was back, big time. The pain in David's stomach was there again, aggravated by the brandy he had drunk.

In future he was going to stick to Heineken or Evian!

As David stood to leave, a sudden thought struck him.

"Sam," he said, "You're talking surveillance with several men for weeks, a private jet. Who's paying for all this?"

Sam looked surprised.

"I thought you knew," he said, "Alex Goldberg hired us weeks ago."

Chap 37

When Sam and his crew got him back to Chicago David became a virtual prisoner in his condo. Although it seemed unlikely that there would be another attempt on his life, Sam was taking no chances. David was never alone. There were only two weeks until the trial, and he spent most of the time watching endless hours of T.V. in his condo.

His first encounter with Alex after he got back was classic.

"Understand you had an interesting trip, Doctor. Got to watch those red-heads, huh?" said Alex with a sly smile.

David was ready for her. "Actually the red hair was a wig. It was worse than that. She was a natural brunette killer, Counselor. They're the most dangerous of the breed."

Behind Alex, Cindy smothered a laugh.

Despite the unusual situation they were in, there was a sense of growing comfort between David and Alex. Cindy was certainly aware of it. She had never seen Alex so loose before a big trial.

Alex's trial strategy was very simple. She planned to put on Robert Brown to tell the jury about his life with Winnie, her illness from the patient's perspective, and what her tragic death had meant to him and their children. An economist would briefly testify about the economic loss to the Brown family caused by the death of a young wife and mother.

She had identified two medical colleagues of David who would tell the jury that he was nationally recognized and respected as an expert in lymphoma. His old mentor from the National Cancer Institute was coming to describe his experiences with David as a fellow in training and junior staff member.

Literally dozens of patients were willing to testify that they had always felt the utmost confidence in David. She had selected four, chosen to give a racially balanced view to the jury.

Most importantly, she had persuaded the current chief of staff of International Medical Center to testify that David had served the hospital for years with no hint of previous scandal or mental health problems.

It had taken very little persuasion. Bud Aaron was a cantankerous sixty seven year old whose bluff manner hid a keen mind.

"Ms. Goldberg," he said when Alex first approached him by telephone about testifying, "I'll be happy to help David."

"He's a fine young man. Can't say that he did a real smart thing injecting that poison in the woman's head. We all screw up from time to time, maybe not in quite so spectacular a fashion. But you don't destroy a fellow's career over it. And then denying it ever happened, and trying to paint him as crazy, that's shameful. Bunch of vipers we've got in Administration now. Anyway they can go screw themselves if they try to mess with me."

Alex's last and most important witness would be David Stern.

Chap 38

David took the witness stand. If he was nervous it didn't show. Alex stood at the lectern. After David was sworn in he sat down and turned to Alex.

Game time.

Alex gave him a brief smile, "Good morning, Doctor, my name is Alex Goldberg and as you know I represent the family of your late patient Winnie Brown. Please state your full name and occupation for the jury."

Once the formalities were past Alex quickly took David through his medical education and qualifications. It was easy to establish that he was one of the foremost experts in lymphoma treatment in the United States, and that he had headed up the lymphoma program at International for more than five years at the time of Winnie Brown's death.

Most importantly for her case against International she showed that David was a full time employee of International.

"Under the terms of your contract it is your understanding that International is responsible for your actions, is it not?"

"Objection," from Herb Walton, "Lack of foundation. The doctor is not an expert in contract law."

"Overruled," said Judge Reagen, "She specifically asked him what his understanding was. Most employees have a pretty good idea of the details of their employment contract. You don't need a law degree for that, Mr. Walton."

This was pretty boring stuff, but necessary for the jury to understand that International was on the line when the conduct of any its employees fell short.

Alex then had David describe Winnie Brown's illness and treatment up till the fateful day.

"So your medical opinion is that at the time of her last treatment in the clinic at International she was free of lymphoma with an excellent chance of cure?"

"Yes," said David.

"And that opinion is held to a reasonable degree of medical probability?"

David nodded in agreement, "Yes it is Ms. Goldberg."

Alex paused. *Now the tough stuff.*

"Doctor, I'd like to turn now to the events of Monday January 8 2001."

David nodded, "OK."

In response to Alex's questions, David then described in detail what happened in the Oncology Clinic. The jury sat engrossed in every detail as David described the tragic accident that killed his patient. At the conclusion of the story David shook his head.

"I made a terrible mistake that I will always regret, and a brave young woman died as a result."

There was silence in the court.

Alex paused for a moment, then continued her questions.

"Now Doctor it's been suggested by the defense in their opening statement that you did not make a mistake."

David listened calmly as Alex continued, "In his opening statement, Mr. Walton told the jury that your belief that you injected the wrong drug is in fact a delusion, a completely false and irrational belief. Mr. Walton has stated that you are suffering from a psychiatric condition that renders your memory, judgment and recollection of the events of January 8 unreliable. Is that true?"

David smiled ruefully, "I wish it were true."

He turned to the jury, "The fact is that I did exactly what I told you."

"They believe him. He's come right out and said I screwed up," thought Alex.

The jury was clearly impressed by David. He had spoken in a straightforward way. No dramatics, no hand wringing. His story had the ring of truth.

Next question. "As far as your mental state is concerned, did you ever seek psychiatric care from Dr. Rubin?"

David shook his head. "No, that was bizarre."

He told the jury the story of the week of meetings to prepare the non-existent grant application.

"And who initiated these meetings?" asked Alex.

David replied, "Dr. Rubin."

"Did you ever seek Dr. Rubin out to treat you or help you in any way?"

David shook his head, "Absolutely not."

At the defense table Herb Walton sat calmly listening to David's testimony. If Herb was in any way concerned by how impressive a witness David was, he certainly didn't show it.

Alex changed tack slightly, "Doctor, have you been promised anything by myself or Mr. Brown in exchange for your testimony today?"

David shook his head, "No."

Alex leaned towards the jury as she asked her next question.

"It is true, is it not that you were in fact a co-defendant in this case? You admitted your personal responsibility and we have settled the case against you as an individual prior to this trial."

Herb leapt to his feet. "Objection, your Honor!"

Both attorneys and the judge huddled together in a sidebar out of the jury's hearing.

Herb was furious, "Your Honor, disclosing the pre-trial settlement between Doctor Stern and the Brown family will inevitably prejudice the jury. Counsel's question was deliberately intended to convince the jury that Stern's story must be true, that he would never have settled otherwise."

The judge raised an eyebrow and looked to Alex who remained calm despite Herb's theatrics.

She calmly replied, "Your Honor I'm really not sure why counsel is so excited. He really has not done his homework. This was covered in your pre-trial rulings. We all agreed that the jury had to know that we had settled with David Stern."

She continued, "Otherwise it makes no sense for us to be suing International only. The only reason International is in the case is because Doctor Stern was acting as their agent. Without the knowledge that we settled with the doctor, anyone with half a brain would question why are they suing the hospital and not the guy who did the deed?"

Judge Reagen nodded in agreement, "She's right Mr. Walton. I did rule that the jury could be informed that the case against Stern had settled."

He smiled briefly at Alex.

"I'm glad at least half of my brain is functioning. I'll instruct the jury as to the significance of this."

Alex smiled to herself, *"Herb was a great performer in court, but sometimes he was a little sloppy in preparation."*

The attorneys returned to their places and Judge Reagen addressed the jury.

"You have just heard that Dr. Stern was originally a defendant in this case, together with International. The fact that Mr. Brown has settled his case against Dr. Stern prior to this trial is of no relevance to the present matter. The details of that settlement, whether

Dr. Stern admitted responsibility or not, or whether International agreed with that settlement, none of these issues should influence your deliberations or final decision."

He paused, "Only the evidence presented in this courtroom should influence your discussions and final decision."

Walton appeared slightly happier after the judge's statement to the jury.

Alex then had David explain to the jury exactly what an accidental injection of Vincristine into the brain or spinal fluid would do. She concluded by having him read the warning label on a package of the drug.

"Fatal if injected intra-thecally," read David.

"And that's just what you did, correct Doctor?"

David nodded, "That's right."

There was silence in the court.

Alex looked over her notes.

"Doctor, since Winnie Brown's death you have been suspended from International. Why is that?"

Over Walton's vigorous objections David was allowed to answer.

"I refused to agree with their cover up story," he said bitterly, "so they said that I was mentally unbalanced."

Alex paused, "Doctor, at any time in your life have you ever been diagnosed with or treated for a mental illness?"

David shook his head, "No."

"Prior to this case, have you ever had your medical license suspended, revoked or had your hospital privileges in any way modified or restricted?"

David shook his head again.

"No."

"Prior to this occasion have you ever had any disciplinary action taken against you by any hospital or medical association?"

"Same answer, no."

"Doctor Stern, since your suspension by International you have not practiced medicine, correct?"

"That is correct."

"Why is that?" asked Alex.

David sighed, "Until this whole issue is resolved I really wouldn't feel comfortable taking care of patients. It's bad enough what I did to Winnie. But I'm also aware of what International has said about my mental health. There will shortly be a hearing before the State of Illinois to assess my mental status. I'm hoping to get back to work after the State gives me a clean bill of health."

He smiled bitterly, "Cancer patients have a tough enough time without having to worry whether their doctor is crazy or not."

He looked straight at the jury. "I want this trial to compensate the Browns for my error, although I know that no amount of money will bring Winnie back. It may be selfish of me, but I also want to finally put all this behind me, as much as I can, and get on with my own life."

For the first time his voice shook.

Alex shot a quick look at the jury. Several were close to tears.

She nodded gravely, "Thank you, Doctor Stern, I have no more questions for you."

"*O.K. Herb let's see what you make of that,*" thought Alex as she sat down.

Chap 39

Herb Walton rose to his feet and walked slowly to the lectern. The crowded courtroom was very still. Everyone realized that this was probably the most important moment of the trial. Alex's examination of David had impressed the jury. Now it was Walton's job to convince the jury that David Stern was not to be believed.

Walton rested both arms on the lectern. He appeared very confident.

"Doctor Stern, you have told the jury your version of Ms. Brown's tragic death. You have no doubt that it happened just as you say, correct?"

"Correct," replied David calmly.

Walton nodded, "Would you agree, Doctor that a bad result, even the death of a patient, does not always mean medical malpractice?"

"I would certainly agree with that," said David.

Walton was low key.

"You've told the jury at great length about your training and experience. During the past fifteen years, as a medical student, resident, fellow and since then would you agree that you must have seen thousands of patients, Doctor?"

"Sure."

"And during that time, especially as a cancer specialist, you've had your share of patients die?"

David agreed, "Certainly. Unfortunately many patients with cancer die of their disease."

Walton continued easily, "In fact isn't it true that about half a million Americans die every year from cancer?'

David nodded in agreement, "That's true."

"And those patients of yours that died from cancer over the years, the fact that the patient died, that doesn't mean there was malpractice by you or any other doctor, correct?"

David nodded in agreement, "Correct."

"Until Winnie Brown?" asked Walton, turning to the jury.

"That's correct."

Walton shuffled some papers.

"Doctor when Ms. Goldberg was questioning you earlier, you told us how Ms. Brown actually had her first seizure while you were in the process of injecting chemotherapy into her brain fluid. Do you remember that?"

"Mr. Walton, I'll never forget it," replied David.

"Explain to the jury, if you would please, how close you were to the patient when she started having the seizure."

"Well, I was right beside her. She was lying on the treatment table and I was standing beside her. My hands were inches from her head."

"And suddenly, she cries out, loses consciousness and has a series of seizures one after the other, correct?" asked Walton, turning towards the jury.

"That's right," said David.

"And you're powerless to stop them. Despite your years of training, all of your medical knowledge, nothing you can do, correct?"

Again David agreed with Herb, "Nothing."

"That must have been a very frightening experience for you, Doctor. There you are, inches from this person, suddenly without any warning she's having seizure after seizure, unconscious, not breathing and close to death. Were you frightened, Doctor?"

"I was," said David quietly.

Walton nodded, "And feeling helpless, correct?"

"Yes."

"Helpless to do anything?"

"David nodded again, "Yes.""

Alex was feeling very uneasy. This sympathetic Herb Walton was as genuine as a three dollar bill.

Where was he going with this?

David was an innocent. He had no idea of what was coming. Alex waited for the roof to cave in.

She didn't have to wait long.

"Doctor, seizures are not uncommon, are they?"

"True."

Walton paused, "Have you ever witnessed a patient actually have a seizure in the past, Doctor?"

David thought for a moment, "Yes, I have."

"I don't suppose there's anything that can prepare you for the suddenness of an event like that, true?'

"Probably not," agreed David.

Walton casually walked over to the defense table and picked up a couple of sheets of paper. As he did so he asked his next question.

"Do you remember the first person you saw have a seizure, Doctor?"

"Let me think," said David, "I don't remember exactly, probably as a medical student or maybe a resident."

Walton paused, "Are you sure about that, Doctor?"

"No, I don't remember exactly," said David.

"Well let's see if I can help your memory," said Walton smugly.

He addressed the judge, "Your Honor, I'd like to introduce this as Defense exhibit number 1."

He handed a piece of paper to David, and casually passed a copy to Alex. She started to read it, but was interrupted by a strangled cry from the witness box.

She looked up startled. David had turned ash-white. For several seconds he closed his eyes, he looked as if *he* were about to have a seizure.

Alex was on her feet.

"Your Honor," she cried, "I would request a brief adjournment, Doctor Stern is clearly unwell."

David was on his feet also.

"You rotten piece of shit! How dare you!" he yelled at Walton who stood with a shocked expression on his face.

Judge Reagen hammered on his desk. "Doctor Stern, be quiet! Ms. Goldberg, get your witness under control at once. I will not have this behavior in my court."

David ignored him.

"I'll break your neck, you bastard!" he yelled at Walton.

David was shaking uncontrollably.

There was nothing Alex could do. She read the piece of paper that had provoked David's outburst.

It was the death certificate for Dana Stern, David's twin sister. Date of death June 23 1978, age 12. Cause of death was listed as asphyxia due to uncontrolled seizures.

"Oh Herb, you slimy bastard," thought Alex.

Chap 40

"Doctor Stern, I will not warn you again. Compose yourself at once," said Judge Reagen sternly. "If you cannot control yourself I will have the court bailiff remove you. Do you understand?"

Reagen addressed the jury, "Let's take a ten minute break."

A shocked jury left the court staring at David who sat mute in the witness box.

Reagen addressed Walton, "Mr. Walton, what is the meaning of this? You've been around long enough to know that every exhibit that you plan to use must be shared with Plaintiff's Counsel ahead of time."

Alex was fuming, "Your Honor, I have never seen this before today,"

She held the copy of the death certificate between two fingers, as if it were infected.

"The whole purpose of this disgraceful episode has been to provoke Doctor Stern into an emotional reaction in front of the jury, which is now hopelessly tainted."

Walton stood in front of the judge. He spread his hands innocently in front of him.

"Your Honor, the defense only came into possession of this document late yesterday afternoon. A copy was immediately hand-delivered to Ms. Goldberg's office."

Behind Alex, Cindy gasped, "That's a lie! I never received anything like that yesterday."

"As for tainting the jury," continued Walton smoothly, "I am as shocked as the court is by Doctor Stern's outburst."

"Please!" Alex rolled her eyes.

Walton was not to be stopped. "I regret that this has caused Doctor Stern emotional distress. I assumed that Ms. Goldberg had prepared Doctor Stern for this document. I also assumed that the death of Doctor Stern's sister so many years ago would no longer be a cause of such severe distress. And I am more than willing to wait as long as necessary for Doctor Stern to compose himself."

"Sure," thought Alex, *"He'd just love the jury to sit outside for an hour or two wondering what the hell David's up to. Wondering how crazy he is."*

Walton continued smoothly, "However what the court witnessed is typical of Doctor Stern's behavior. And your Honor knows that we have numerous witnesses from International, and expert psychiatric testimony to confirm that. So far from tainting the jury, the outburst, regrettable though it was, has actually given the jury an accurate picture of Doctor Stern's true mental state and behavior."

Judge Reagen drummed his fingers on his desk as he pondered. "Ms. Goldberg, any response?"

Alex shook her head, "No, your Honor."

Alex reasoned that there was no point in trying to fight it now. No judge wanted to declare a mistrial without a solid reason. If she could prove that Walton lied about delivering the death certificate, then that would be the time to go for a mistrial.

"Very well," decided the judge, "we go on. However,"

He turned to a pale David Stern who sat with his head in his hands in the witness box.

"There must be no more reactions from you Doctor Stern, is that clear?"

"Yes," mumbled an obviously still shaken David Stern.

The jury returned and was seated. They all looked uncomfortable. Alex was aware that several members were looking at David in an entirely new light.

Walton was very smooth. Like all good fighters, he knew when he had his opponent on the ropes.

"Doctor, I apologize if my last question upset you." He paused, "And I deeply regret that I need to explore an area that is clearly a source of continued distress to you."

"The hell you do," thought Alex who sat unable to do a thing as her star witness self-destructed.

Walton continued, "Before our break, I showed you a document. Please tell the jury what that document is."

David answered in a monotone. He was very different from the calm self assured professional of twenty minutes earlier.

"This is the death certificate of my twin sister, Dana Stern."

"And again I apologize for having to explore such a sensitive area, but please tell the jury the circumstances of her death."

David controlled himself with an effort.

"Dana suffered from seizures all of her life. Her first occurred when she was eighteen months old. They were fairly well controlled by medication, but she never went more than three months without one."

Still that flat unemotional monotone.

"You were with her when she suffered her fatal seizure, correct?"

"Yes I was."

"Was there anyone else present?"

"No, just me."

"I'm sure you felt quite helpless, a twelve year old boy watching his beloved twin sister die in front of his eyes, unable to do anything to save her, correct?"

"I'm sure I did Mr. Walton, but that has nothing to do with Winnie..."

Walton interrupted David's response.

"Thank you Doctor, you've answered my question."

He turned to the jury but addressed his question to David.

"So Doctor Stern, let's be clear about this. For over twenty years, you have lived with the memory of your twin sister, your only sibling, dying in front of your eyes of uncontrolled seizures. You were unable to help her, unable to save her. Is that an accurate picture?"

David nodded, unable to speak.

"Let the record reflect a non-verbal affirmative response." said Walton.

Walton shuffled some papers.

Let the jury think about that for a minute.

"I'm almost done Doctor, and I apologize again for stirring up such painful memories. Don't you see the similarities between the death of Winnie Brown and Dana Stern?"

"Not at all," said David, "I killed Winnie Brown."

"Thank you, Doctor. You've answered the question," said Walton, cutting off David's answer.

At that moment there was probably no-one in the court room who believed David. Even Alex had serious doubts.

Alex tried to rehabilitate David on re-direct examination, but it was uphill all the way. It was hard to see him as a credible professional after his emotional outburst. Walton's cross-examination had been disastrous for Alex's case, and she knew it.

All those in the courtroom who knew David were shocked by what they had seen and heard. Most importantly the jury had seen David out of control. They had witnessed with their own eyes behavior very consistent with the picture of David that International was trying to portray. Powerful stuff.

Could they believe him after what they had seen?

Walton's story that David blamed himself for Winnie's death, so similar to that of his twin sister, certainly had the ring of truth. Walton had hit a grand slam, and he knew it.

After Alex completed her re-direct the judge looked to Walton.

He shook his head, "Nothing further Your Honor."

Herb was already looking forward to his first martini of the evening.

David was excused by the judge and left the jury box, his head low.

"He looks beaten," thought Alex. *"That was as bad as it gets today."*

"Very well." said the judge, "we'll recess for the evening. Tomorrow morning nine thirty."

Reagen gave his usual admonition to the jury not to discuss the case until all the evidence had been heard. Once the judge and jury left the courtroom Walton broke into a grin from ear to ear.

Alex walked up to him. "Herb, I just want you to know I'm going to investigate exactly who delivered the death certificate to my office and exactly what time it was delivered."

She lowered her voice, "I know you lied today in open court. That document was never delivered to my office during office hours. If I can prove it, I will personally ram those fancy gold cufflinks so far up your ass, that you'll shit gold for a week."

Walton lost his grin in a hurry.

"If you run a lousy ship, that's your problem, Counselor," he muttered.

Without another word Alex walked from the courtroom.

This round went to Walton, probably a knockout.

Chap 41

Alex walked slowly with Cindy and Sam McClendon the three blocks to her office. No-one spoke until they were all seated around the desk in Alex's office.

"Well, that was not a good afternoon," said Alex. "Shit, Walton's got me doubting Stern myself. We were sandbagged in there. I hate to say it but Walton handled it perfectly. Did you see the look of surprise on his face when David blew up?"

She shook her head, "I'm done. Tomorrow morning I'm going to rest our case, and let Walton put on his defense witnesses. Let's see what lies he's going to show up with. We'll keep Melissa Walters for rebuttal."

She exhaled loudly, "Herb's an unethical bastard, but I'm afraid he just won this case for his client. There's no way that that jury will ever believe David Stern now."

Sam stretched his long frame, "It's too soon for the autopsy, Alex, the patient's not dead yet."

Alex shook her head, "Sam, you know me, I'm not by nature pessimistic. This patient may not be dead, but she's pretty damn terminal."

Sam was persistent, "You know Alex the fat lady may be tuning up her voice but she's not singing yet."

Alex smiled, "What is this? *Cliché time?* She may not be singing, but it's awful close, Sam. Especially when the jury hears from all of the International people who are going to swear that David's nuts."

She yawned, "I'm beat. Time for some rest, I think."

Sam stood up, "I'm going to check in on David. He must feel like crap."

Alex nodded, "Poor guy, I can't blame him for not telling me about his sister. He probably didn't think it was relevant. But you know that's just the kind of stuff that Walton would find out and use."

Cindy had sat silently listening to the conversation, Finally she spoke.

"For what it's worth, Alex, I believe Doctor Stern. We've all spent a lot of time with him. I don't accept for one second that he made up the whole story. I don't think that what happened to his sister had anything to do with Winnie Brown. If he said that he injected the wrong medicine then that's what he did."

"Alex you have to believe him. You have to prove that he told the truth."

Alex looked at that them both in silence.

There was no more to say.

Chap 42

The next morning Herb Walton was still smirking from his triumph of the day before. He was too much of a professional to let the jury see it, but as he and Alex made their way into court he whispered to her.

"Got your boy doped up this morning, Alex? Don't want him foaming at the mouth in front of the jury again, do you?"

Alex shot him a look full of contempt but said nothing.

David sat in the rear of the court, looking grim. Alex looked over to him as she sat. They smiled briefly at each other.

When Judge Reagen had the jury brought in and seated, he looked to Alex, who stood.

"That concludes the plaintiff's case your Honor."

Judge Reagen nodded briefly, "Very well."

He turned and addressed the defense table. "Mr. Walton."

Walton stood, immaculate as always. "Your Honor, the defense calls as its first witness Dr. Frank Crandall."

During the next four hours the jury learned that Crandall was the head of the Department of Pathology at International, that he had been recruited from Harvard, and had authored over four hundred scientific papers during a thirty year career.

They also learned that he had spent several years working in London at the Hammersmith Hospital where he had apparently developed an upper class English accent. Despite his mid Western roots the accent still clung to him twenty years later.

He favored English country attire, heavy Harris tweed sports jacket and wool shirt and tie, with cavalry twill trousers and brown brogues.

"What a pompous asshole. All he needs is his horse," thought Alex acidly.

Walton treated every word of Crandall's testimony with awe and reverence, as the doctor described to the jury the results of the autopsy that he had performed on Winnie Brown.

Crandall described in detail finding lymphoma in the brain and surrounding tissues. Walton produced several large blow-ups of color slides of the brain tissue. Crandall demonstrated the lymphoma cells to the jury. He explained that lymphoma in the brain is often resistant to chemotherapy treatment because the brain is protected by the blood brain barrier.

Alex had to admit that Crandall was a powerful witness. He obviously knew his stuff and the pictures of the tissue samples with overwhelming numbers of cancer cells clearly impressed the jury. She was going to have a hard time discrediting this guy.

Walton was drawing to a close.

"And so, Doctor Crandall, let us summarize what you found, just so there's no confusion here. At the time of autopsy you found extensive lymphoma in Ms. Brown's brain and meninges, the tissues that surround and support the brain, is that correct?'

Crandall nodded, "That is correct."

"Sufficient in your opinion to cause seizures of the type that the patient experienced before her death?'

Another nod of agreement from Crandall. "Yes."

"And you found no evidence of the type of brain damage that would have been produced by the accidental injection of chemotherapy that Doctor Stern claimed to have done?"

Crandall shook his head, "None at all."

"And your conclusion, held to a reasonable degree of medical probability, is that Ms. Brown died as a result of lymphoma in the brain, correct?"

Crandall nodded, "Yes."

"And that's how the attending physician Doctor Keating signed the death certificate, correct?"

Again Crandall nodded his agreement, "Yes."

Walton stepped away from the lectern.

"Thank you Doctor Crandall. I have no further questions for you."

"Shit," thought Alex, *"I've got my work cut out here."*

Crandall made an impressive witness for the defense.

Judge Reagen looked at his watch, and turned to the jury.

"It's now twelve fifty," he said, "we'll take our lunch break now, and then start Doctor Crandall's cross-examination. We'll restart at two."

After the judge's usual instructions to the jury not to discuss the case among themselves the jury filed out. Alex sat at the table, deep in thought. She had nowhere to go with Crandall. Walton knew it too. He looked at her with a smug smile on his face.

"Need some help there, counselor?" he grinned.

Alex would not let him get to her.

"Actually I do," she replied, "I'm having difficulty writing my complaint to the Bar Association about your little stunt yesterday. Remind me, is *sleazy asshole* spelt with one z or two?"

Walton scowled darkly.

"It's easy to score points off him like this," thought Alex, *"but how the hell do I get to Crandall on cross?"*

There was no easy answer to that question.

When court re-assembled, Alex tried to impeach Crandall, but couldn't do it. The witness readily agreed that he was an International employee, but vigorously denied that he would falsify results of any medical test to satisfy the company or defend it in a lawsuit.

She was able to show that Crandall, like most of the Department heads at International, owned several thousand shares of company stock. *But so what?*

By the time Judge Reagen adjourned for the weekend at four o'clock Alex had pretty much run out of ideas and questions. She decided however not to finish her cross-examination of Crandall until Monday morning.

Maybe inspiration would strike during the weekend.

Chap 43

All day Saturday David sat in his apartment, reading Winnie Brown's medical records. Alex had provided him with a complete copy of the thousands of pages that Winnie's treatment had generated during those long months of treatment at International.

Something bothered him about Crandall's testimony, but he couldn't put his finger on it. He knew Crandall was lying, although David had to admit he had sounded pretty persuasive on the stand. David was convinced in his heart that Winnie had no residual lymphoma in her body when she died, and certainly none in her brain.

But how to prove it?

Much as David hated to admit it, Alex's analysis of the case was correct. When she first heard the details from David, she had correctly predicted that International held all the cards. Their pathologist had done the autopsy in their hospital. Who could disprove the results?

It appeared that Robert's decision to have Winnie's body cremated had robbed him of any chance of obtaining justice. Although Alex hadn't admitted it to him, David knew that Crandall's testimony was the most crucial of the defense's case. He looked and sounded the part, and his scientific credentials couldn't be challenged.

Most important he and Keating were the only people present at the autopsy. The regular autopsy room staff had been excluded. To someone looking for conspiracy, that fact was by itself suspicious. But the jury would not be convinced by that, especially with the autopsy findings that Crandall had presented.

David felt very badly about his outburst. He had fallen right into the trap that bastard Herb Walton had laid for him. David knew that based on what they had seen with their own eyes, the jury could very well be convinced that he had imagined the whole thing because he was all wrapped up with Dana's death.

He read on into the evening, plowing through hundreds of pages of medical records and testimony. Apart from a one hour break for soup and a sandwich, and the nine o'clock news on TV he kept at it.

At eleven thirty, weary and dispirited he went to bed. He couldn't sleep. His stomach was bothering him. At two in the morning, he gave up trying to sleep. Pulling on his robe, he made himself a cup of tea.

As he sat at his kitchen table, drinking the tea, he remembered something Alex's uncle had said to him a few months ago.

"David," Rabbi Shuster had said quietly, "don't be intimidated by the opposition. Remember, you knew the patient better than anyone. You were her doctor. Use that information to help you."

Suddenly it came to him.

"Holy shit."

He feverishly searched through Winnie's medical records, until he found the page that he wanted. He sat and looked at it. Here was the proof that Alex needed. David had found the evidence that could prove that Crandall was a liar, and that Winnie had not died of lymphoma in her brain.

It was two thirty Sunday morning. David didn't hesitate. He went to the phone and called Alex. She answered after one ring.

"What are you trying to do, Doctor Schweitzer?" she asked when she heard his voice, "cause an epidemic of insomnia?"

"Who are you kidding?" he said. "I know you weren't sleeping. Listen to me Alex. I can prove that Crandall lied on the stand. I can prove that the pictures he showed the jury with lymphoma cells in the brain couldn't have come from Winnie Brown."

There was a long silence.

"I'm coming round now, O.K.?" she said.

He gave her his address. Thirty minutes later he buzzed her into his building. A few minutes later she knocked quietly on the door. She wore jeans and a thick red sweater under a wool coat of the same color.

They sat at his kitchen table. David's stomach felt like fire but he didn't care. He explained his discovery to Alex, and showed her what she had to see. She listened carefully and asked only one question.

"Exactly what do we need to do to prove beyond any doubt that you are correct?"

David told her what had to be done.

She hugged herself against the cold and fatigue she felt. Her eyes were red rimmed and surrounded by deep shadow.

"I hear you," she said, "I don't doubt you, and for what it's worth I think you did a brilliant job of working it out."

She shook her head, "Our problem is time. From what you've told me it will take a minimum of one week to get the proof that Crandall lied. We don't have one week. He's back on the stand at nine thirty Monday. I have to be able to nail him then."

Frustration burned in David's stomach.

"Can't you get a week's delay?"

Alex shook her head, "Not a hope in hell."

She thought hard.

"Are you sure there's no other way to get him?" she asked.

It was David's turn to shake his head.

"I have to give it to them," he said, "They really covered their tracks well."

They stared at each other in frustration.

Alex looked pensive, "You know if I can't nail him then we'll lose this case."

There was a long silence. She shivered. "It's freezing in here," she said. "Do you have anything hot, maybe soup?"

David nodded and pointed to a cupboard full of cans. He was too tired and frustrated to speak. Just when it seemed that they could finally win the case, to simply lose because of lack of time was too much. He was angry with himself for failing to think of the answer sooner.

"Sit down, I'll find it," said Alex.

She rummaged through his kitchen.

"Obviously a gourmet you are not," she said, shaking her head.

She finally found a can of mushroom soup, opened it and filled two mugs. She nuked them in the microwave for a couple of minutes and brought them to the table. David looked and felt terrible.

"Hey," said Alex, trying to cheer them both up, "you have to admit, I open a can as well as anyone I know."

They drank the soup in silence for a few minutes.

"What's the matter with you?" she asked.

David's face had turned a greenish color.

"Don't like my cooking, huh?" said Alex, "if you don't like the soup just don't drink it!"

Suddenly David dropped the mug and vomited all over the kitchen table. He groaned, clutched his stomach and lay down heavily on the floor. He vomited again, this time bright red blood.

"Oh no," said Alex.

She ran to the phone and called Sam McClendon.

"Call 911," he said, "I'll be there in ten minutes."

Sam got there just after the ambulance. David lay shivering on the floor. Since Alex made the call, he had vomited three more times. The amount of blood on the floor seemed enormous to her.

The paramedics were fast and efficient.

"Obvious G.I. bleed, major one." the older of the two explained, "he's in shock now, pulse 150, blood pressure 80/50. We'll have to stabilize him before we move him."

With Sam's help they got him on the gurney. Within a few minutes they had a saline I.V. running, wide open. Despite several blankets, David was shivering uncontrollably. Beneath his oxygen mask, his lips were pale. Alex was terrified that he was going to die in his own kitchen. She felt his hand. It was ice cold.

"Pulse is down to 120, BP 90/50. I don't think we can do much more here."

The younger of the paramedics had checked David's wallet. "His insurance card says International. Let's roll!"

Sam and Alex exchanged glances. "Not International" they said simultaneously.

The older paramedic shrugged. "O.K. we'll go to County, it's only a few minutes more. We'll call them from the ambulance."

"I'll follow you," Sam said to the paramedics, as they wheeled the gurney with a barely conscious David to the service elevator.

Sam pulled out his cellular phone and turned to Alex as he left. "I'll have two of my guys meet us there. Don't worry, I'm sure he'll be fine."

Alex sat in the chair and hugged herself, as she stared at David's blood on the floor. Far below she could hear the ambulance siren receding in the distance as it carried David away.

She was overwhelmed with emotion. David had given her the key to victory, but would he live to see her achieve it?

Chap 44

Eight hours later David was lying in his room at Cook County Hospital. For the second time in just over a month he had a tube in his nose and Sam McClendon sitting by his side.

His mouth felt like sandpaper and his belly hurt, but he was grateful to be alive.

Carla Moore, the chief surgical resident at County sat casually on David's bed, swinging her right leg. Her pink surgical scrubs complimented her smooth cafe au lait skin.

"Gosh, she looks like a high school cheerleader," thought David.

He felt very old. Carla explained to them both what she had found.

"You were pretty shocked when you got here," she said, "it took four units of blood to stabilize you and get you to the O.R. You had a large duodenal ulcer which had eroded into a major arterial branch. It had also perforated. I under sewed the vessel and then patched the ulcer. We've got you on an I.V. H2 blocker now."

"It was a big ulcer," she continued, "I'm surprised that you hadn't had some symptoms prior to this."

David felt too sick to be embarrassed. He had been experiencing for months the classic symptoms of a duodenal ulcer which had nearly killed him. And he had assumed it was all just stress.

Carla concluded, "Anyway you're going to be fine."

She looked at her watch, "I've got to go. Any problems they'll call me. See you later."

With that, the young surgeon strolled out of the room with a casual wave to her patient. Sam stepped out of the room with her. They spoke for a few minutes in the hall.

"I've got three messages from Alex," Sam came back into the room.

"First, she says don't worry about court tomorrow. She's working on something. Second, Cindy will arrange for a cleaning crew to go in to your apartment."

Sam grinned, "And third, Alex says don't worry. If they screw up here and you die, she'll sue the ass off them."

Despite himself David laughed. It hurt.

Chap 45

Nine thirty, Monday morning David lay in Cook County Hospital sucking ice chips. His belly hurt, but he didn't care. A telephone message from Alex via Cindy told him all he needed to hear.

"Great detective work. I'm going to run with it."

Two dozen roses delivered that afternoon from the same source did wonders for his morale.

They took out the Foley catheter collecting his urine on Monday evening. That was a relief. They took the tube out of his nose Wednesday morning. That was a greater relief.

Sam McClendon stayed with him for much of his hospital stay. David drank a little skim milk and took his Zantac. They watched a lot of T.V. The Bulls without Michael were now the mutts of the N.B.A. The Knicks beat them by thirty points at the Garden.

David went home on Thursday morning. By then the case was all over the newspapers and the T.V. networks.

Monday in court started with Alex requesting a one week delay in the trial because of David's illness. The judge was sympathetic, but unmoved.

"I had an ulcer once," he said, "it hurt like the dickens. But the motion is denied. Doctor Stern is no longer a defendant, and he has testified already. So I don't see any reason to delay the trial and inconvenience the jury. We'll continue."

Herb Walton looked smug.

Despite Judge Reagen's denial of her motion Alex was neither surprised nor particularly concerned. All Sunday afternoon and evening she had worked with Cindy to lay out her strategy.

She had a plan.

Everybody rose as the jury filed in. The judge addressed the jury.

"Ladies and gentlemen, I'm glad to see that you all made it back. I hope you had an enjoyable weekend."

The judge continued, "When we recessed on Friday, Ms. Goldberg was cross-examining Dr. Crandall."

Alex rose, as Charles Crandall was recalled to the witness stand. Judge Reagen reminded the doctor that he was still under oath. Crandall nodded his understanding

"Good morning, Dr. Crandall" Alex started politely, "I think I only have a few more questions for you."

Crandall seemed to relax at these words.

Alex looked over her notes. "You've told us in detail about your autopsy findings. You stated that you and Dr. Keating were the only physicians present during the post-mortem examination, correct?"

Crandall nodded, "That is correct."

"You also testified that no autopsy technician was present?"

"That is correct."

"And you told us that was not the usual procedure in your department?"

Crandall nodded, "That is also correct. In this case, because of Doctor Stern's behavior at the time of the patient's seizures and subsequently in the I.C.U., I felt it important that only medical staff should be present at the autopsy. There was enough gossip about this case in the hospital already. I didn't want any more rumors coming out of my department."

Alex nodded, "Very understandable, when a doctor's reputation and career may be on the line."

Alex was very agreeable with Crandall. He appeared to relax even more, and expanded several answers. Alex let him get used to talking a little more than usual.

She had him explain how samples of each tissue were preserved in paraffin blocks, sliced very thin with a special knife called a microtome and then mounted on glass slides to be looked at under the microscope by the pathologist.

"Doctor, if you didn't have the usual autopsy technician with you, who prepared the tissue samples for the blocks and slides?"

"I did," said Crandall.

Alex was impressed, "Really, but you're the head of the Department!"

"That's correct," said Crandall, "but I've always insisted that every one of our doctors in training learn full autopsy procedure, so that they can complete all of the technical processes that are used in the Department if need be. I follow the same rules myself."

"So, Doctor Crandall, if there were a problem with any slide or tissue sample with Winnie Brown's autopsy examination, it would be you who were responsible?"

Herb Walton was on his feet with an objection.

"Lack of foundation, your Honor. There has been no evidence presented to indicate a problem with any autopsy material."

Alex responded. "Your Honor, it's a hypothetical question."

"I'll allow it," said Judge Regan.

"You may answer the question," he instructed the witness.

Crandall frowned and looked thoughtful "In answer to your question, hypothetically speaking, if there were ever a problem with a tissue sample, then whoever the technician was who worked on that case, they would be responsible."

"However," he added, "We pride ourselves on our professionalism in my Department. We don't make those kind of mistakes."

Alex nodded her understanding. "Thank you doctor. Just a few more questions, and then we're done."

Alex took a minute to look over her notes, although she knew exactly where she was going.

She looked up. "In his direct examination Mr. Walton had you describe your research achievements. You've written over three hundred scientific papers, correct?"

Crandall stiffened, "Four hundred."

Alex smiled, "I'm sorry, over four hundred. That's very impressive. I read your bibliography. I must apologize, there are some terms that I didn't understand. Perhaps you could enlighten me."

"Certainly." Crandall was more gracious now.

"I see you've written a lot of articles on P.C.R. What's that?"

"P.C.R. stands for Polymerase Chain Reaction. This is an elegant laboratory technique which allows scientists to identify the presence of specific protein molecules in organic material. Using P.C.R. we can actually measure microscopic amounts of protein in different tissues. It is a research tool that has numerous applications."

He had adopted his lecturing professor mode and Alex encouraged him.

"That's amazing," she said, "So you are an expert in this field?"

"I developed the technique when I was at Harvard."

(Not entirely true.)

"And is it accurate?"

He looked at her coldly. "Yes, very."

"Apart from yourself, who are the foremost experts in the field?"

He warmed up a little. "Well, apart from myself, probably the three best known workers are Higgins in Boston, Rutherford in London and Haju in Tokyo. They all worked at one time in my lab at Harvard."

"Well they'll all have the stuff later this week," thought Alex.

"Just give me a moment, Doctor, to look over my notes."

Alex shuffled papers for a moment or two, then looked up. She asked the next question casually. Behind her Cindy held her breath.

"Doctor there was one other area I wanted to clarify. During your direct examination you showed the jury the cancer cells, the lymphoma cells that you found in the specimens you took from Winnie Brown's brain and meninges. Do you remember that?"

Crandall nodded, "Yes, I do."

"So this was material that you obtained from the patient at the time of autopsy?"

Crandall nodded again, "That is correct."

"This was not some archival material from storage or a teaching library?"

Crandall flushed angrily, "Absolutely not."

Alex nodded and turned to Cindy, "I wonder if we could put up that big picture that Mr. Walton had, Defense exhibit number 14."

The exhibit was brought out.

Alex smiled at Cindy, "Thank you."

She turned back to the witness. "Now Doctor Crandall, I apologize if my questions seem unsophisticated, but remember I'm not a doctor, and neither are the members of the jury."

Crandall smiled as if to say, "I understand."

Herb Walton did not smile. He felt very uneasy.

"Where the hell was the bitch going with this? Was she fishing or did she know something?"

Alex asked, "First, the tissue specimen shown in Exhibit 14 was made from tissue you obtained at the time of Winnie Brown's autopsy, correct?"

"Correct."

"No chance of error?"

Crandall shook his head, "None."

Alex continued, "Absolutely no chance of confusion between Winnie Brown and any other patient?"

Walton felt definite alarm.

Crandall shook his head again. "Absolutely no chance of error or confusion."

Alex nodded, "O.K. fine. Doctor, if you would please, show the jury the lymphoma cells in this picture."

Crandall identified the cancer cells for Alex and for the jury.

"Thank you. Doctor."

Alex pointed at a small blood vessel. "Tell me, what are these pretty things here?" Are these lymphoma cells also?"

Cindy held her breath.

"No, Ms. Goldberg," Crandall said in a patronizing tone, "those pretty things are red blood cells in a capillary, a small blood vessel."

"How does the blood get there?" asked Alex.

Herb Walton had to stop this.

He rose, "Your Honor, I must object to this entire line of questioning. This is cross-examination. In my direct examination there was no mention of blood cells or blood vessels. This has no relevance to any issue in this case."

The judge turned to Alex. She was ready.

"Your Honor, when the defense introduced this exhibit as part of their evidence, they opened the door to allow us to question their witness about any and all aspects of the material."

The judge nodded his agreement, "Objection over-ruled. You may answer the question Doctor."

Crandall briefly described the circulation of the blood.

Alex continued to press, "So Doctor, the blood that is present in the brain is the same blood present everywhere in the body, in the heart, kidneys, muscle, liver?"

"Yes, Yes." said Crandall impatiently.

"*He still doesn't see where she's going,*" thought Cindy, "*he still thinks she's just asking naive medical questions. What an arrogant asshole!*"

Alex turned and faced the jury, while directing her next question to Crandall.

"Doctor, and again I apologize for asking questions that must seem very naive to you. What is it that makes red blood cells red?"

Cindy held her breath again.

Crandall answered the question, "Hemoglobin, Ms. Goldberg, Hemoglobin makes red blood cells red."

Alex felt a huge weight fall from her body. With that single word, delivered in a condescending tone, Crandall had lost the case for International.

Although he would remain unaware of his fate for a few more minutes, Crandall had also destroyed his career and that of the other conspirators.

Alex was relentless, "Hemoglobin is the red pigment present in human red blood cells, correct?"

"Yes," said Crandall.

Alex turned and looked directly at the jury, but addressed her question to Crandall.

"Doctor Crandall. Was there anything special about Winnie Brown's hemoglobin?"

Frank Crandall went as white as a ghost. It was as if all of the hemoglobin had suddenly been removed from *his* face. In that moment, he suddenly realized how stupid he had been to underestimate this young woman.

Herb Walton silently fumed. He didn't know what the Goldberg bitch knew about the hemoglobin, but it was obviously something crucial. He doubted that Crandall knew. *Pompous, arrogant bastard!*

As his witness sat silent, Herb Walton realized that his legal career was over. If any of the others talked, then he would certainly face jail time.

He rose, "Your Honor, Doctor Crandall appears unwell, could I suggest a brief recess?"

Judge Reagan looked at Herb Walton for several long seconds.

"Counselor," he said quietly, "the bailiff will give the doctor a glass of water, and we'll continue."

Chap 46

"Doctor, you must answer the question," said the judge.

Crandall shifted uncomfortably in his seat.

"No, I am not aware of anything special about Mrs. Brown's hemoglobin," he said.

Alex handed the witness a copy of the medical records.

"Doctor, I refer you to page 764 of Ms. Brown's certified medical record."

An enlarged copy of the page was brought out by Cindy for the judge and jury to see.

"You will note," continued Alex "that on September 13 1994, a test of Ms. Brown's blood, hemoglobin electrophoresis, showed 39% hemoglobin S. Do you see that Doctor?"

Crandall looked at the lab report in the medical record.

"Yes I see it."

"What is the significance of that result, Doctor?"

"It means that she had sickle cell trait," answered Crandall reluctantly.

"For the benefit of the jury, Doctor. What you are saying is that the hemoglobin, the red pigment in Winnie Brown's blood was different from that of most Americans, correct?"

"Yes," said Crandall, who looked very uncomfortable.

Walton fumed silently.

"And the difference is that Ms. Brown's hemoglobin was abnormal, of a type present in many African-Americans. Sickle cell trait is an inherited condition, is that correct Doctor?"

"That is correct."

"And this abnormal hemoglobin is called hemoglobin S, correct?"

Crandall nodded reluctantly, "Yes."

Alex turned once again to the jury but directed her question to Crandall.

"Isn't it true, Doctor, that the presence of hemoglobin S can be identified by P.C.R. examination of blood or other tissue samples?"

Crandall sat silently, simply nodding his head.

"Doctor," said the judge, "you must respond verbally. The court reporter has to have a spoken answer to record."

Crandall pulled himself together with an effort. "I'm sorry your Honor. The answer to the question is *yes.* P.C.R. will identify the presence of hemoglobin S in a tissue sample."

"Doctor, would a P.C.R. examination identify the presence of hemoglobin S in tissue obtained at autopsy?"

Crandall smiled bitterly, "Yes Ms. Goldberg, P.C.R. would do the job just fine."

Herb Walton was on his feet. He knew it was a lost cause, but he had to go through the motions.

"Your Honor," said Walton, "I object to this entire line of questioning and ask that it be stricken. This is quite irrelevant and goes beyond the scope of cross-examination. Ms. Brown's blood was never an issue in this case, and was not brought up in my direct examination of this witness."

Judge Reagen turned to Alex for her response. She was ready.

"Your Honor, Dr. Crandall identified red blood cells on the pathological slides that he examined and showed to the jury, and therefore questions about the patient's blood are an appropriate area for cross examination."

She paused, "As for relevance, if the court will be patient for just a few minutes I believe the relevance of the hemoglobin issue will become very clear."

Several jury members sat up straighter.

This was interesting.

Judge Reagen obviously thought so too.

"Objection overruled," he said. "Carry on Ms. Goldberg."

She continued, "Dr. Crandall, you have testified that according to her medical records a significant proportion of Ms. Brown's blood contained an abnormal protein, hemoglobin S, consistent with sickle cell trait, correct?"

Crandall nodded, "Yes."

"You also told us that P.C.R., a highly sensitive lab test that you invented, which is now widely used in medical laboratories all over the world, would be able to accurately identify the presence of hemoglobin S in the tissue specimens obtained at Ms. Brown's autopsy, is that correct?"

"Yes."

"Doctor, a few minutes ago you told the court that the blood that circulates through the brain is the very same blood that circulates through every other tissue of the body, correct?"

"That is correct."

"No difference?"

"None."

"So the blood in the brain is identical in every respect to the blood in the rest of the body, correct?"

"Yes."

Alex paused and took a quick look at the jury. *They were with her.*

"The blood in the brain would have exactly the same amount of hemoglobin S as the blood in the rest of her body, correct Doctor?"

Crandall licked his lips, suddenly very dry, "Yes."

"So P.C.R. testing of every tissue obtained at the time of Ms. Brown's autopsy would be expected to show identical results as far as the concentration of hemoglobin S is concerned, correct?"

Crandall paused, and looked at the judge who sat impassively. "Yes," he finally answered.

Alex paused and turned to Cindy who with great theatrics passed her a bright red folder. It contained Cindy's recipes for the annual lunch of her children's P.T.A.

Alex gazed thoughtfully at a recipe for lasagna.

"Can't beat basil," she thought.

Crandall looked at the folder as if it had leprosy.

"As well you might Doctor," thought Alex.

She flipped through the pages in the red folder.

"Home made pizza, spare ribs, Boston cream pie. Gee, Cindy did you ever hear of cholesterol?"

Alex closed the folder and looked directly at Crandall.

"Doctor," a pause, "if I were to tell you that each tissue sample taken from every major organ at Winnie Brown's autopsy tested using P.C.R., your technique, tested by three separate experts, the three experts you identified as the best in the world. If I were to tell you that each and every one of those tissue samples showed the presence of hemoglobin S in the same percentage, 39%."

She paused and turned to the jury for dramatic effect.

"Except for the samples obtained from the brain tissue and meninges, the only tissues that showed lymphoma. P.C.R. testing of the brain and meninges showed 100% normal hemoglobin. Would you be surprised?"

The court held its breath. Crandall remained silent.

"Answer the question, Doctor," said Judge Reagen.

Finally Crandall spoke, "No. I wouldn't be surprised."

His shoulders sagged. No bluster, no arrogance now. Crandall was beaten.

Alex was relentless. "Dr. Crandall it isn't a question of surprise, is it? You *know*, don't you, that the brain tissue that you reported to be that of Winnie Brown does not contain any hemoglobin S?"

There was a long pause. Finally Crandall answered in a near-whisper.

"Yes, I do."

Alex pressed on, "And the reason that you know this is because you switched samples, didn't you Doctor? Those pictures of brain tissue that you showed this jury, full of lymphoma cells, those pictures were not from Winnie Brown. They were from another patient with lymphoma. Isn't that correct?"

Before Crandall could answer the judge interrupted.

"This would seem like a reasonable time to stop for today."

Most members of the jury and the people sitting in the court looked surprised and disappointed.

It was only eleven o'clock.

"We'll recess now," said the judge.

The court-room buzzed as the jury left, following the judge's admonition not to discuss the case among themselves.

After the jury was gone, Judge Reagen turned and addressed Crandall.

"Doctor Crandall, you are aware that you have been testifying under oath. I must remind you that untruthful testimony leaves you open to charges of perjury, which can carry severe criminal penalties. You have the right to refuse to answer any question which might incriminate you. My advice to you is that before you continue with your testimony in this case, you should consult with an attorney."

"I have recessed now and will delay starting tomorrow, to allow you time to do so. We shall re-convene at eleven a.m. tomorrow."

With a hard look at the defense bench the judge continued, "My advice to Doctor Crandall may also be relevant to other potential witnesses for the defense, and others in the court."

Herb Walton appeared fascinated by his fingernails.

Alex handed the red folder back to Cindy.

"Thanks Cindy," she whispered, "Great recipes, but maybe a little too much cheese in the lasagna."

All in all a useful morning's work.

Chap 47

After court Alex walked over to her office with her client, Sam and Cindy. They sat in her office. She took off her shoes with a sigh. She hated heels.

"Let me explain what this morning was all about Robert," she started after Cindy had brought them all lunch, tuna sandwiches and drinks. Coffee for Alex and Sam, Cokes for Cindy and Robert.

"What you are hearing now is a preview of my closing argument for the jury," she said with a smile.

She addressed Robert. "You understand that all along International has denied that Dr. Stern did anything wrong when he treated your wife. Although he himself testified that he made a grievous error, and injected the wrong drug, the hospital has all along claimed that he injected the correct drug, the ARA-C into the Omaya. They claim that your wife died from the effects of lymphoma. Their explanation for Dr. Stern's testimony is that he is mentally unstable, and is suffering from delusions that he committed a fatal error."

Robert nodded. He understood all this.

Alex continued, "Their explanation is that the trauma of seeing your wife's seizures triggered memories of fatal seizures that Doctor Stern witnessed in his twin sister."

She shook her head. "They sure did a good job of painting him as emotionally unstable."

There was a long silence as everyone remembered David's reaction the previous week.

Alex continued, "The autopsy findings that Crandall described to the jury on Friday reported lymphoma cells in the brain, which of course supported their case that Winnie died as a result of her lymphoma. The only doctors who had access to the autopsy were Dr. Keating and Dr. Crandall, both International Doctors, so it wasn't at all surprising that the autopsy result confirmed the International position."

She shook her head, "There is no way that both Dr. Stern and Dr. Crandall were telling the truth. Their stories are mutually contradictory."

"We knew that Dr. Stern's story was in fact true. Our problem was not working out what happened. Clearly there was a conspiracy to manipulate the facts in this case, to make it appear that David Stern was deluded, that Winnie died of lymphoma, and that the fatal injection never occurred."

"Those slides showing lymphoma cells in the brain couldn't have come from Winnie's autopsy. They had to have got them from another patient."

She smiled, "Our problem was how to *prove* that happened. That's where the sickle cell trait became so crucial. It gave us a way to prove without any doubt that the slides showing lymphoma in the brain could not have come from Winnie."

She smiled at Cindy.

"I don't actually have the proof yet, but we will soon enough. But Crandall didn't know that, and he didn't call our bluff."

Sam McClendon laughed, "Never play poker with her, Robert. I found that out the hard way."

Alex blushed. "Anyway it's moot now, because Crandall folded, and all but admitted under oath that he switched the tissue."

She continued, "Tomorrow I plan to have him expose the whole conspiracy. Crandall knows it, Herb Walton knows it and the judge knows it too."

She looked at her watch. "Incidentally that's why the judge stopped court so early and advised Crandall to retain counsel. The judge is a fair man. He's giving Crandall time to get some legal advice. If Crandall follows that advice he'll almost certainly recant his prior testimony tomorrow."

Alex leaned back in her chair, "You're about to see this entire conspiracy crumble, I expect."

Robert had one question, "I understand everything you said, Alex. That thing with the sickle cell was brilliant. Winnie had been told about it years ago. She was told it wasn't serious, that it didn't mean anything. How did you work it out, Alex?"

Alex shook her head. "Robert," she said quietly, "I didn't work it out. David Stern worked it out. He called me in the middle of the night Saturday, just before he got sick. If it were not for him, you and I would have lost this case."

Cindy broke the silence, "What do we do now, Alex?"

"Well, that's what we have to decide," said Alex.

She turned to her client, "Really, Robert, I need you to tell me what you want to do. I can only advise you of what's likely to happen."

She continued, "We'll win this case now, no question of it. You saw what happened today. Crandall believes I have the result of P.C.R. analysis of the autopsy tissue showing that he switched tissues. He's terrified, with good reason that he'll go jail for perjury, conspiracy and obstruction of justice."

She smiled, "You know, I never actually said that I had the results of the P.C.R. studies. But he knows what he did, tampered with evidence and lied about it under oath. He knows that P.C.R. would prove it beyond any doubt. He wasn't smart enough to call my bluff."

She stood up and started pacing around the office.

"After David Stern explained it all to me, Cindy and I spent the better part of Sunday contacting the three guys that Crandall identified as the best at P.C.R. We got their names from Crandall's bibliography. They've all co-published with him. We Googled them for their current addresses."

She turned to Cindy, "We're FedExing the tissue blocks to them today, right?"

Cindy nodded, "They're on the way as we speak."

Alex continued, "Excellent. We'll have those results within a couple of weeks. They'll certainly need them for the criminal trial."

She looked at her watch again.

"Anyway, for now Crandall's probably spilling his guts to his attorney. When I continue to cross-examine him tomorrow, I suspect he'll tell the truth even though it means incriminating himself and several other people in a criminal conspiracy to falsify evidence and obstruct justice."

"He really doesn't have any other option, now," she shrugged.

She laid her arm gently on Robert's.

"Robert, I want you to know that if I call Herb Walton now, and demand twenty million dollars, he and I will haggle, but we'll agree within five minutes on at least ten million dollars. That's in addition to the million that we already have agreed on from Doctor Stern. It's a huge amount of money, and if you want I'll be very happy to make that call for you."

Robert Brown looked at Alex. "If we accept their offer, what happens to the court case?"

Alex shrugged, "It would be over."

Robert shook his head, "Alex, you know this case was never about money. If we settle now, then the hospital doesn't have to admit anything, does it?"

Alex shook her head. "Usually I'd say that you're correct. An out of court settlement generally requires both parties to remain silent about the terms of the agreement, with neither side admitting responsibility."

Robert started to speak but Alex held up her hand.

"But wait a minute Robert, "she said. "Thanks to Doctor Stern you can have it both ways in this case."

Robert looked puzzled and Alex explained.

"You saw the judge in there this afternoon. Believe me, what happened here will go to the Cook County District Attorney. There'll almost certainly be criminal charges against Crandall and whoever else was involved in this conspiracy. So even if International tried to buy your silence with a settlement, I don't think that they can."

She smiled, "Even if you accept an offer from them now, they will not be able to keep this case quiet. It may not all come out now, but it will come out at the time of the criminal case."

"As your attorney I have to give you the best advice I can. You can leave my office this afternoon with a guaranteed eight or ten million dollars, and every chance of having the truth come out in open court within a year."

Robert shook his head again. "No way. I want this jury to hear it all now."

"Do you want to sleep on it?" Alex asked.

Robert shook his head, "No way."

Alex nodded, "O.K. It's your decision, and I respect it. I just wanted you to know what all your options are. I really don't think that the jury will fail us now, but it's possible. I hope that you get the kind of statement that you want in open court."

Cindy had sat listening silently. She spoke now.

"Robert, think of your kids. There would be no shame in taking their money now, and waiting for the criminal case later."

Robert shook his head.

No," he said firmly, "I want this over now. I want to hear this jury say clearly that my wife died because this doctor screwed up, and the hospital knew it and tried to cover it up."

"O.K." said Alex, "I understand you. But Robert you have to realize that the statement you want might be very expensive for you and your children. Even if the jury does say exactly that, there is no way to guarantee you that they'll award you anything like ten million dollars.

Robert nodded, "I understand."

"O.K. then, said Alex with a smile, "We'll just have to see what we can do for you tomorrow."

Robert Brown stood up. The meeting was over.

As Sam, Robert and Cindy left the room Alex reached for the telephone. Cindy heard her ask for David Stern's room at Cook County Hospital.

Chap 48

Next morning Alex was woken at six o'clock by the ringing of her bedside telephone. As she opened her eyes she glanced at her alarm clock and smiled.

"Good morning Herb," she said.

Herb Walton's voice lacked its usual confidence. "Alex, can we meet at your office for breakfast?"

Alex thought for a moment, "O.K. Herb, seven thirty. I've got coffee. You bring doughnuts or muffins."

She hung up. This promised to be an interesting day.

She spent longer than usual in her shower. She had slept only four hours, a little less than her usual when on trial. She stood in the shower and let the hot water wash away her weariness.

She did not feel nervous during trials. She was always confident of her ability to deal with whatever happened. However this morning she felt uncharacteristically edgy.

As she was drying her thick hair, she finally realized what was bothering her. It was David. She cared about him and his feelings. This was new, and scary.

In the past Alex had always demonized the opposition. The defendant doctor was always an object of scorn and contempt. More than that, he or she was simply another example of the incompetent and uncaring physician who had killed her parents and Marsha, and so traumatized Alex.

As such the defendant doctor deserved and received no pity from Alex. For Alex there was only one deserving of sympathy, her client...the victim.

For the first time, with David Stern a shade of grey had entered into Alex's world, up till now populated only by villains and heroes, the blackest of the black and the whitest of the white.

She physically shook her head, as if to put such thoughts out of her mind. She would not lose her competitive edge. She owed as much to Winnie Brown.

She dressed with care. On the critical days of a trial she always wore what she and Cindy called her *nail-'em-to-the-wall outfit,* a dress or more commonly a suit in a dark color that emphasized her professionalism and dedication to the gravity of the day.

It was as if her very appearance would say to the jury, *"We have serious business today. Please listen carefully to me."*

Today she chose a medium length dress with a muted blue and purple paisley pattern. The only jewelry she wore was a long heavy gold chain necklace, a gift from her parents. Her exquisite legs were sheathed in tights of the palest blue. She wore black patent shoes with the hated heels.

She walked the five blocks from her apartment to her office. It was one of those perfect spring days in Chicago with blue skies and wind from the North. At seven in the morning the air was still chilly, and she wore a light wool coat. The high was expected to reach fifty-eight.

She arrived at her office with plenty of time to spare, found Cindy's special blend and made a large pot of coffee.

Herb was punctual. Immaculate as always, today he wore a midnight blue single-breasted suit from Saville Row. His shirt was pale blue with white collar and white French cuffs. He wore an Italian silk tie with a hand painted abstract design and heavy gold cuff links. The only outward sign of strain was the deep circles under his eyes.

As requested he had brought donuts (three kinds) and muffins (raisin and chocolate chip.)

They sat in Alex's office and drank coffee. While Alex chose her second muffin (*no contest, chocolate chip again*), Herb started to speak.

"There is no question, Alex, you did a great piece of detective work here. I haven't been able to speak to Crandall since yesterday, but it's clear to me that there has been a conspiracy, obviously instigated by Crandall to falsify evidence here. I'm shocked, of course."

There it was, the twitch!

"So you were part of it, you slimy bastard," she thought.

She said nothing and her face revealed no emotion as Herb continued.

"I've spoken to Frank Houston, and he is just as shocked as I am."

"I'll bet," thought Alex. She said nothing.

"Houston wants this whole business wrapped up as expeditiously as possible. We are prepared to make a very generous settlement offer, with the understanding that there would be no public acknowledgement of wrong-doing by either side."

Alex still had not spoken and Herb was beginning to squirm.

"Look Alex, I really need to know what your client wants. International will go up to five million dollars. What does your guy want?"

Alex finally spoke, "Herb, I discussed a potential settlement offer with Mr. Brown. It's not about money. He wants a public acknowledgement by the hospital that his wife died because of David Stern's error, and that subsequent to that error there was a conspiracy within the hospital to conceal the true facts."

Walton continued, "O.K. Alex, tell me how much does he want? We'll agree to any reasonable counter proposal. Houston absolutely wants this settled today."

Alex shook her head. "Herb, I don't think you understand, Robert Brown is not looking for money here. He wants that public statement."

Alex watched as Herb's face showed disappointment, anger and finally, fear.

He stuck his face as close to Alex as he dared. "Listen to me counselor," he snarled, "That black bastard doesn't know who he's dealing with. You tell him that he can have a check for five million dollars today. Christ! He's a truck driver! He'd have to drive a truck for five hundred years to earn that kind of money. Does he have any idea how many new women he can get with five million bucks?"

Alex said nothing, but simply continued looking at Herb without expression.

Herb calmed down. "Listen," he pleaded, "I'll get him a private apology from Houston. We'll fire Crandall, Keating, O'Rourke and Piper today. We have to settle this thing now. You know Houston just won't tolerate this kind of publicity."

Alex finished her coffee and her second muffin, carefully wiped her lips with a paper napkin, and looked at Herb.

"I'll certainly communicate your offer to my client, but I don't think he'll accept."

Herb started to interrupt, but she stilled him with a gesture.

"You know the old joke. *If someone says it's not the money, it's the principle of the thing; then you know it's the money.* Well Robert Brown seems to be the exception to that rule."

"I never thought it was a very funny joke anyway," she said, almost to herself.

She stood up. Breakfast was over.

"Herb, thank you for coming over and thank you for the eight hundred calories. I'll speak to my client and call you in your office by ten thirty. We're due in court at eleven, right?"

Alex was correct. Robert Brown rejected the offer. She was wrong however about the court time. It was two in the afternoon before court finally re-assembled.

Much had happened since yesterday's recess. At one thirty the judge met in chambers with all of the lawyers and brought them up to date.

When the jury was seated, Judge Reagan looked around the crowded courtroom. There was electricity in the air. Alex Goldberg sat with her client. She looked calm. Herb Walton looked as if he had the mother of all heartburn.

"As well you might, Mr. Walton. This is certainly your last professional appearance before the bar," thought Reagan.

All eyes were on the judge as he addressed the jury.

"Ladies and Gentlemen, I apologize for the prolonged recess, and the delay in starting today. Your patience is appreciated. Let me explain what's been going on."

He turned to the witness box.

"Dr. Crandall wishes to amend some of his prior testimony," said the judge.

Crandall had wasted no time in following up on the judge's advice. He had contacted his brother-in-law, a real estate attorney who had immediately put him touch with Mike Hawkins, one of the top criminal defense attorneys in the city. They met that evening in Hawkins' office, two blocks from Judge Regan's court.

Hawkins was fifty two years old. He was six foot four and weighed two hundred and thirty pounds. His bright red hair was now flecked with silver. He wore it long, down to the collar of his hand-made silk shirts. The biggest disappointment of his life was that the Boston Celtics considered him too small and too slow to be a power forward. So he went to Harvard Law School instead.

Hawkins listened to Crandall's story in silence, making a few notes with his fancy gold pen. Finally when Crandall was finished with his story, Hawkins leaned back and thought for a moment before he spoke.

"My advice Doctor is simple. Tell the truth in court tomorrow. You have been discovered. Any further lying will only make your position much worse."

He paused, "In one sense you're lucky, because of all those who were involved in this conspiracy, you're testifying first at trial."

He shook his head. "From what you've told me, it sounds like you've all perjured yourself at your discovery depositions, although I obviously haven't read the transcripts yet."

"As I said, you're fortunate in that you have the first opportunity to rectify the situation, as you're testifying first here. That may work in your favor, at the time of your own trial."

Crandall sat white-faced as Hawkins continued, "There will be criminal charges against you all, without a doubt."

"I'm pretty sure that I'll be able to work out a deal for you with the District Attorney if you are willing to testify against your co-conspirators. I can't guarantee that you won't face some jail time, though."

He shook his head, "Perjury, conspiracy to manufacture false evidence, obstruction of justice. These are all serious charges."

Hawkins continued, "If you agree I'll speak first thing tomorrow to Judge Reagan, and tell him that you wish to recant your earlier testimony. You really have no other choice."

Doctor Crandall reluctantly agreed, and so Mike Hawkins now sat in court.

In front of the jury and the packed courtroom Judge Reagan took Doctor Crandall through his earlier testimony. For the next four hours, with only a short break, Doctor Crandall told the true story of the events that occurred after Winnie Brown's death.

As Crandall answered the judge's questions, revealing everything to the attentive jury and silent court, Alex had a sudden irreverent thought.

"Shit, I stayed up till two o'clock last night preparing for this, and he's spilling it all without me. I could've gone to a movie!"

Chap 49

According to Crandall's testimony, there were six people involved in the plan: Piper, the hospital director; O'Rourke, the head of hospital security; Keating, the head of the cancer program; Rubin, the head of psychiatry; Crandall himself, and Herb Walton.

Crandall described in detail the events of that fateful day. After hearing of the patient's collapse in the clinic and David Stern's reaction to it, Stuart Keating visited Winnie Brown at four thirty in the evening in the Neurology I.C.U. She remained unresponsive, her heart rate irregular and blood pressure unstable. She was brain dead.

The prognosis was hopeless.

Keating went directly from the I.CU. to David Stern's home. At eight that evening Keating called Harold Piper at home with very disturbing news. He had just arrived home from visiting Stern. His reason for going to David's home was ostensibly to make sure that David was O.K. In reality he wanted to find out how David would react to the cover-up that he was already devising.

Keating told Piper that Stern was adamant that he had caused the disaster, and that he feared that Stern would not co-operate in any cover up. It was agreed that Keating and Piper would meet at eight the next morning in Piper's office. O'Rourke also attended. Keating had already seen Winnie in the I.C.U. and confirmed that she was brain dead.

The first steps in damage control were taken. David Stern would not be allowed any further access to his patient. Keating would continue as her attending physician. O'Rourke reported that all evidence relating to the chemotherapy administration had already been secured and would be immediately destroyed.

As it was inevitable that the patient would die, it was agreed to bring Crandall into the plan. Crandall and Keating agreed that they alone would conduct an autopsy if Robert Brown gave permission. If Robert refused an autopsy, fine. Then there would then be no physical evidence to support Stern's admission of guilt.

These plans were carried out that day. Winnie was disconnected from life-support at two o'clock that afternoon and pronounced dead shortly thereafter.

Keating explained the importance of an autopsy to Robert Brown as they sat in the I.C.U. family waiting room.

"We really want to find out as much as possible about why Winnie died, Robert," he said. "You know how brutal these lymphomas are. We want to learn as much as we can about them. It's too late to help Winnie, but hopefully we'll learn something to help other patients."

A grieving Robert readily agreed to an autopsy.

The autopsy suite was secured by O'Rourke, and Crandall and Keating conducted the post-mortem at seven that evening. The results showed massive destruction of brain tissue due to the Vincristine injection. There was no evidence of residual lymphoma anywhere in Winnie's body, including the brain.

Alex felt her gut wrench when she heard this.

Crandall and Keating prepared and labeled all of the tissue samples from the autopsy. Everything was locked away that night by Security. After the autopsy was completed, the two doctors sat in Crandall's office, where they shared a single malt Scotch. The defense theory of death due to lymphoma evolved from their conversation.

"It was really rather clever, and certainly clinically plausible," said Crandall, with a trace of his previous arrogance.

"Idiot," thought Alex.

In the courtroom, Keating's newly acquired criminal defense attorney scribbled furiously.

By the end of that evening Keating and Crandall had agreed on the medical details. The next morning the two doctors once again met at eight o'clock with Piper and O'Rourke in the hospital director's office. Also present was Herb Walton who was introduced by Piper as a legal consultant who had special expertise in sensitive medico-legal affairs.

When asked specifically by the judge, Crandall shook his head, "No, there was no-one present from the general counsel office of the hospital."

"Thank goodness for that", thought the Judge, *"only one lawyer going to jail on this one."*

Crandall continued his testimony. At the meeting in Piper's office, the events up till that point were reviewed, and Herb Walton offered his analysis.

He congratulated those present for excellent damage control. His view was that the only potential problem was David Stern. If he could be brought into line, then it was all over.

Walton proposed a two-track approach. He would like to meet with Stern, and get a feel for where he stood. If he could be brought in, fine. If not they would have to totally discredit him, so that no-one would believe his testimony.

"Herb actually looks green," thought Alex.

Several jury members were staring angrily at Herb. Alex thought they were probably remembering how convinced they had been during Herb's cross-examination of David.

It was Keating who suggested bringing in Cheryl Rubin, the head of Psychiatry. Keating knew David better than anyone else in the room at that meeting. He didn't expect David to agree to the cover-up that they were concocting. He knew that David felt terrible about what he had done. Keating believed that they could use this to their advantage, and manufacture a valid psychiatric story out of it.

Under the judge's direction Crandall continued his testimony. Herb Walton welcomed Keating's suggestion enthusiastically. Cheryl Rubin's name was added to the list of those invited to a nine o'clock meeting scheduled the following Monday in Piper's office.

More angry looks from the jury for the defense attorney who sat with his head bowed.

"Jesus, if I lose this case, I should be sued for legal malpractice," thought Alex, *"What should I ask the jury for here? Michael Jordan's salary or house? Shit, maybe I'll just ask for Michael Jordan!"*

She focused her attention on Crandall who continued to testify in a flat, unemotional voice. He needed little prompting from the judge.

While Cheryl Rubin was being brought up to speed, David was called and asked to come to Piper's office at eleven o'clock. He arrived promptly. Crandall described how Walton had threatened David, and how Rubin had helped David from the room.

"Classic bad cop, good cop," thought Alex.

Crandall started on another topic, but Alex was on her feet.

"Your honor, if I may ask one or two questions for clarification here?"

There were no objections from Herb Walton, who looked as if he would not have objected if Alex had claimed that David was a reincarnation of Honest Abe Lincoln.

Alex asked Crandall, "Doctor, was Doctor Stern ever told that he had indeed injected the wrong drug, but you had decided to defend the case with the fabrication that you had agreed upon?"

Crandall shook his head, "No. Stern didn't know the plan. We were very careful. Whenever he was present, the case was discussed as simply one of recurrent lymphoma in the brain causing fatal seizures. The true facts of the case, and how we switched materials at the autopsy were never discussed in front of Doctor Stern. We knew he wouldn't go along with the cover-up."

"So, his refusal to go along with you was because he was convinced that he had injected the wrong drug. Even though it would hurt him, he wanted compensation for the Brown family, he wanted the truth to come out?"

"Come on, Herb, isn't that calling on the witness to speculate about Doctor Stern's frame of mind? A first year law student would object to that one!"

Silence from Herb whose face was now the color of putty.

"Yes," from Crandall.

Alex turned to the judge, "Your Honor, a few more questions, if I may."

Reagen nodded and Alex continued, "Doctor during the meeting you just described, or any subsequent meeting, did any participant raise any objection to the plan that you have outlined?"

Crandall shook his head, "No."

"Did anybody say even once, *'We can't tamper with evidence. We can't commit perjury, we have a moral and a legal responsibility to Winnie Brown's family. We can't mess with Dr. Stern's head?'* Did anyone ever ask the question about any of these issues, *'Is what we are doing here wrong?'* "

Crandall looked shame faced, "No."

There was a long silence. Several of the jury members shook their heads in obvious disgust.

Judge Reagan looked enquiringly at Alex as if to say, *"Any more questions?"*

"Thank you, no more questions for now, your Honor" said Alex, sitting down.

Under the judge's questioning Crandall resumed his description of the conspiracy and subsequent events.

Keating's prediction proved accurate. It rapidly became clear that David Stern would not co-operate with the defense plan. Crandall and Keating concentrated on securing the scientific evidence while Rubin and Piper worked to set up the evidence of psychiatric illness in David Stern. Herb Walton's role was to prepare the legal defense should Stern continue to refuse to cooperate.

The autopsy report that Crandall dictated graphically described the appearance of lymphoma in the brain. Robert's decision to have Winnie's remains cremated was a bonus. There was now no way to refute Crandall's report. All that remained to do was make sure that the tissue blocks and slides showed the same results.

Crandall and Keating had no problem finding autopsy material from another patient with a similar lymphoma to Winnie Brown's. It was then easy for them to re-label the blocks and slides with Winnie Brown's identifying hospital number. When they were finished the available evidence clearly indicated that Winnie's brain tissue was involved by lymphoma.

The doctors and the hospital were untouchable.

While the scientific evidence was being secured, Rubin and Piper worked on David Stern. He was so guilt-ridden by Winnie's death, that it was easy to suspend him on medical grounds, diagnosis severe depression with secondary delusions. Like any good lie, there was an element of truth in this. David was certainly depressed.

Cheryl Rubin had no problem in getting David to visit her office under the guise of seeking his input for a Psycho-Oncology grant application she planned to write.

If David was puzzled by the amount of time they spent in seemingly casual talk, and the slow progress on the grant proposal he didn't question it. Perhaps David thought this was how psychiatrists always did things, or maybe his critical faculties were so traumatized by Winnie's death that he did not see what was happening.

Rubin made sure that they were frequently seen together. By carefully dropping a word here and there regarding David's condition, and her concern for him, Doctor Rubin made sure that the whole hospital knew that David was very disturbed and was under her psychiatric care.

David was completely unaware of how he was being manipulated.

"If psychiatrists can't play mind games, then who can?" Crandall asked the court with a sly smile.

No one smiled back.

Judge Reagan, the former prosecutor took Crandall through all of his previous testimony, testimony carefully elicited by Herb Walton. After reading each question, Reagan then read Crandall's response, and followed with a brief question

"True or false, Doctor?"

After the sixth "False," Alex kind of tuned out. Judge Reagan was doing her job magnificently.

The effect of these constant admissions of perjury were having an almost hypnotic effect on the jury and most of the spectators.

Judge Reagan's repetition of the transcript, and Crandall's responses came to an end.

The judge then addressed Alex, "Counselor, thank you for your forbearance. Now that the witness has had the opportunity to clarify his prior testimony, you may now continue your cross-examination. It is nearly six o'clock, however and I think it best that we adjourn for the evening. We will start at nine sharp tomorrow."

As the jury filed out, it was as if the entire room let out its breath all at once. Alex walked over to the judge as he rose from his seat. She spoke quietly to him as he stood up.

"You know, your Honor, if you ever get tired of lording it over us from up there, I could use you as my associate any time. You were killer!"

Reagan was too smart to think that Alex would try to gain an advantage by flattering him. He had too much respect for her integrity. But still, it was nice to get a compliment from a good-looking woman.

He smiled as he whispered, "It's nice to know I haven't lost my touch. I used to put away sons of bitches like him all the time."

Nodding gravely to the court, his Honor walked to his chambers for a well earned glass of wine, thinking to himself, *"Killer, hah!"*

Chap 50

When court resumed next morning, it was Alex's turn. She approached an obviously nervous Crandall, who sat in the witness box.

"Doctor, you told us yesterday that your initial testimony was in fact untrue. You conspired with other doctors at International Hospital, members of the International administration and Mr. Walton to falsify evidence, correct?"

Crandall nodded, "Yes."

"Doctor, why did you do this?"

Crandall shrugged, "Piper told us that there was no way that International would admit to serious malpractice by any of its doctors."

"Do you have any reason to think that the decision to fight the Brown case by falsifying evidence came from Mr. Piper alone or anyone else in the International organization?"

Herb Walton was on his feet, "Objection, your Honor. That calls for speculation from the witness.

The judge agreed, "Sustained, rephrase the question Ms. Goldberg."

"Doctor Crandall, did you hear anything said at any meeting that made you think that Mr. Piper had made the decision himself to fight this case, or was he taking orders from higher up?"

Walton was on his feet again," Same objection, your Honor."

The judge shook his head," That one I'll allow. Answer the question, doctor."

Crandall licked his lips nervously. "At our first meeting Piper did say that he had been told that there was no way that

International would settle this case, but he didn't say who he'd spoken with."

Alex smiled to herself. *She had what she wanted.*

"O.K. Doctor, let's move on. You have admitted you lied previously, why should the jury believe that you are telling the truth now?"

She wasn't making this easy for him.

Crandall shifted in his seat. "I know I'm in serious trouble. You proved that the brain slides were switched."

"Thank you, Doctor Crandall!" thought Alex.

"My lawyer has told me that I have to tell the truth now, or it will be harder for me."

Alex thought that this certainly had the ring of truth. The jury would see all of the conspirators trying to save their own asses. International was going to smell to High Heaven.

"So Doctor Crandall, you have no doubt that the cause of death here was the inadvertent injection of Vincristine into the Omaya reservoir by Doctor Stern?"

Crandall nodded, "Yes. There is no question about it."

"Now Doctor you told the court yesterday that when you performed the autopsy, you found no evidence of residual lymphoma anywhere in Ms. Brown's body. Is that correct?"

"That is correct."

"So without this fatal error on the part of Doctor Stern, an International employee, Ms. Brown would have been cured of her disease."

Crandall nodded reluctantly, "Yes."

"And that opinion is held to a reasonable degree of medical certainty?"

"Yes."

"Thank you Doctor C. Let's see Herb Walton deal with that one," thought Alex.

"Doctor, I know you are not a psychiatrist, but you have worked with Doctor Stern for many years, and you know all of the facts in this case, better than anyone else. You saw the patient's brain at autopsy. You switched the slides. When Doctor Rubin in her discovery deposition claimed that Doctor Stern was suffering from a delusion when he claimed to have injected the wrong drug, do you agree with her diagnosis?"

The Judge allowed the question over Walton's objection that Crandall was not a psychiatrist.

"Ms. Goldberg," replied Crandall, "Doctor Stern is not and never was deluded. That brain was destroyed, devastated by the Vincristine."

He paused, "Dr. Rubin knows that he's not deluded. It happened just like Stern said it did."

She turned back to the witness and paused for a moment.

"One more thing, Doctor. Do you know anything about the recent attempt on Doctor Stern's life?"

Crandall looked like he'd been punched in the gut. He turned to the judge and almost pleaded.

"You have to believe me, I knew nothing about that."

"O.K., Doctor," said Alex. "No more questions from me."

The judge looked at the defense table. Herb Walton shook his head. No questions from him. There was no way he could repair the damage done to the defense case by his own star witness.

Doctor Crandall was excused. As he stood up, he averted his eyes from the jury. That was fine with them, none of them wanted to look him in the face.

Chap 51

After Dr. Crandall, the defense case collapsed completely. Walton called Doctor Rubin. His plan to have her testify regarding David Stern's mental state blew up in his face.

She testified that in her opinion David was mentally healthy. She believed that his feelings of remorse and guilt following his error were natural under the circumstances. There was no evidence of delusion or any mental illness.

Walton was faced with either accepting her testimony, which supported Alex's case, or impeaching his own witness. He chose the former. His direct examination of Dr. Rubin was very brief.

On cross examination, Alex pointed out to the jury that Dr. Rubin had testified under oath during her discovery deposition. In that deposition she had stated that David was suffering from a serious psychiatric illness. She also expressed the opinion that David should not be allowed to treat patients because of his mental illness.

Rubin explained the discrepancy between her earlier testimony and her opinions today. Earlier she had been convinced by Crandall and Keating that there was no cancer in the brain. Based on that, she thought that David's insistence that Winnie was cancer free and that he had caused her death was the expression of a serious delusion.

Knowing as she did now that David was in fact correct about the cause of death, well, this allowed her to change her opinion one hundred and eighty degrees and still remain credible. Alex greeted this tortuous explanation with obvious skepticism, which was apparently shared by the jury.

After Alex had established that Rubin saw no evidence of psychiatric illness in David, the doctor visibly relaxed. She clearly thought that her testimony was over. She was wrong.

"Doctor," asked Alex, "you have testified that David Stern was your patient, and that you saw him a total of five times in one week, correct?"

Rubin nodded, "Yes."

"Doctor, other doctors refer patients to you, do they not?"

Rubin nodded, "That is correct. Most often times, a family doctor or internist will decide that a patient requires psychiatric help, and refer the patient to me. Although sometimes a patient will call up and ask to be seen, without a referral from another doctor."

Alex nodded, "I understand. By the way who referred Doctor Stern to you?"

Rubin paused, "Ah... Doctor Stern was a self-referral."

"So no other doctor referred Doctor Stern?"

"Correct."

Alex continued, "Doctor, I see from your resume you have an international reputation in the area of Alzheimer's Disease, specifically new drug treatments for this condition, correct?"

Play to their ego, it rarely failed!

"That is correct," replied Dr. Rubin.

"Doctor, Isn't it true that for the past six years or so you have restricted your practice to patients with Alzheimer's Disease only?"

Rubin agreed, "That is generally true."

"So Doctor Rubin, if I called you up and said, *'Doctor I'm depressed and I'd like to see you.'* I wouldn't be able to get an appointment, would I?"

Rubin hesitated, "No. My secretary would probably refer you to one of my colleagues who has a special interest and expertise in depression."

Alex continued, "And that's one of the advantages of a large academic center, isn't it? You get the benefit of a doctor with special expertise in whatever problem you may have, right?"

"Correct."

"Unless your name is David Stern, correct Doctor?" asked Alex.

"Excuse me?" stammered Doctor Rubin.

Alex once again turned to face the jury, while directing her question to the witness who was actually squirming in her chair.

"Let me put it another way, you just told the jury that anyone calling up and saying, *'I'm depressed, can I please see Doctor Rubin.'* would be referred to another doctor. Correct?"

Rubin reluctantly nodded, "Yes, that's true."

"And you just told us that no other doctor referred Doctor Stern to you, correct?"

Again Rubin conceded that this was true.

Alex was relentless, "Isn't it true, Doctor Rubin, that during the past six and one half years the only patient that you have treated with a diagnosis other than Alzheimer's is Doctor Stern?"

"I....I'd have to check," said Rubin.

"I have checked, Doctor," said Alex sweetly.

"Well you're probably right, then."

"Doctor, I want to be fair to you," said Alex, "when you have checked, and if you find any other non-Alzheimer patient that you have treated, please let the court know."

Rubin nodded, "O.K."

"Yeah, right," thought Alex, *"The Cubs will win a world Series before we get that."*

"Now Doctor, assuming that Doctor Stern was in fact the only patient without Alzheimer's that you have seen, what made him so unique that you agreed to see him, when he asked?"

"Well, he was an attending physician on the staff of the hospital."

"Doctor isn't it a well known fact that doctors, and lawyers (this was said with a small smile), and many other professionals quite frequently avail themselves of psychiatric help?"

"Yes, that's true. Professional people often function under significant amounts of stress."

"Like right now, Dr. Rubin?" thought Alex.

"Probably the only people who can afford your fees, right Doctor?"

The courtroom laughed with this attempt to break the tension. Judge Reagan made a benign comment that if Alex was going to make an issue of doctor's fees, he wished to make the observation that he had rarely seen an attorney driving a used Chevy.

All of the lawyers present dutifully responded to this outstanding expression of judicial wit.

Alex continued, "There are over five hundred attending physicians currently at International hospital. Is it likely that David Stern is the only one who has been treated in your Department?"

The cardinal rule of cross-examination is never ask a question if you don't know what the answer will be. Alex had the names of two doctors at International who had signed affidavits that they were patients of other psychiatrists there. David was not without his supporters.

Rubin answered, "I'm sure that there are other doctors on staff who are or have been patients in our department."

"Nothing wrong with that, is there Doctor?"

Certainly not," answered Doctor Rubin stiffly, "there is no stigma attached to psychiatric treatment."

"Well Doctor I'm still puzzled, when Doctor Stern approached you, and asked for psychiatric help, as you claim, why didn't you refer him to one of your colleagues, like Jensen or Peters both of whom are nationally known as experts in depression? They are already treating several of your medical colleagues, and you have referred many non-Alzheimer patients to them in the past. So why not refer Dr. Stern to one of them?"

There was no response from Rubin.

Alex paused and turned to the jury for emphasis, "I ask again Doctor Rubin, what was so special about Doctor Stern?"

Rubin was flustered, "I.......I.... He was very upset. We had just finished meeting with the hospital administration, and Mr. Walton, and..... Doctor Stern was very upset."

"Was this the meeting that took place on the Monday after Winnie Brown's death?"

Rubin nodded, "Yes."

What time did the meeting end?"

"About twelve noon."

"What time did Doctor Stern arrive at the meeting?"

"Eleven."

"What time did you arrive?"

Rubin answered cautiously, "I don't remember, maybe a little before eleven."

Alex raised an eyebrow, "Are you sure?"

"I....I really don't remember."

"Well let me help you refresh your memory," said Alex with a sweet smile.

"Ms. Diabetes, look out Dr. Rubin !" thought Cindy.

Alex picked up a sheet of paper from the table. "Doctor, I have here a copy of your appointment book for the day in question. You had both a nine o'clock and a ten o'clock patient that morning. But Doctor Rubin, you didn't see the ten o'clock. When he arrived your secretary told him and his wife that you had been called to an emergency.

"Now your patient has Alzheimer's, and he can't remember, but his wife remembers. She had come twenty miles to see you, and she was pretty ticked off because you weren't there. Your secretary remembers the scene real well. Aren't good secretaries worth their weight in gold?"

Behind Alex, Cindy simpered.

"Doctor Rubin isn't it true that at approximately nine fifteen on that morning you received an urgent call from Mr. Piper's office and were summoned to an emergency meeting, where the Winnie Brown/David Stern case was discussed."

"You immediately left your office and your nine o'clock patient, and went to that meeting, where it was suggested, either by you or another attendee that you develop evidence to indicate that David Stern was suffering from a psychiatric illness that would seriously impair his credibility? Isn't that true Doctor?"

Rubin squirmed in her seat, "On the advice of counsel, I refuse to answer on the grounds that I may incriminate myself."

Alex appeared disgusted with this response, although it was really ideal for her purposes.

She shook her head, "I'm beginning to wonder if this is a medical malpractice trial, or a Mafia movie."

"Objection!!' shrieked Herb Walton.

"Sustained. Ms. Goldberg, you know better than that," said the Judge who did not appear too outraged.

"I'm sorry your Honor."

"Doctor Rubin, here's a question that you can answer. Why didn't you bill Doctor Stern for the five therapeutic sessions that you claim you had with him that week?"

Dr. Rubin hesitated. "Ah......professional courtesy."

The real reason of course was that a bill or submission to insurance might have alerted David to what was going on.

Alex appeared skeptical of Rubin's answer. She followed up with her next question. "Your department does that often, treats other doctors for free?"

Alex knew that, as a matter of policy the department of Psychiatry at International, like most doctors in the age of insurance reimbursement, did not offer that degree of professional courtesy. They may waive a deductible, or reduce a bill by twenty per cent, but free care, no way.

Rubin had to admit that once again David Stern was treated in a manner completely different from any other patient in the department. When asked why, she had no explanation.

Alex faced the jury again, "Doctor did you have any prior knowledge of the plot to kill David Stern?"

Rubin seemed to shrink from the question. "No," she whispered.

There was a long silence in the courtroom. Those watching the jury later reported a variety of reactions. One lady in the back row fingered the large cross she wore around her neck. Several members of the jury were very pale. The silence lasted only twenty seconds, but seemed much longer.

Alex continued, "Doctor I'm still puzzled by one thing. You claim you were Doctor's Stern psychiatrist, correct?"

"That is correct."

Rubin was hopelessly entangled in lies. She waited desperately for this nightmare to be over.

"As such, you were concerned about his emotional health, correct?"

"Of course."

Alex nodded, "Well Doctor, please explain to us all. Your patient is suspended by his employer. His entire professional career is in ruins. Traumatic, yes?"

"Possibly."

"Possibly? Well you're sure going to find out, lady. Maybe I'll ask you that question again in about a week!"

Alex was angry for David. From her calm demeanor you'd never know it.

"Your patient Doctor Stern, whose emotional health is your concern, has seen his career end under very adverse circumstances. Then he undergoes a terrifying experience. He is almost murdered. Which would be tremendously traumatic for the most stable person, right?"

"Yes."

"He comes back to Chicago. Within a few weeks he suffers another life-threatening experience, a massive gastro-intestinal bleed which requires emergency surgery, correct?"

"Yes."

"Also a terrifying experience, yes?"

"Probably."

Alex made no attempt to hide her scorn.

"Well Doctor. Please explain to this court. If your relationship with Doctor Stern was really that of caring psychiatrist and patient, why is it that despite all of these tremendously traumatic events, you have made no effort to see or speak to Dr. Stern since the second meeting in Mr. Piper's office two weeks after Ms. Brown's death, well over a year ago?"

Doctor Rubin burst into tears. Alex turned and walked away, shaking her head.

"Let the record reflect that the witness gave no response to the last question," said Alex.

"I have no further questions."

"That's the problem with lies," thought Alex, *"They always trap you in the end."*

Herb Walton declined the opportunity to re-examine the witness. A sobbing Doctor Rubin was helped by the bailiff from the witness stand. Her career as a conspirator, and as a doctor were over.

Judge Reagan ordered an early adjournment. It was only three thirty but the jury had been kept late on Tuesday evening, and they welcomed the break.

Alex counted the day a fair success. Herb Walton looked bilious.

Chap 52

Thursday morning, Piper and O'Rourke testified in quick succession. After the drama of Rubin's testimony, it was back to business without emotion. Their direct testimony was simply a description of the scene after Winnie's collapse in the Oncology clinic and her terminal care in the I.C.U.

On cross-examination both denied all of Crandall's allegations. There was no conspiracy, according to their testimony. They admitted that they had met with the individuals indicated by Doctor Crandall, but these meetings were to control the rumors that David Stern's outburst had started. Piper had no explanation for why records of these meetings were not kept.

The exclusion of all but the two doctors from the autopsy suite was to prevent further rumors, he explained, and to reduce the Brown family's suffering.

Alex asked why Doctor Rubin was included in these meetings. Piper's explanation was that Doctor Stern's behavior had been erratic for some time. Several of the medical staff had raised concerns about his psychiatric health following his outburst shortly after Winnie had her first seizure. It was therefore advisable to have input from the head of Psychiatry.

Piper admitted that he couldn't remember the name of the doctors who had voiced concern about Doctor Stern's mental health, and was unable to find records of any formal complaint about him in his more than five years of service at International.

Piper denied any contact with anyone from International's corporate head office regarding Winnie Brown, until the lawsuit was filed. He had made the decision to contact Herb Walton on his own. Piper had no knowledge about the murder attempt on David.

O'Rourke firmly denied destroying any evidence in this case. Alex asked if he had ever falsified evidence while serving as a police officer. O'Rourke was clearly spooked by the question. He had no idea what Alex might know, but he was damn sure he wouldn't be hung out to dry like the ass-hole doctors. He respectfully declined to answer the question on the grounds of self-incrimination.

Alex smiled to herself. She had no hard evidence against him of previous wrong-doing, but her hunch had paid off. The jury's anger was clear. No further questions.

Walton had nowhere to go.

"That concludes our case, your Honor. We have no further witnesses at this time," he said, sitting down.

Walton had originally planned to have Dr. Richard Keating add his expertise as a cancer specialist to confirm Crandall's testimony that Winnie Brown died of lymphoma in the brain. Crandall's retraction yesterday made it obvious that this would not happen.

Walton did not call Keating. Alex did. He was her first rebuttal witness. His testimony was important to Alex to show the depth of the conspiracy at International.

Keating refused to answer any question relating to the conspiracy described by Crandall on the advice of his counsel on the grounds of his Fifth Amendment right against self-incrimination, a promising start for Alex.

Alex was able to show from his discovery deposition that Keating had previously testified under oath that he was present at the autopsy, and that there was extensive lymphoma demonstrated in Winnie Brown's brain at the post-mortem examination. Alex pointed out that this opinion disagreed with Doctor Crandall's amended testimony that there was no lymphoma in the brain.

In response Keating claimed he could not actually remember what the state of the brain was. The jury obviously didn't believe him. The patient had seizures and was determined to be brain dead. Clearly the brain was the most important organ to be studied at the autopsy, and Keating couldn't remember?

Alex suggested that maybe Dr. Keating should consult with Doctor Rubin, as she, Alex, believed that amnesia was an early symptom of Alzheimer's disease.

The court laughed, Keating and Walton did not.

Keating's explanation for why he, the head of Oncology was functioning as an assistant in the autopsy room at seven o'clock in the evening, was that he was interested in lymphomas.

Alex asked him why, if he was so interested in lymphomas, had he not attended, let alone assisted at any one of the other one hundred and twenty seven autopsies of lymphoma cases which were performed at the hospitals in Washington D.C., and Chicago where he had worked during the previous eighteen years? He had no answer to this question.

Walton had no questions for Doctor Keating, who left the witness box with obvious relief.

Alex decided that she didn't need to use Melissa Walters as a rebuttal witness. After all Cheryl Rubin had testified that David Stern was sane and had no delusions, so what was there to rebut?

She did, however have one further rebuttal witness.

"Your Honor," she said calmly, "I have one further rebuttal witness. I wish to call Mr. Walton."

Walton was on his feet in a flash. The judge called all of the attorneys forward. An acrimonious sidebar discussion ensued. Walton was livid.

Red-faced he whispered, "Your Honor, this is outrageous. It is unthinkable for Ms. Goldberg to attempt to force opposing counsel to testify. It's a cynical attempt to impeach the defense here. Clearly attorney-client privilege applies to anything she may wish to question me about."

Alex countered, "Your Honor, the defense's own witness, Doctor Crandall has freely testified to the existence of a conspiracy here. Sworn testimony by that witness implicates Mr. Walton. Several other witnesses have refused to testify because of the possibility of self-incrimination. I would like to explore with Mr. Walton any information he can supply regarding this conspiracy."

The judge listened carefully to the arguments.

He addressed Alex first.

"No, counselor," he said after a few minutes deliberation. "All of the witnesses you mentioned are employees of International, Mr. Walton's client. Attorney-client privilege does apply."

He turned to the defense attorney, "Calm down Mr. Walton. You don't have to testify here."

Alex smiled to herself. She hadn't expected for a minute to get the slimy bastard on the stand. The jury had watched for almost five minutes while Herb Walton argued vigorously to avoid having to testify under oath. Although they hadn't heard the words, they had a picture of what was going on. Alex had got what she wanted again.

The judge adjourned at three thirty. Closing arguments would start at nine o'clock Friday morning. The case would go to the jury tomorrow. It was coming down to the wire.

Chap 53

No poker for Alex this Thursday evening. At nine o'clock she sat at her kitchen table with a cold cup of coffee at her elbow. The legal pad in front of her was blank. All around were discarded sheets of paper. She was having a hard time putting the words together.

This was a new experience for her. She was usually very fluent with both the written and spoken word. She had been frequently complimented for her closing statements. For some reason tonight was different, and she didn't know why.

She was wearing jeans and her Bulls tee shirt. Her face was scrubbed clean, and her hair pulled off her face in a pony tail. She was barefoot. She frowned when her phone rang.

"Who the hell could it be at this time," she thought.

It was Jerry, her doorman." Good evening Ms. Goldberg. Your pizza is here."

"Jerry, I didn't order pizza," she told him, irritated that her concentration was broken.

"Not that it's getting me anywhere," she thought.

She heard Jerry talking to the deliveryman. Voices were raised. Jerry came back on the phone.

"He has your office number, said Cindy ordered it for you."

Alex smiled, *"Cindy! What a sweetheart, she knew that I'd be working late tonight."*

"OK Jerry," she said, "you can send him up."

A few minutes later Alex answered her doorbell.

David Stern stood there holding a large pizza box.

Her first thought was, *"I look terrible."*

Her second thought was how pleased she was to see him.

David asked meekly, "May I come in?"

Alex said nothing. She simply stood aside and allowed him to enter.

"I got deep dish, OK?"

Alex found her voice. "Sure Cindy," she said dryly.

David laughed. "It worked, didn't it?"

"Do you have any milk?" he continued.

Alex looked at him. He looked better, still very thin and pale, but definitely better. *Mind you, last time she saw him he was lying in a pool of blood on the floor of his kitchen!*

"Help yourself," she gestured to the refrigerator.

He did. Deep dish pizza and coffee for Alex, cold milk for David.

"How are you feeling? Should you really be out so soon after the surgery?" Alex asked.

David made a *so-so* gesture with his right hand. He had only been discharged from the hospital that morning.

"I'm O.K, as long as I don't laugh or cough too hard. How are you?"

He had this disconcerting way of turning attention back to her. She would learn later that this was not because he was trying to divert attention from himself. He was just very interested in Alex Goldberg.

They ate, or rather she ate and he drank his milk in a comfortable silence for a few minutes. David was smiling.

"What's so funny?" she asked.

"I was just thinking, when I first met you, you wore the same tee shirt."

He laughed, "Do you remember that day? I thought you were nuts!"

She had the grace to blush. David thought the added color in her cheeks made her look stunning. He was already in love with her, a fact that he had only recently admitted to himself.

"Well! Doctor Stern," she said with mock severity, "you may not remember exactly what your first words to me were but I do."

It was David's turn to blush.

He laughed, "I remember what I said. I don't have Alzheimer's, even if I was Doctor Rubin's patient."

The reference to Rubin sobered them both up. Tomorrow was going to be a big day.

"Incidentally," continued David, "I heard you were just brilliant today."

"I must tell you Alex," he took her hand, "I could just sit and look and listen to you all day. You have such a presence in that courtroom."

Alex lowered her eyes, "Thank you," she said.

"Those eye-lashes!" he thought.

"I'm planning to come to court tomorrow," he said.

Alex was concerned. "Are you sure you're up for it? You're just out of the hospital."

"Wouldn't miss it for anything," he smiled. "Anyway I was sitting at home thinking about you, and I just knew you wouldn't have eaten tonight. So I decided to do something about it."

He waved at the legal pad, "So how's it going?"

She frowned, "Not well. I usually have no problem with closing arguments, but for some reason right now I can't get it together."

She continued, talking almost to herself, "You'd think that it would be easier than usual here. I mean, they've shot themselves in the foot so many times. I've never seen a case where the other side is in such disarray. Every one of their key people is probably going to be indicted for perjury and conspiracy, including the defense attorney!"

David said quietly, "I think I know what your problem may be."

She looked at him with a raised eyebrow.

"What a face!"

It was his turn to speak reflectively.

"In a curious way you may be doing exactly what I did wrong with Winnie."

Alex looked puzzled and he explained.

"You may be trying too hard."

They had left the kitchen and moved to her living room, without a word having been said. They sat on her couch. Almost without realizing it, she snuggled into his arms. It just felt so right. David's arm was around her, his hand gently stroking her dark, lustrous hair.

David was speaking softly to her, "It's funny how an experience like this really knocks you back on your heels, makes you re-examine everything. Maybe the psychotherapy I got from Rubin has made me more introspective."

She started to sit up to protest that last remark but he stilled her with a gentle pressure.

"I was joking, you're not the only one who can make bad jokes, you know."

He gently stroked her shoulder as he continued, "You know all that psychobabble that Walton put together about Dana having seizures before she died, affecting my reaction to Winnie?"

Alex nodded. She could not remember when she had last felt so relaxed, and in less than twelve hours she had to give a major summation for a judge and jury, with nothing prepared yet!

David continued, "Well it was garbage, I certainly would never blame myself for something I didn't do, but there was just a spark of truth in it all."

Alex sat up and looked in David's eyes. She feared for him, for what he was saying. What she saw calmed her immediately. She saw the face of a man who was at peace with himself.

He smiled at her, "The truth is this. I probably tried too hard for Winnie, I've probably tried too hard for patients all my life."

He held up a hand to quiet her disagreement. "Hear me out. Did you ever think that if Winnie had been treated by any other oncologist, she might still be alive?"

Alex was mystified and he explained. "You see, all the other staff doctors there have the oncology fellows or nurses administer the chemotherapy. I'm the only one who gives his own chemo. It's a small thing, but its a reflection of my wanting to do everything possible myself."

He smiled, "I'm not saying it's wrong, but it's certainly a little quirky of me. You know I don't take the personal involvement to crazy extremes. I'm not there twenty-four hours a day and I don't break into a million pieces when patients die. They die all the time in oncology. I know that intellectually, and I can handle it emotionally."

Alex had never heard David speak about himself so much. She liked it.

"I'm sure," he went on, "that all this comes from Dana's death. I don't need analysis to know that my choice of career was all because of Dana."

He continued, "There's nothing wrong with having originally chosen to do what I do because of Dana, but that was then, and now is now. It's not fair to any patient for me to be even subconsciously fighting for Dana, when I should only be considering the patient's needs. I should be fighting for the patient and the patient only."

He shrugged. "I suppose you could argue what does it matter what the motivation is. If I'm subconsciously motivated to fight harder because of my sister's death, so what. It's a bonus, take it."

He shook his head, "But that's wrong, because that kind of over-commitment can lead to Winnie Brown tragedies, or their equivalent."

He leaned back. "I've learned a valuable lesson here. I'll fight for my patients one hundred per cent, because they deserve that. I'm not going to fight for them one hundred and ten percent because of my needs, because the patient could be harmed in all sorts of subtle ways."

He paused, "Doctors, I guess like lawyers should always be objective. Sympathetic, empathetic even, but objective. Because otherwise mistakes can happen and people get hurt."

David continued softly, "I have learned from all this. When it's all over, my approach to how I practice medicine will be different."

Alex realized that this was the first time she had heard David talk about the possibility of practicing medicine in the future. She was very happy to realize that he was finally recovering from the trauma of the past twelve months.

"I like hearing you talk about yourself," she said softly, stroking his hand.

"I wasn't just talking about me, you know," he said. "I told you this tonight for a very good reason."

Alex looked puzzled and David laughed.

"You must be one of the smartest people I have ever met, but there's a certain lack of insight....."

He stopped as he saw tears well up in Alex's eyes.

"I'm sorry," he said.

He gently kissed the tears away. Gently he turned Alex around until they were looking directly into each others eyes.

"Look," he said, "I know a lot more about Alex Goldberg now than I did the last time I saw you wear that shirt."

Despite herself, Alex smiled.

"I told you about Dana tonight because, in a sense, you and I have had very similar experiences. Your uncle told me what you went through when you were a law student."

He shook his head, "I can't imagine how terrible that must have been for you."

Tears welled up in Alex's eyes again and he held her tenderly.

"We both strive to do everything we can for our client or patient because we are trying to overcompensate for the past. That's what I meant when I said your writing block tonight is maybe because you are trying too hard. Maybe you want too much to win this one big for Robert and Winnie Brown. You want to punish International for trying to cheat Winnie's family out of what is rightfully theirs, and that's O.K. That's what you should be doing."

"Then there's the more personal stuff. International and Herb Walton in particular have offended your sense of professionalism. They have brought dishonor to a system and a profession, actually two professions, that should adhere to higher standards."

Alex nodded. *David really had a way of expressing her thoughts very clearly.*

"You also want revenge for those dear to you who were victimized by careless and dishonest doctors."

Alex was in tears again.

"My parents and my friend Marsha" she whispered.

She gripped David's hand, "And also my David," she said fiercely, "they tried to kill you! They terrorized and hurt you."

She nodded, "You're right, this is very personal for me."

"It's O.K. as long as you can recognize it, but don't focus on it," said David.

"I care for you deeply, and I sense how these cases must hurt you. You know you are so good that you don't have to give one hundred and ten percent of yourself to win."

"Please, Doctor, don't refer me to Psychiatry at International," begged Alex.

David replied with a straight face, "Not unless you get Alzheimer's. They've a great doctor there for that."

They laughed and held each other, bound by deep understanding and growing love.

Alex gently disengaged herself.

"David," she said, "it's now eleven o'clock. You've been very sick. You need to rest. I need to work, and I need to get some sleep."

They stood up from the couch.

"Maybe you're right," she mused, "this is personal for me at many different levels. I'm not going to write out the whole thing. I'm going to simply write down the key legal points, and speak without notes."

David nodded, "You know best. I saw the jury. They know you're the only honest one there. I think they'll respond when you speak from the heart. You have a big heart."

Arm in arm they walked to the front door. They gently kissed good night.

Alex sat at the table. Despite her words to David, she worked steadily until nearly three a.m. Both words and tears came freely. At three she climbed into bed.

She was ready.

Chap 54

Alex rose at seven thirty. Her first thought on waking was last night's conversation with David. She knew that they had crossed a very significant line. Apart from her uncle and Cindy, David Stern was the only person who knew how Marsha and her parent's deaths had affected her.

That he had brought her to a new level of consciousness about her personal losses was fine with her. She was very grateful that he had done it in such a sensitive manner.

Perhaps she had done the same for him.

After a long hot shower, she toweled her thick hair dry. The lemon scent of her shampoo and the thick cotton towel reminded her of her childhood, when her mother would towel her hair dry, and hold her tight in her loving arms.

She felt tears well up. Her emotions were raw today.

Not today. She needed to be strong, for Winnie and Robert, and for David.

She wrapped herself in her favorite robe, an old pink terry cloth, and made herself coffee and oatmeal. She scanned the Tribune as she ate her breakfast. There it was, front page in big type,

"Growing Scandal at International as Doctors take the Fifth!"

Her coffee grew cold as she read the story. It was factual, albeit a little sensational. As she filled her cup with fresh coffee, she reflected on the piece. Not really over-sensational. After all, several doctors and administrative staff at the flagship hospital of a major hospital chain had participated in a conspiracy to obstruct justice.

Alex thought to herself, *"I'd better dress pretty special today. If the jury comes back quickly, I may be on the evening news."*

Just then the phone rang. It was David.

"Seen the newspaper, yet? You'll look great on TV tonight."

"How do you do that?" she laughed, "honestly, I was just thinking the very same thing. I'm going to dress up in case they do interviews."

"How did I know what you were thinking? I'll tell you a secret," he said, "but you have to promise not to use it against me. I receive messages from aliens in outer space all the time. That's how I knew you probably hadn't eaten last night, and that you liked deep dish."

Alex laughed again, "I know your alien. She weighs about 185 pounds and lives in Bridgeview with her husband Kevin and two kids."

David laughed, "Well, you may be right about that. I just called to wish you all the best."

"Thank you, David."

Alex dressed with extra care, midnight blue wool dress, mid calf length heavy gold chain necklace, black patent pumps. Her hair was drawn back from her face with a dark blue headband, light make-up.

The weather was fine for early April, light clouds with a high expected to be close to sixty. Any other day, she might have walked to the Daley Center. Not today.

Robert, the daytime doorman had a smile and a cab ready for her.

"Good luck today, Ms. Goldberg. You give them what for."

All of a sudden she felt close to tears.

"Thank you, Robert. I'll do my best," she said.

It was the same as she made her way through the crowded concourse at the Daley Center. Lots of smiles, lots of expressions of good luck from many of the sheriff's officers at the security gate, from the staff she shared the elevator with. Alex felt as if she were carrying the responsibility for a lot more people than simply her clients.

In a sense she was.

The court was crowded. She saw her uncle, Rabbi Shuster and his new wife. Brief wave and smile. Jim Davis was there, looking as distinguished as ever. They embraced briefly.

"We missed you at the game last night. Finally gave me a chance to win a few hands!" he said with a smile.

"Seriously though, I've been following this case carefully, as you might imagine. I'm very proud of you. You'll not be surprised to know that many of your colleagues are outraged by some of the revelations here. A rotten apple can reflect badly on the entire barrel. Let's get together for lunch when all this is over. Good luck today, although I doubt you'll need much luck."

She was surprised to see several of her old clients. They all greeted her with smiles and waves. James Duncan raised his only arm in a boxer's salute of triumph. Alex remembered the asshole surgeon who was responsible for the other arm. It was a different room, same building when she nailed him, eighteen months ago

Looking round the room Alex saw David. Their eyes met, a little half smile. She again felt close to tears.

David seemed to sense that her emotions were fragile. He held out his wrists, as if to say, *"OK, put the cuffs on now."*

She rolled her eyes but David's little joke had its intended effect. She felt herself smiling, felt a little looser.

The crowded courtroom rose as Judge Reagan entered. He nodded good morning to the attorneys. The jury were brought in and seated.

"Ms. Goldberg," said the judge.

Alex rose.

What was it David had said last night? Objective. Be sympathetic, empathetic but objective.

Chap 55

The silence in the crowded courtroom was absolute.

"May it please the court," Alex began formally, her voice low.

She addressed the twelve members of the jury and the two alternates, eight men and six women who would soon decide this case. The jury sat at attention. Several had pencils poised over notepads. They took their responsibility seriously.

"Ladies and Gentlemen, this morning I would like to take you for a walk."

That got their attention!

"Not a walk outside in the sun. For that we'll all have to wait a little longer."

This was said with a small smile. Alex was pleased to see smiling responses from more than half of the jury.

"Instead we'll take a walk together through the Winnie Brown case"

"Many of us have taken walks in unfamiliar places. It's best to do so with a guide to keep us on the right track, and point out interesting places or objects. That's what I'm going to do today. I'll be your guide, because none of you are familiar with the details of medicine or the law."

"Of course," added Alex with a smiling gesture towards the bench, "there's a chief guide here to make sure I don't lead you up the garden path."

That got a few chuckles.

She continued, "It can be difficult for a jury of lay people to sort out everything they've heard during a trial."

She paused and pointed a finger at the defense table, at Herb Walton.

"It's particularly difficult in this case, where witnesses have changed their story and refused to tell all they know."

A pause for emphasis, "Where evidence has been tampered with and falsified."

This last was said looking straight at Herb Walton. He flushed angrily and seemed to be on the point of standing to interrupt, but settled back in his chair without saying a word. Herb and Alex both knew that most judges gave counsel a little more latitude during closing arguments. She'd take all she could get, and then some.

The audience was hanging on her every word. David watched and marveled at her skill. He felt as he did watching a surgeon make a complex procedure look simple, or an expert skier effortlessly dance down a steep mogul run.

Alex was enjoying herself. Despite the high stakes, she genuinely enjoyed the process of summarizing complex cases for the jury. She was too modest to realize that she was blessed with a rare talent. She possessed the combination of a first rate analytical mind, and the ability to effectively communicate her ideas to those less gifted or sophisticated.

She continued for the jury, "Let's start with the facts that no-one disputes. Everyone agrees that in August of 1999, at the age of twenty-nine, Winnie Brown was diagnosed with a cancer of the lymph nodes, called large cell lymphoma."

Alex slowly and methodically described the process of diagnosis and treatment, and Winnie's response, up till the day before her death.

"Everything that I've told you so far are medical facts, documented in the medical records, and testified to by Doctor Stern, Ms. Brown's treating physician."

Alex emphasized that for several months before her last treatment, the clinical records reflected that the patient was in a complete remission, completely free of any sign of cancer.

"Nothing has been produced by the defense to suggest that the clinical records were inaccurate, or that Doctor Stern was wrong in thinking that the patient was well on her way to being cured of cancer by December of 2000. The complete absence of any sign of cancer in Winnie Brown in December is another medical fact, not challenged by the defense."

"Both the patient and her doctor expected the treatment of January 15th 2001 to be her last. Tragically it was, but not in the way that Winnie or Dr. Stern expected."

Alex paused. *What came next was rough.*

"Instead of going home to her husband and twins that evening when her chemotherapy was completed, Winnie Brown tragically died. She died the following day in the intensive care unit of International Medical Center after suffering repeated seizures and lapsing into irreversible coma."

Alex had been on her feet for nearly thirty minutes, speaking without a break and without referring to her notes. Jo Glen, a freelance artist sitting in the courtroom quickly sketched Alex's profile, as she leaned forward to make a point to the jury.

"Great for T.V. news," thought Jo.

Little did she realize that her sketch would be on the cover of TIME magazine within a week.

After a few sips of water, Alex was ready to continue. Mouthing a silent *'thank you'* to the bailiff who had thoughtfully provided the water, Alex turned back to the jury. Several members of the jury were in tears. Alex herself felt close to choking.

She continued, "Winnie Brown had never had a seizure in her life before. Her first seizure occurred during the administration of her chemotherapy. More specifically it occurred immediately following the injection of chemotherapy into her Omaya shunt, into her brain fluid."

"Her doctor," she turned and looked at David, "Dr. David Stern has testified under oath that he accidentally injected the wrong chemotherapy drug into her Omaya reservoir. Instead of injecting ARA-C into the brain he injected Vincristine into the Omaya with immediate disastrous results."

She paused, "It was a terrible error on Dr. Stern's part."

Another pause, "a fatal error".

David sat quietly in his chair. He showed no emotion as Alex continued. Alex was glad to see his composure. He really seemed to be at peace with himself.

Alex reminded the jury that both drugs were colorless liquids that appeared identical when drawn up in the syringes. She also reminded them that because of staff shortages that day David was alone with his patient when the disaster occurred.

She threw up her hands in an expression of futility.

"Once that fatal error occurred there was no hope for Winnie Brown. Her death was inevitable. She was rendered brain dead by the toxic effect of the Vincristine, a fact freely stated by Doctor Stern and confirmed, albeit reluctantly, by Doctor Crandall."

A long pause and a look at the defense table. "Confirmed by Doctor Crandall only after his earlier lies had been exposed."

Turning back to face the jury, Alex continued. "You have heard that Vincristine must never be injected into brain fluid. That there is no treatment for the devastating brain damage caused by Vincristine when injected incorrectly. And indeed Ms. Brown died as soon as life support was withdrawn."

Alex walked over to the jury box, and stood with her right hand extended, pointing at the defense table. Her voice was low but everyone in the crowded courtroom hung on her every word.

"I said earlier that David Stern committed a fatal error, and that is true. A fatal error that he freely admitted, and has done everything that he can to rectify."

Alex paused and then said very thoughtfully. "But there were actually two fatal errors in this case."

Several members of the jury looked puzzled and Alex explained,

"The second fatal error was committed by the senior doctors and administrators at International," another pause, "and their legal advisors."

The last was said with a withering look at Herb Walton who refused to meet Alex's eyes.

Alex continued, "International's fatal error was simply this. Unlike David Stern who had the courage and honesty to admit his mistake, International refused to accept the truth. Rather they embarked upon a carefully planned pattern of lies and deceit."

"They probably convinced you for a time at least that Ms. Brown had died of lymphoma, and that David Stern was suffering from a mental illness and therefore could not be believed when he told you what he had done."

Alex paused, "Think for a minute what in their arrogance and greed these people did. Simply so that they would not have to admit culpability and pay compensation to Winnie Brown's family."

She ticked off the following on the fingers of one hand.

"They committed perjury and falsified medical records. They had a whole procession of people conspire to tell you under oath that David Stern was mentally unstable. They suspended him."

Despite herself, Alex's voice rose. "They denied Doctor Stern's other patients, all of whom are suffering from cancer, his services, the services of a dedicated cancer specialist who knew more about their illness than any other doctor."

She turned to the judge, who sat impassively. "They concocted a whole false story, full of lies for this trial."

She paused, "All for what? So that they wouldn't have to pay the Brown family the compensation that they knew was rightfully theirs."

Several members of the jury were shaking their heads as Alex continued.

"Make no mistake, every one of the conspirators knew the truth. They knew all along that David Stern spoke the truth when he told them of his error, just as he spoke the truth to you a few days ago."

"Less than one month before this trial David Stern survived an assassination attempt." Here Alex's voice faltered for a second.

"And so they tried to destroy him here in this court-room. You saw and heard how Mr. Walton used the tragic death of Doctor Stern's twin sister, when they were twelve years old, to cynically and dishonestly provoke him, to make him react emotionally so that you would question his mental health, and therefore his entire testimony."

She looked at the jury, "Do you feel you were manipulated?"

Several heads in the jury box nodded vigorously.

"You should feel manipulated." said Alex, "because you were. We all were."

She turned once again to Judge Reagen who sat expressionless.

"The entire system was shamelessly manipulated. Your time and the court's time needlessly occupied, and for what reason? Simply because International would not admit their liability and pay compensation to Robert Brown and his family for their grievous loss."

She turned back to the jury. "No amount of money will bring back Robert Brown's beloved wife. No amount of money will give her twins the mother they lost, but that is the only form of compensation that you, the jury can offer the Brown family."

Tears were flowing freely now, both in the jury box and elsewhere in the court, as Alex stopped to compose herself.

"There is however another way that you can compensate Robert and his family."

Several members of the jury looked questioningly at Alex.

"David Stern has apologized in word and action to the Browns. International has not yet done so."

Alex fixed the jury with a look full of passion and conviction. She pointed her forefinger at them for greater emphasis, and spoke very slowly.

"You have the opportunity to say to International. *Your arrogance is unacceptable. Your duty is to serve your patients and your staff, to serve the entire community honestly and honorably. Medical care is a sacred trust. Break that trust at your peril.*"

She sighed and raised her arms, "You've heard during these long days of the trial of the economic loss due to Ms. Brown's premature death. You've heard about the financial value of a wife's companionship, and a mother's love."

She spoke very softly, "I don't want to cheapen Winnie's memory, by trying to put a dollar figure on all this. I know Robert Brown, and I believe him when he told me that for him, this case is not about money. I trust you to do the right thing in that regard."

"More important than money is that the Brown family hear you say that the attempted cover-up was an insult to Winnie's memory, and that International's behavior was outrageous and unacceptable."

"You have the opportunity to punish International for their outrageous behavior. That's what *punitive* damages are all about, *punishment.*"

She shrugged her shoulders and said, "I'm a simple lawyer. I really have no idea how you punish a multi-billion dollar company, so that they get that message. Once again I am simply going to rely on your good sense, and the guidance of the court."

She looked each jury member in the eye, as she concluded, "On behalf of the Brown family, and from the bottom of my heart thank you for your attention throughout this trial, and thank you for listening to me now."

She sat down as the room let out its collective breath.

The judge turned to the defense table. Herb Walton rose to his feet, buttoning the jacket of his tailored Armani jacket.

He knew it was a lost cause but he had to go through the motions. He spoke for five minutes, the shortest final argument he had ever made, while studiously avoiding the jury's eye.

His basic argument was that only one International employee, Crandall, had admitted any wrongdoing, and he assured the jury that International would take immediate steps to rectify that situation.

Walton concluded his argument. "No-one has *proved* that Winnie Brown died because of a drug injection. You haven't seen with your own eyes the brain damage that Dr. Stern claimed he inflicted."

"Dr. Crandall now says that was the case, but Crandall admits that he lied to you before under oath. So which of Crandall's stories is true? You all saw with your own eyes how irrationally Doctor Stern acted. Can you really believe either one of them? Can you be sure what caused Winnie Brown's death?"

His final words to the jury were, "People die of lymphoma every day, and you have already heard that Ms. Brown had stage four disease, the worst you can have. That's why she died. Tragic but hardly the fault of International."

He sat down without looking directly at the jury.

Judge Reagen gave the jury its final instructions, and they filed out to deliberate.

The trial was all but over.

Chap 56

Alex had a routine that never varied. At the end of every trial, whenever the jury left to consider their verdict she took a cab to Shalom Funeral Park in Maywood, near Brookfield Zoo.

There she visited her parents' grave. It didn't matter whether it was ninety degrees or nineteen, there she would stand for an hour or more and pour out her heart. Today was no exception.

There was one difference however. She was not alone. With her was David Stern.

Alex carried her pager and cell phone. Two hours into the jury deliberations her phone rang. It was Cindy.

"Sorry to bother you, Alex. I just want to let you know that the jury has sent out a note for the Judge. They had a question about punitive damages. It's looking good."

Alex smiled briefly, "Thanks Cindy. I'm coming back now. See you in an hour or so."

By the time Alex and David made it back to the Daley Center, the word was out that the jury had reached a verdict. The courtroom quickly filled to capacity, as the jury entered the room. Several of the members of the jury looked close to tears as they sat down.

Judge Reagen asked the foreman of the jury to hand their verdict to the clerk of the court, who then passed it up to the judge. He calmly read the verdict without showing any emotion, and instructed the foreman to read the verdict.

John Kowalski was seventy-five, but looked about sixty. The retired postal worker had a strong sense of fair play, a fact that had Herb Walton known it, would certainly have kept him off this particular jury.

It was therefore with pleasure that he spoke.

"Your Honor, the jury finds for the plaintiff in this case, and awards the Brown family five million dollars in compensatory damages."

He then turned towards the defense table. Looking directly at Herb Walton he spoke again.

"We also award the sum of one hundred million dollars in punitive damages against International."

"We also agreed that all legal costs should be paid by International," he added.

At Alex's side Cindy whispered, "Gotcha!"

The court exploded with noise, quickly stopped by Judge Reagen's gavel.

"Thank you for your service," he said to the jury. "Before discharging you, I wish to make several observations. First it is clear to me that you were correct in your verdict. Ms. Brown died as a result of the inadvertent injection of the wrong medication into her brain, a tragic and regrettable error that Dr. Stern freely and courageously admitted to. As such it is fit and proper that compensatory damages be paid to the Brown family by Doctor Stern and his employer."

Judge Reagen paused for a moment then continued. "It is certainly true that the amount of punitive damages that you have awarded in this case is an enormous sum. This court has previously criticized excessive jury awards."

He turned to a sick looking Herb Walton. "However in this case I am not inclined to reduce the award. I agree with the jury that the behavior of International's employees has been outrageous. They refused to admit their liability and instead attempted to perpetrate an illegal cover-up. In doing so they needlessly increased the distress that this tragic accident caused the Brown family."

Robert Brown cheered silently as the judge continued. "This type of behavior by any corporation is unacceptable. It's particularly disgraceful when the corporation is a health care provider, responsible for looking after people's health and welfare. International would do well to closely examine the corporate culture which allowed such actions to occur."

Reagen turned to David Stern who sat pale-faced in the court. "The conspiracy also caused tremendous distress to Doctor Stern." He paused, "If there is anything positive at all in this tragic incident it is the behavior of Doctor Stern. Instead of agreeing with and participating in this sordid and illegal cover-up, he insisted on telling the truth. Despite suffering the loss of his job and severe attacks on his personal and professional reputation as a consequence, his insistence on sticking to the true story is the major reason why justice has been served today."

The judge concluded, his face grave. "I view with particular concern the apparent attempt to subvert justice through manipulation of evidence and perjury. All of the relevant evidence and a full copy of the transcripts of this trial will be sent to the Cook County District Attorney."

With a rustle of robes the judge left the court.

Robert Brown walked over to David and held out his hand. "Doctor Stern, you acted like a man. I'm grateful to you for that."

David was too choked to speak. He simply nodded and grasped Robert's hand.

Alex put her head down on the table and wept.

As the court emptied, Alex sat and sobbed for ten minutes, her head in her hands. Cindy ran interference with the hordes of reporters who wanted a piece of her boss, promising them a news conference later that evening.

The room was finally empty and silent. Alex became aware of a whimpering sound coming from the far corner of the room. She looked up. David was wedged against the wall. His eyes were closed, his face pale.

She rushed over to him. "David what is it, are you bleeding again?"

He shook his head, "No it's not that, it's my.... It's my...." he whispered.

"Your what?" Alex almost screamed.

"It's my ass," said David, "You nailed it. You nailed it to the wall!"

Alex shook her head. "Asshole."

She laughed through her tears, "You had me worried sick."

They left the court-room together.

Chap 57

The trial with its sensational verdict ended in the second week of April. Alex, David and Robert Brown were deluged with invitations from radio, television, Time Magazine, Newsweek and People. Even Playboy called Alex with a proposal. Cindy blushed when she heard Alex's response to that one.

Thursday of the following week, Alex took a call from Frank Houston, the C.E.O. of International. The next day she met with Robert.

Alex, Cindy and Robert sat around her desk, with coffee for Robert and Alex. Cindy as always had diet Coke. John Rowland was also present, looking quite dapper in a new Brooks Brothers suit, his first in five years.

International had paid his fees in full.

Alex laid it out for her client. "Well Robert, this is what International wants to do. They can appeal the case, but their chances of success are slim. Judge Reagen runs a very tight ship and I certainly don't see any grounds for a reversal on judicial error."

"If International loses an appeal, they'll generate more bad publicity, and add more legal fees. They'll also have to pay interest on the one hundred and five million they currently owe you throughout the time of the appeal."

Cindy corrected her, "Actually one hundred and six million when you include David's million."

Alex nodded. "You're right Cindy. Anyway Robert, I spoke to Houston. I was pretty blunt with him."

Cindy rolled her eyes. "Your actual words were, *'your guys got their asses caught in a wringer'*, Alex."

Alex blushed, "Well maybe I was a little too blunt. Anyway Houston doesn't want the added publicity of an appeal. He wants this over now. He's agreed to pay you the full amount of the award, compensatory and punitive damages."

She continued, "He's also ready to issue a public apology to you for the actions of those responsible, and fire them."

She shrugged, "That's really a no-brainer. He really has no other option. They're already suspended and they're all going to be convicted in a criminal trial unless they plea bargain it out, which is actually more likely."

She shrugged again, "Either way International wants them out."

"What about David?" asked John.

"Well" said Alex, "I did bring that up."

David was never far from her thoughts now.

"He actually has a good case himself against International for slander, don't you agree John?"

Rowland nodded as Alex continued, "And for wrongful dismissal. I mean they labeled him crazy and suspended him. And we know that was all a crock. He can make a strong case that they have prevented him from working, that they screwed up his future job prospects."

Alex looked kind of smug.

"She's got something cooking, I know it," thought Cindy.

"Come on out with it, what have you done Alex?"

"Well," said Alex, "With the head of Oncology at International probably going down for perjury and conspiracy, it occurred to me that David Stern could fill that position just fine. That might even make any lawsuit of his against International moot, right John?"

She looked round the table with a broad smile. "And Houston agreed. If he brings David back on board it would certainly help International's image which is a tad tarnished right now."

John smiled, "Works for me."

Cindy said, "Why don't you get David on the phone right now.

Alex picked up the phone and dialed David's home. When he answered, she told him her news. After listening to his answer she slowly replaced the receiver with a puzzled look. They all looked at Alex expectantly.

She looked at them and shook her head.

"He said no," she said.

Chap 58

The following Monday Alex and Cindy had a surprise visitor. David Stern came to their office at eleven fifteen.

When David walked into the office, Alex was trying to read a long brief from the other side in a breast cancer case that had been going on and on for years, it seemed.

"Hi Cindy, you're looking as svelte as ever." said David as he breezed in.

He had gained back nearly ten pounds since his surgery.

Cindy simpered as David gave her a hug. Alex rolled her eyes.

"And what can we do for the heroic young *unemployed* doctor today?" she asked, putting aside the papers she had been trying to read.

David didn't answer her. He simply closed the door to her office, pulled her from her chair and kissed her full on the lips. After a few moments he felt her start to respond. There was a discreet knock at the door. Cindy was already in the room.

"Ah, excuse me doctor, she said, "I didn't know you made house calls."

"Only when the patient is very sick, and the need is great, Cindy," said David with a smile.

"And whose need would that be, Doctor?" asked Alex dryly.

"No matter," said David with an airy wave of one hand, "I have come to rescue you both from the drudgery of your toil, and take you to lunch. And as my employment status may be changing soon, it's on me."

Alex raised an eyebrow, but David would say no more until after they had ordered lunch. Chinese, two blocks from the office.

Despite Alex's hundred million plus win, she was still a pretty basic person.

"I met with Frank Houston, yesterday," David said casually as they were served egg rolls and fried rice.

David had tea only. His surgery was still too recent.

"One of these days I've got to tell Alex I can't stand Chinese," he thought.

He continued. "I've agreed to take the International job, and drop any thoughts of a lawsuit on several conditions. And Frank agreed."

Alex gave him her cynical look. *"Frank* is it now?"

David waved airily, "Well you know how it is when we men of the world get together."

Cindy started looking a little uncomfortable but Alex laughed, "Don't worry Cindy, he can't help being an asshole."

David smiled at Cindy. "Don't pay any attention to your boss. Anyway Frank and I had a long conversation. And actually, my taking the International job is still conditional."

Alex said nothing, she merely raised an eyebrow.

David took her hand, his face serious. "If I'm going to rejoin International I need to know that that Winnie Brown is finally at rest. I also have to know that there will be no more questionable practices. That's why I took you ladies out to lunch today."

"I knew it," said Alex. She shook her head at Cindy. "That's how it is with doctors. They always want something."

"Shut up, Alex," said Cindy, "go on, David."

"Well," said David looking smug, "I need Robert Brown to agree to one of these conditions, and Alex to agree to the other."

He explained, "I suggested to Frank Houston, and he agreed, that we name the cancer center at International the Winnie Brown Cancer Center, and set up a fund for research and treatment of cancer in minorities. We agreed on twenty million for start-up funds."

He sipped his tea and suppressed a shudder.

"Why didn't they serve decent American tea instead of this cat's pee?"

"You know, don't you that highest cancer death rates in the world are in African American males right here in the USA?" he added.

Alex smiled broadly, "I'll call Robert this afternoon. I can't imagine he'll refuse. That's a lovely idea. You said there were two conditions?"

David looked a little nervous. "Well, this one's a little closer to home. I pointed out to Houston that he could rehabilitate International's name more effectively if he took a strong position regarding business ethics."

Alex looked curious, "What'd he say?"

"Well, I think he saw the value from a business perspective of being seen as one of the good guys. So he has agreed to fund a Center in Business Ethics at a major university. I suggested maybe Northwestern or University of Chicago. He's got his people looking into it. What do you think Alex?"

Alex shrugged, "What do I think? I think it's a great idea."

David smiled, obviously relieved. "You agree? Good, that's settled then."

Alex was puzzled, "You don't need my agreement for that."

David smiled and said, "To name it the Morris and Leah Goldberg Center for Business Ethics we do."

Cindy was ecstatic, "Oh Alex."

Alex gripped David's hand tightly, "Thank you David, but my client still gets his money, right?"

David looked offended, "Honestly Alex, we didn't even discuss that."

Alex smiled broadly, "Then I agree, and thank you David, I'm very touched."

She leaned over and kissed him gently on the cheek.

David smiled, "Well that's settled then. I'll call Frank this afternoon. Maybe he and I can do lunch later this week."

Alex rolled her eyes. You really are going to be insufferable. I know it."

Alex and David walked out of the restaurant hand in hand. Cindy walked a few steps behind them, grinning from ear to ear.

Chap 59

Spring gave way to summer. David Stern returned to International and immediately threw himself into his work. True to his word Frank Houston established the Winnie Brown Cancer Center, and poured money into it. David's time and energy were consumed in rebuilding the Oncology department.

Alex often felt a certain emotional letdown after a big trial. It was as if all of her energy and emotions were focused on the task at hand. Once it was over it took her some time to bounce back. It was no different after the Winnie Brown trial.

Robert Brown had a strong support group in his immediate family. He wisely followed Alex's advice, and established a trust fund for the twins. With that done, Alex felt that her job was over.

With such a massive settlement for her client, Alex's own financial future was more than secure, a fact that Cindy took pleasure in pointing out to her boss.

The massive publicity resulting from the International case generated many new referrals. Several told such heart rending stories that Alex had to accept them. The work threatened to swamp her. After much prompting from Cindy, Alex finally agreed to take a partner to share the load.

Cindy was delighted. John Rowland was a great choice.

David and Alex kept seeing each other regularly; a fact that once again pleased Cindy immensely.

After a few months, however Cindy sensed problems. Alex seemed more irritable and the glow that she would always exhibit when David's name came up seemed to have vanished.

It all came to a head one steamy day late in August. Alex was sitting at her desk, trying for the third time that day to respond to her opponent in yet another screwed up surgical case

Cindy was quietly humming to herself as she watered the plants in Alex's office.

Alex threw down the letter, "Cindy will you please shut up. How can I concentrate with all that crap going on!"

Cindy was startled. "I'm sorry Alex. I didn't realize I was bothering you."

Alex burst into tears. Cindy rushed over and hugged her.

"Tell me, what's really bothering you, Alex? This isn't like you."

Alex sniffed, "I don't know. I just feel shitty."

Cindy was alarmed, "Is everything O.K. with you and David?"

Alex shrugged, "Not really. I don't know why. I love him. You know how fine he is. But recently everything he says and does irritates the crap out of me. I don't get it."

Cindy grinned slyly. "Maybe that's it. You're not getting it."

Alex had made it clear to David. He'd had a major blood transfusion, and until he checked out negative for any disease that could be transmitted in blood or any other body fluid, there would be no sex, period.

Alex rolled her eyes. "Come on Cindy. Give me some credit. I'm thirty-three years old. I'm not some horny twenty year old."

Cindy didn't say a word, but simply grinned at Alex. No more was said.

Later that week Cindy took delivery of three dozen beautiful long stemmed red roses. She carried them into Alex's office.

"Aren't they beautiful, Alex. I wonder who they're from? "

There was a card attached. Alex took it out and read, *"Go to the FAX machine."*

She rolled her eyes. *"O.K. Doctor, you want to play games?"*

Alex walked over to the office FAX machine. A long message was just scrolling out.

"I don't believe it," laughed Alex as she read the message.

It was a copy of blood tests dated three days earlier from International Hospital. Patient name, David Stern.

"Hmm. Let's see. H.I.V. negative; R.P.R., that's syphilis negative; Hepatitis B and C negative; Cytomegalovirus negative. Yellow fever negative, *yellow fever?*"

That was David's little joke.

Across the bottom of the lab report David had written, *"Dinner 7.30? Wear something special."*

Cindy and Alex looked at each other. Cindy wore a wicked grin.

"Well I suppose I can expect your mood to improve quite soon."

Alex wagged one finger at her. "Cindy, if you say one more word, even one word, I guarantee you will never work again. Never. Do you understand?"

"Yeah, yeah Alex whatever you say," said Cindy.

She didn't say another word, but she didn't stop leering.

That night, seven thirty David was buzzed up to Alex's apartment. She opened the door. She wore the jeans and the Chicago Bulls tee shirt she wore when they first met.

She looked fabulous.

David wore jeans and a pink Brook's Brothers button down shirt. Loafers with no socks. He carried a large pizza in a box.

David looked at Alex. "Perfect." he said.

Alex closed the door behind him. They tore at each other's clothes.

"Wait, wait," he said, "let me put the pizza down."

Somehow they made it to Alex's bedroom, undressing each other on the way. She was even more beautiful naked. They made love frantically. Afterwards they lay together in each other's arms.

David stroked her hair, "Finally. I've dreamed of this moment ever since I first saw you."

Alex couldn't help it. "So you're pleased I'm not *Mr.* Goldberg after all?"

David smiled, "Alex you're truly an evil person. But it's my goal in life to help people, and I will therefore help you become a better person."

Alex was too relaxed to roll her eyes. "Thank you Doctor. And how exactly do you plan to do that?"

David didn't say a word. They made love again this time more gently, exploring each other and growing ever closer in their love. Afterwards they slept.

At three fifteen, Alex woke and nudged David. "Are you hungry?"

He grunted in response.

They sat at the kitchen table eating micro waved pizza from paper plates.

"Alex," said David, "I have to tell you something and I hope you won't be angry with me."

Alex looked concerned, "What is it?"

David looked away. "You know those lab tests I sent you yesterday? Well I cheated. I rigged the results so that they would all be negative."

Alex looked at her lover, her exquisite eyes narrowed. Then she relaxed and sighed.

"That's O.K. David, I know you doctors falsify lab tests all the time. You wouldn't have done it if it weren't important to you. It doesn't bother me at all."

David broke into a broad grin. "I knew you'd understand," he said happily.

She threw her plate at him.